ENEMY BROTHERS

Also by Constance Savery

The Reb and the Redcoats
Pippin's House
Welcome, Santza
The Good Ship Red Lily
Dark House on the Moss
Magic in My Shoes
Emeralds for the King

ENEMY BROTHERS

CONSTANCE SAVERY

BETHLEHEM BOOKS · IGNATIUS PRESS
BATHGATE, N.D.   SAN FRANCISCO

Text © 1943 Constance Savery

Cover art © 2001 Carol Phenix
Title page illustrations by Henry Pitz
Cover design by Davin Carlson

First Bethlehem Books printing March 2001

ISBN 978-1-883937-50-8
Library of Congress Catalog Number: 00-108548

Bethlehem Books • Ignatius Press
10194 Garfield Street South
Bathgate, ND 58261
www.bethlehembooks.com

Printed in the United States on acid free paper

Enemy Brothers

Contents

Enemy Brothers

1

Out of the Gray North Sea

A YOUNG MAN in Air Force blue stood by the window of a hotel lounge, staring out at a gray world: the gray streets of a gray town under a gray sky with a gray sea beyond it. Streets and sky and sea had to be taken on trust; for all that could be seen was dense gray mist.

"And the sea sighed and the fog rose up sheer,
A wall of nothing at the world's last edge,"

murmured the young man. He turned back into the empty room and sat down by the fire. Taking a folded sheet of paper and a tinted photograph from the end-flap of a shabby leather pocketbook, he studied them closely.

On the paper was a child's colored-pencil drawing of a house with a high peaked roof. Red and blue flowers sparkled in window boxes; a balcony with curly balusters decorated every story; fluted pillars flanked the front door; and pargeted plaster urns, laurel wreaths and fat dangling tassels filled the space between one window and the next. A dachshund sat under a linden tree on a grass plot in which heart-shaped beds had been cut for roses. Tree, flower beds and dog appeared to be sliding down a steep hill toward small garden railings near the foot of the sheet. The airman's half smile died away as he looked at the photograph.

It showed the head and shoulders of a boy of ten, with

1

the name *Tony* written beneath in a woman's upright foreign hand. The little face that laughed up at the airman might well have belonged to a younger brother: the likeness between them was not confined to their dark-brown hair and blue-gray eyes. Had a dozen years been taken from the elder's age, it might not have been easy to tell them apart.

The airman's keen gaze rested for some moments on the boy. Then, sighing, he returned photograph and sketch to the pocketbook. "Poor old Tony!" he muttered. "I wonder what you've become."

He sat for a long time, deep in thought. Then he glanced at his wrist watch, flung himself back in the chair and within two minutes was asleep, his head pillowed on his arm. Flames crackled on the hearth; beyond the glass doors figures flitted to and fro in the entrance hall; from the unseen harbor came muffled sea sounds. Half an hour later two midshipmen hurled themselves into the room. Wide awake in an instant, the sleeper started to his feet.

The newcomers stood looking at him reproachfully.

"And is that all the welcome you have for two young heroes, Flying Officer George Dymory Ingleford? Your beloved brother Ginger and his dearest friend Lancelot rush into your arms, fresh from their valiant exploits—and what sort of welcome do they get? None whatever; 'cause you're asleep, at this hour of the day! You lazy beggar, Dym!"

The young man grinned. "Sorry," he said. "I'm tired."

"Been busy lately?"

"Much as usual. What have you been up to?"

They looked at him with mock severity.

"We're the great strong silent Navy; we don't rush about,

shouting the names of the places we've visited lately. We leave the R.A.F. to do all the talking. We've been dodging round here, there and everywhere in the icy North Sea— Icy North! Ugh!"

Two more easy chairs were drawn up to the fire. Dym rang the bell for coffee. The brothers looked into each other's eyes and smiled. It was their first meeting since the outbreak of war.

"All well at home?"

"All well."

"Decent of you to come all this way on a bare chance of meeting me, Dym. Must have cost you a fortune."

"Well, what could I do when I had a leave and a whisper that you might be here at a given time? It didn't cost me anything. Cousin Olive insisted on franking me—"

"She's an old trump."

"She is," Dym agreed, speaking as though words and thoughts had drifted apart.

"What's up, Dym? Still sleepy?"

"No. I was only thinking that I should have come, whatever the cost." He laughed.

"I'm honored."

The airman fidgeted with the lapel of his tunic. "No, you're not. You'll call me superstitious when you hear that I had a queer feeling I had to come. As if"— he paused, and his eyes went to the seaward windows—"as if someone called me here."

"Called you here? What on earth do you mean?"

"I don't know."

It was Ginger's turn to grin.

"Sounds like softening of the brain, old man. Who do you suppose was doing the forsaken merman act? Not me,

I assure you, and certainly not old Lance. We're jolly glad to see you, but we didn't call."

"No," said Dym, with a laugh and a shrug, "neither of you. I can't explain—but I knew I had to come. Ring the bell again, Ginger."

The waitress brought coffee and cakes and banked up the fire with driftwood. Little salty flames of blue, purple and green danced round the rusty nails in it. Outside the windows the fog pressed closer.

"Can't think how you managed to get ashore in the morning," said Dym as he poured out the coffee. "Didn't expect to see you till this afternoon."

"So you probably would have," said Ginger, "if the Skipper hadn't told us to take the German prisoner ashore and buy him some clothes."

"Prisoner? What have you done with him?"

"Left him in the hall to wait for us, under a joint guard composed of porter, receptionist and giggling maids."

"Quaint way of dealing with prisoners, isn't it?"

"Well, he isn't an ordinary prisoner. He's only twelve."

"Twelve!" said Dym, startled.

"Picked up in mid-ocean on board a motorboat packed with young Norwegians escaping to England. They were workers in a chemical factory that had been commandeered by the Germans. The plucky chaps set fire to their own factory by night and made a dash for England in a motorboat belonging to their German masters. They bumped across a deadly mine field straight into us; their petrol and stores were just about exhausted—"

"But the German boy?"

"Oh, it's a long tale. Surely you don't want to hear it now?"

Once more Dym's eyes sought the fogged glass. "Yes," he said.

"Here goes, then. One of the Norwegians was Olaf Eriksen, the son of the ex-manager of the factory. Only fifteen; he'd had a bad time. His father had been clapped into prison for refusing to serve under the Germans, who put in men of their own instead—Quislings. Well, that proved a failure, so the head of a chemical works in Germany was sent out to take their place. He brought his wife and son with him and billeted himself and family on the Eriksens. The wife wasn't bad, but the son was a thoroughgoing little Nazi, as fanatical as they're made. He bullied Olaf's little brother and sister, and spied on Olaf. Made a good thing of his spying, too. He found out that Olaf belonged to a secret patriotic association for schoolboys and informed the authorities. Olaf just had time to get his mother and the kids into hiding lest they should be made to suffer for his so-called sins. Then he joined the others in their flight. If he hadn't gone he'd have found himself in a concentration camp."

"Plucky lad! And your small prisoner?"

"Mixture of revenge and prudence on the part of Olaf's friends, I'm afraid. Olaf himself didn't know about it till they were standing out to sea. Fact is, the other Norwegians didn't intend to leave Little Hitler behind; every child in the place went in terror of the young monkey. So they carried him off when everybody was busy trying to save the factory from going up in flames—and, after some hair-raising days inside a German cockleshell, the boy found himself a prisoner on a British man-of-war."

Dym kicked the nearest lump of driftwood and stared into the sharp blue spires of flame. "Poor little chap!" he said.

"You wouldn't be so sympathetic if you knew our Little Hitler," said Ginger. "From what we've seen of him it isn't hard to believe that a week ago he was a swaggering, blustering, detestable little bully. He's arrogant still, in spots, though he's been partly tamed by fright and by the tossing he's had since he put to sea. There's not much of him left now, barring a sort of white determination to go down with the swastika flying. I don't know what he thinks is going to happen to him in England. You can see that he's been stuffed with awful stories about the British. I fancy that death by slow torture is about the best he expects."

"Poor little chap!" said Dym again. "What's his name?"

"Eckermann—Max Eckermann."

"Ah!"

"You don't mean to say you've met him on your travels before the war?"

"No, I didn't mean that. Go on."

"But you spoke as if you'd found a missing bit in a jigsaw puzzle," protested Ginger, eying his brother curiously. "Something slipped into place then; I'm sure it did. What did you mean?"

"Tell you later. Go on."

"The Skipper turned Olaf and Little Hitler over to the gun room and made the lot of us responsible for their health and happiness. Olaf's had the time of his life. He's wild to join the Navy—ours or his, it doesn't seem to matter which! He and the rest of the Norwegians will be off as soon as we've got into touch with their authorities—there'll be dozens of people ready and willing to look after them till the war's over. As for Little Hitler—well, there's no love lost between him and his fifteen nursemaids, that's all I can say."

"He's game, though," said the silent Lancelot suddenly, between two mouthfuls of bun.

"Yes, that's his best point," Ginger agreed. "The Norwegians say he fought like a young tiger before they got him on board the motorboat—and he's fighting-mad still, whenever he has the strength for it. Luckily for all concerned, he's the world's worst sailor, and has spent most of the time on board more dead than alive. But he was game even then—he took his punishment without whimpering. He stood up to the Skipper yesterday, too. I had the luck to be present at the interview as a kind of unofficial prisoner's friend.

"The Skipper told me to bring Little Hitler down to the after-cabin—he wanted to find out whether the boy had any friends in England. He's much too small to be shipped off to a camp for young male enemy aliens. The Skipper thought his people might have friends among the German women who have been interned here. But they haven't—as far as we can make out. Little Hitler was as cautious as you please, wouldn't say an unnecessary word. Instead of answering questions, he began demanding to be sent back to Germany at once! He said that his detention was a breach of international law. Must have invented that for himself, for I don't suppose there has ever been a case like his before. Shows he's got brains, doesn't it? Don't believe the Skipper knew himself whether Little Hitler was right or wrong. Do you?"

"No," said Dym, "but that point needn't detain us. Get on with your story."

"So he told Little Hitler, as comfortingly as he knew how, that the British Government couldn't undertake to send him home because the German Government wouldn't grant safe-conducts for ships carrying children. 'We're responsible for your safety, Max,' he said, 'we can't let you run the risk of being torpedoed on the way home.' It took him a long time to say all that; for he speaks German badly, if you know what I mean. The Skipper told him that he would have to make the best of a bad job. He couldn't go home at present; but the British Government would find him a temporary home, probably with other Germans. Little Hitler didn't seem pleased. He grumbled till the Skipper lost patience and told him straight out that it was no good storming about a trouble he had brought on himself by bad behavior.

"Little Hitler drew himself up, looked the Skipper squarely in the face, and said in English, without any trace of an accent, 'You have no right to speak to me like that. I am German.' None of us had the slightest idea the kid could understand English, let alone speak it almost as easily as you or I! Hullo, Dym! What's wrong? You jumped as if a mine had blown up a yard away."

"Did I?" said Dym. "Sorry."

"It's my belief," said Lancelot solemnly, "that the Skipper rather likes Little Hitler. He hates people to be afraid of him—the boy certainly isn't or, if he is, doesn't show it."

"Yes, he likes Little Hitler, but wants to get rid of him as soon as he conveniently can," said Ginger. "He can't keep him on board and doesn't know where to park him while he's getting in touch with the authorities. He's been sounding the married officers to find out whether they have wives brave enough to house Little Hitler for a week or two. But they're turning a blind eye to his blandishments; they say etiquette demands that the Captain's wife should be asked first, and hoping she'll rise to the occasion."

"She won't," said Lancelot. "I've seen her. She's young and as timid as a kitten. The mere sight of Max would scare her stiff."

"Euphemia wouldn't mind—" Dym began.

"Not on your life!" said Ginger. "That's carrying kindness too far. After all, England's bristling with orphanages and child-adoption societies—the Skipper will find a way out somehow. It's his business."

"I can't help feeling sorry for the little beggar," said Dym. "He's just Tony's age—"

"Yes—I suppose he is," said Ginger. "It's funny how you always contrive to remember everything about poor little Tony. But you needn't waste your pity on young Max. He's all right. The Skipper, with a thousand more important things to think about, is doing his best for him. That's why we're here now. He gave us some money and told us to take the boy ashore and buy anything we could find in the way of warm clothes. The unlucky little wretch was caught and carried off while he was in the middle of dressing for a Hitler-Youth meeting. They took him just as he was and, two days later, handed him up our accommodation ladder in nothing but a rug wrapped round his uniform. We couldn't buy much—just an overcoat, a pair of knickers and a crimson pullover. And we've had our trouble for nothing, he says he's not going to cover up his precious uniform. He'd rather freeze. Well, we couldn't have a shindy in the shop, so we marched him along here still in his fancy dress—"

"And left him in the hall for everybody to stare at!" said Dym, springing to his feet. "Kind of you, upon my word! I'm going to bring him in for some coffee."

"Sheer waste of money," said Ginger. "He probably won't be able to eat the cake, and he's as likely as not to throw the coffee cup at you for your pains. Oh, we'll come with you to protect you. You're not used to Little Hitler yet. He isn't above kicking and scratching and makes no distinction between friend and foe. We've had our work cut out, I can tell you, to keep him from flying at the Norwegians whenever he saw them."

They went into the hall.

On a chair by the porter's office sat a boy in the regulation uniform of the *Jungvolk:* black shorts, brown shirt, and black neckerchief drawn through a braided leather holder. His bare arms and legs were purple with cold; his face was set hard for endurance. Dym looked—stood still—looked again. Then he turned to his brother. "It's Tony!" he said, very quietly indeed.

The captive flung up his head and stared at the airman steadily and defiantly. "Tony is not my name. I am Max Eckermann."

2

The End of a Quest

SOME HOURS later two men sat together in a room in the Naval Barracks behind the misty gray town.

"And you seriously think," said the elder, "that Max Eckermann is your brother Anthony, kidnapped ten and a half years ago, when he was eighteen months old?"

"I do," Dymory Ingleford answered gravely.

"Let me run through your story again. A little while before your father's death, you and your brothers and sister were staying at the seaside with your mother. One day a woman, who had been watching you as you played on the sands, came and spoke to your mother. She introduced herself as Anna Keller, a former schoolmate. Your mother remembered her?"

"Yes, she was one of the senior girls when my mother went to school in Switzerland."

"She took particular notice of Tony. Having played with him for the rest of the morning, she returned in the afternoon and again devoted herself to the boy. She told your mother that she had been married for many years, but had no child. She suddenly and hysterically begged your mother to allow her to adopt Tony. On your mother's prompt and firm refusal, she rushed away without saying good-bye or giving her married name. A day or two later Tony disappeared. It proved impossible to trace him?"

"Yes. You do understand, sir, that we did everything we could?"

"You?"

The pilot colored and laughed. "Not then, sir. I was only eleven. My people, I mean. They did everything they could, but—I told you that my father was killed in a car accident a few weeks later, while the search was still going on."

"Yes, you told me that."

"And I told you how Mother—"

The Captain's grave, sympathetic nod told the speaker there was no need for him to go over the story of the mother whose hold on life had been shaken by the double loss of husband and child. "The twins were barely a month old—my father and mother were both dead—my sister Margaret had been crippled for life in the accident that killed Father. Thomas, our eldest brother, had his hands full—no one could have done more for us all. But he hadn't the time or the ready money to continue the search for Tony. He was obliged to leave off. You don't blame him, sir? Honestly, he couldn't have done more than he did."

"No, no, I don't blame him. He had the certainty that the little brother was happy. You told me that, as a schoolgirl, Anna Keller had mothered the little ones with unusual tenderness. Your mother remembered her chiefly for her love of children?"

"Yes."

"Twice in the ten years a photograph of Tony was sent to your home."

"Yes. The first photograph came when Tony was six years old. I suppose some remnant of conscience induced her to send it."

"You had no clue—photographer's name, postmark, anything of that sort?"

"One clue. There was a smear across the back of the card, above the Tony. It looked as though someone, probably a child, had written and then rubbed out his name. Two letters were still fairly clear: a small *a* in or near the middle of a short Christian name and a small *n* almost at the end of a longish surname."

"H'm! That gives you two letters of *Max Eckermann* in their proper places, doesn't it? No other clue?"

"Nothing worth calling a clue. As the packet had been mailed from Paris, we had copies of the photograph inserted in the French as well as the German newspapers, but without effect. It wasn't a professional photograph. Amateur, and very good too."

"The publication of the photograph didn't frighten her out of sending a second?"

"Well, she didn't send another till August 1939, about three days before war was declared. She must have known then it was safe to do us a kindness—we wouldn't be in position to reward it with inquiries and advertisements!"

"And the second photograph?"

"It was accompanied by the sketch I showed you."

"I should like to look at it again."

For the second time Dym handed over the photograph.

"H'm, yes. It bears a marked resemblance to our young friend Max, a very marked resemblance— You're like him too, you know. I noticed the likeness when I first saw you. It did not strike your brother Reginald?"

"Apparently not, except for one moment when Tony reminded him of someone, he couldn't think who."

The Captain looked searchingly into the face of the young pilot who had carried with him the picture of the little lost brother. "I want to hear more about your attempts to trace him. You told me that from fourteen onward you went to Germany as often as you could— What made you so anxious to find him?"

"Mixture of motives, sir. First and foremost, I'd promised Mother that I would try to find him—then there's something alluring about a quest or a lost cause—and, after all, I'm his eldest full brother, so in a way I feel responsible for him."

"Your father was a widower with five children when he married your mother? Your half-brother Thomas is the eldest of the first family; you are the eldest of the second?"

"Yes. At first I couldn't do more than wander from place to place, learning the language and something of the people among whom Tony lived. I learnt a lot I should never have had a chance to learn in any other way. Some of it made me anxious to find Tony before it was too late. When I was older and could tackle the job better, I found the German officials kind and helpful, though they laughed at my wild-goose chase. Just before the war I got a clue at last."

"You were able to get in touch with an old member of the staff of your mother's Swiss school. Somebody who was able to put you on Anna Keller's track."

"Yes. The school had changed hands toward the end of Mother's time there; it didn't long survive the change. Everybody belonging to it had been scattered to the four winds some years before her marriage. But I succeeded in tracking down old Mademoiselle Leblanc, who remembered hearing that Anna Keller had married a wealthy business man—she'd forgotten his name—in the town that Max Eckermann comes from."

"You were on the point of following up your clue when the war came?"

"I was on leave, sir, and just about to cross from Switzerland to Germany, but a friend who was in a position to know told me a recall was expected at any hour. He warned me that if I went on with my plans I should be caught up in the whirlwind and interned in Germany till the war was over. It wasn't possible to risk that for my private concerns. I had to choose between Tony and—what had to be done."

"So you returned to England."

"I came back; yes."

In the silence that followed, Dym unfolded the colored drawing.

"I was wondering, sir," he said, "whether you would ask Tony to draw a picture of his home. A resemblance between the drawings would hardly amount to proof of his identity—but the coincidence would be curious, wouldn't it? I could get some colored pencils in the town."

The Captain took the sketch into his keeping.

"The other photograph and the letters that passed between my father and the English and German detectives are in my lawyer's hands," said Dym, "with the records of what I tried to do. I left them with him at the outbreak of war. There will have to be some sort of investigation of my claim to Tony, won't there?"

"Undoubtedly. In the meantime we are still where we were. You and your family won't want the boy until his identity has been established."

"Mayn't he come home with me now, sir? There's no

need, as far as we are concerned, to wait for the result of the investigation."

"You mean that you are sure you are right?"

"I am quite sure."

"You're not afraid of introducing a mixture of hurricane and spitfire into your hitherto peaceful home?"

The pilot shook his head, smiling.

"The rest of your people? Are you entitled to speak for all? What about your eldest brother? Aren't you going to consult him?"

"There's no need. I know what Thomas would say."

"Well, I'd be thankful to anybody who'll take the boy off my hands," confessed the Captain. "My married officers are turning deaf ears to hints that I want a temporary refuge for him, and my own wife says she's afraid to have him in the house with our two small children and three evacuées."

"Tony's all right, sir, really." There was a note of resentment in the airman's voice. "It's only the training he's had. It can't have gone very deep yet."

"I don't know. That training has been nothing if not thorough. Well, good luck to you."

"Then I'll take Tony with me, thank you, sir."

3

What They Told Max

"MAX! THE SKIPPER wants to see you," said Ginger Ingleford.

The boy slid off the long padded bench that skirted the gunroom wall. A visit to the Captain was alarming, but it would at least give him something fresh to think about. His thoughts had not been pleasant since meeting the British airman in the hotel. True, the stranger had been kind to him, kinder than anyone he had met since the shores of Norway vanished in gray smoke fantastically wreathed about pillars of midnight flame.

Flying Officer George Dymory Ingleford had not laughed at the prisoner in *Jungvolk* uniform tied to a chair by an ignominious handkerchief. With grave courtesy he had unfastened the knot, saying in good German, "A very cold day, isn't it? Come and get warm by the fire." After that there had been hot coffee to drink in comfort near blazing logs. He could have had two cakes as well. But he hadn't felt hungry since the first awful hour in the motorboat. Despite the fun and laughter in front of the fire, he had been on his guard; he had felt that the flying officer was watching him. And the explanation of the mysterious words "It's Tony!" had not satisfied him either.

The unknown Dym had volunteered a half explanation. "Sorry I startled you," he had said. "The fact is, Max, you're

17

extraordinarily like someone I know, someone I haven't seen for a long time."

Again it had seemed wiser to ask no questions. But there had been something strange in the look that passed between Dym and Ginger, something strange in their few low-spoken words as they waited for a fresh supply of coffee, in the way they went into the entrance hall together, talked to one of Ginger's officers who had just come in, and then telephoned to somebody from the hall. He had felt sure that in some way the talk and the telephoning had to do with him.

Now, hours after the picket boat had fussed its way back to the ship, he was still unable to shake off the memory of that most unexpected, most unwelcome greeting. Any change from brooding and puzzling could not fail to be a change for the better.

Ginger looked his charge over. "There's no time to get your face washed or your hair decently brushed, but at least I'll spare you another clean handkerchief. Mind you behave better than you did last time you honored the Captain with your presence."

He marshaled his charge to the door of the after-cabin. Sitting at his desk, the Captain smiled at his visitor.

"Come in, Max. I want to ask you some questions."

Max stiffened. "I will answer no questions."

"I'm not going to ask anything about the war work done at your father's factory. These are questions about yourself and your people. You understand what I am saying, don't you? I wonder how you learnt to speak English so well. You must have worked very hard in school."

"No. Not very," said Max.

"I've always been told that German boys work hard at school. Don't they?"

"Vater says they did, when he was a boy. Now there are out-of-school activities that have to be done as well. School work alone is not important. Besides—" He paused, looking doubtfully at the questioner.

"Well, then, how did you learn English if you didn't work hard at school?"

Max hesitated. "I had English playfellows," he said. "An English family lived next door for nearly six years. They went to England just before the war."

"Their name?"

"Their name doesn't matter now. They are British, and my enemies."

"I want their name, Max. You can have no reason for concealing it."

"I forget."

The Captain put down his pen and looked straight at Max. The gaze of the blue eyes was not to be defied.

"Their name is Cavendish," said Max, rather breathlessly. "Mr. and Mrs. Cavendish and Geoffrey, Michael and David. But I do not remember where they live now. I think I should know the name of the place if I saw it written down in a—in a—" He stumbled, groping for a word.

"In an atlas or a gazetteer? We won't trouble about that now. Have you always lived in Germany?"

"No, not always. When I was very little my father and mother were in South America, where I was born. Afterward we went to Japan. We did not come home till I was almost five."

"You told me," said the Captain, looking at the notes made during Max's first visit to the cabin, "that you were an only child, that your father's name was Heinrich Eckermann. But I didn't ask you for your mother's maiden name.

What was your mother's name before she married your father?"

"Anna Keller," Max answered promptly.

The Captain made another note. "Your mother has traveled a good deal, hasn't she? Did she ever go to Switzerland? I'm very fond of Switzerland myself."

"Lots of times. She was at school there, in a house with wistaria above the lake in Lausanne. I've seen it."

"It is a school still, then?

"No, it's a hotel now."

"I expect your mother had English friends at that school, hadn't she?"

"I don't know."

"Has she ever visited England?"

"I don't know."

"Tired of answering questions?" said the Captain goodnaturedly. "Just one more, if you don't mind. Fond of drawing?"

"Yes."

"Well, then, suppose you sit here and draw me a picture of your home. Not the Norwegian house you've been living in lately, but your own home. Here are some colored pencils. You may keep them if you like."

The shadow lightened on the boy's set face. He put out his hand for the pencil and paper. "I may do it here? Really? Not in the gun room? They would laugh."

"Yes, I want you to do it here."

It was the pleasantest half hour Max had spent in the last five days. He liked the clean, warm, airy cabin, made homelike by a bowl of pink hyacinths on the Captain's desk, and he liked handling the pencils that had *Bavaria* stamped on them. Besides, the Captain was amusing. He said that he himself couldn't draw and proved his words by drawing his own house for his prisoner to see. It was just such a house as the babies drew in the kindergarten: a square box with four square windows, a door and two chimneys, each with a neat curl of smoke. "That's the best I can do," said the Captain, laughing.

Max laughed with him for politeness' sake, though inwardly he was shocked that an important man like the Captain made a fool of himself. "Vater does not draw," he said kindly, "nor does Mutti; but they are both very keen on photography. Perhaps you are good at that?"

"Not brilliant," said the Captain. "Your parents do a good deal of it, then?"

"Yes, they make beautiful photographs."

"Ah," said the Captain thoughtfully, "that's interesting. Ever take you?"

Max retreated suddenly into his shell. "Yes. Herr Kapitan, the point of the green pencil is broken. May I sharpen it over your waste-paper basket? Thank you."

The drawing grew apace. Men with gold stripes on their sleeves came to speak to the Captain; in the passage outside the cabin a marine sentry marched to and fro. At the desk the Captain received reports, wrote letters, studied typewritten sheets.

"I have finished," Max said at last, regretfully.

"Bring it to me, please."

The Captain saw before him a house with a high peaked roof, window boxes in red and blue, balconies with curly balusters, fluted pillars, and a decoration of urns, tassels, laurel wreaths and pilasters modeled in high relief on the walls. But the railings now enclosed a garden that did not run steeply downhill, and there was no dachshund on the lawn among the roses and linden trees.

"It's very good indeed," said the Captain.

"It is an old house," said Max apologetically; "they do not build them like that today. Tante Bettina's house is quite different. It has a built-in air-raid shelter."

"I prefer old-fashioned houses," said the Captain. "Yes, an excellent piece of work, Max. You didn't put in any of your pets, though—dogs or cats or anything of that sort. I suppose you have some?"

"Not now," said Max, "it's difficult to feed them. We had a dog till just before we went to Norway last November. He died."

"What kind of dog?"

"Kunz was his name. He was a dachshund."

"They are nice little dogs," said the Captain, slowly unfolding a sheet of paper. "Seen this before, Max? You have improved in your drawing lately, haven't you?"

Max gazed at the paper in amazement. "How did you get that?"

"You know it, then?"

"Ye-es. It is a picture I drew for Mutti a long time ago."

"Your mother sent it to a lady who used to be at school with her in Switzerland. Your mother had English friends, Max, though she did not talk to you about them. Shortly before the war, she sent your sketch of the house to England with this photograph—Do you remember it?"

"Yes, it is—" As if struck by a sudden thought, Max broke off, turned the card and looked at the back. "There is a mistake," he said sharply. "This is the photograph of a boy very like me, whose name is Tony. My name is not Tony; I have already said so. You can see for yourself that I am Max Eckermann—look, here is my identity disk."

The Captain nodded reassuringly. "Don't be frightened," he said, "there is nothing to be afraid of. Surprised, aren't you, to find that you have English friends—relatives, perhaps—of whom you have never heard?"

"I have no English relatives," said Max indignantly. "I am not English."

The Captain drummed lightly on the desk, his eyes on Max.

Max spoke again, still defiantly, "If my mother had English friends, they would not call me Tony. It is not my name. I am not Anton, not Tony. I am Max." He twisted the card in his fingers, uneasily. "Who gave you this photograph? Was it that man in blue, the airman, Midshipman Ginger's brother? Who gave it to him?

The Captain answered, "Yes, he gave me the photograph and your sketch. His mother, who died a long time ago, was the lady to whom your mother sent them, not knowing that her English friend was dead."

"Why didn't she know?"

"Mr. Ingleford will tell you that himself. He kept the photograph and the drawing because he is also one of your unknown—we'll say friends."

It was as far as the Captain dared venture. Max had lost his home and all he held dear; this was certainly not the time to tell him that nationality and kindred were forfeit too. That must come from the airman with the grave, steady eyes; it was a matter with which no stranger could meddle.

"Now I'm going to put these papers into an envelope and seal them for the old gentlemen in the Government offices to read by and by. I took down the particulars on your identity disk last time you came to see me—yes, here they are. That's shipshape, isn't it?"

Notes, sketch and photograph were slipped into a large envelope marked *On His Majesty's Service*. Max spelt the words over while the Captain was sealing the flap. Then he said, questioningly, "Flying Officer Ingleford is going away tonight? I heard him say so."

"Yes," said the Captain, "he is going away tonight. Did you know that he had come to meet his brother for the first time since the war began?"

"That is what Midshipman Ginger told me. He cannot come back again?"

"No, he won't be able to get leave to come here again. His home is a long way off. Why do you ask? Do you wish to see more of him?"

"No, I don't. I have said that I do not want English friends."

"He would be a good friend to have. Do you know anything about his home or his people?"

"No."

"He and Midshipman Ginger are members of a large family. Their mother and father died more than ten years ago, and their home, the *White Priory*, now belongs to their eldest brother Thomas, who brought them up. Thomas is what is sometimes called in England a squire or gentleman farmer. From what I have heard today his is a cheerful, kindly household. There is a good elder sister whose name is Euphemia, and there are brothers and sisters not far from your own age."

Max said stiffly, "That is very nice for Flying Officer Ingleford and his brother, but it does not concern me."

"Well, Max, it concerns you more than you might suppose. You know I have been trying to find someone to take care of you for a few days until a permanent home is found for you. Mr. Ingleford, hearing of my difficulty, has kindly offered to take you home with him and leave you with his brothers and sisters when he goes back to his station."

"No! You promised that I should be sent to live with Germans—"

"Not at once, Max; you are forgetting. I told you there was bound to be some delay first."

"I do not wish—"

"No, I daresay you don't," said the Captain, with more sympathy in tone than in words. "You've had enough of traveling from place to place, haven't you? But I'm sorry there's no way out of it. I can't keep you on board and I must find you a home. Going to the *White Priory* won't be as bad as being handed over to another set of strangers. You know Reginald Ingleford already—"

"I don't like him."

"And you have met his brother Dym," went on the Captain, disregarding the interruption. "You liked Dym, didn't you? He is older than Reginald and—more sensible."

Max considered. "Flying Officer Ingleford is better than that Ginger," he said, "but I do not speak of liking my enemies. It is all one to me whether they are strangers or not. I don't want to go to the *White Priory*."

"Why not?"

The haunted look showed in Max's eyes again. "I would rather not go to my mother's English friends. If she had wanted me to know them, she would have talked about them to me. She always told me everything. Is there no other place to which I could go?"

Max looked hard at the Captain, measuring his slender strength against the other's quiet determination. With a sigh he accepted defeat. "How long must I stay there?" he asked heavily.

"I can't say. A fortnight probably. These papers"—he tapped them—"will have to go to London for consideration. Then you will be told where your future home will be. That clear?"

"Yes," Max answered, dispirited, despondent.

The Captain's blue eyes were full of pity. "That's all for the present, my boy. I'll see you again before you start. Can you find your way to the gun room by yourself? Good. And will you tell Midshipman Ginger that I wish to see him at once?"

Slowly and reluctantly Max made his way back to the gun room. In the doorway he paused and drew himself up, preparing to face any or all of his fifteen guards. Olaf would be there, too, not the tense, tight-lipped Olaf of former days but a new, laughing, uproarious Olaf who had been adopted into the gay band of midshipmen, an Olaf who talked with them on equal terms and took his fair share in the ragging and fooling that went on among those English boys. It was harder to meet Olaf than any of the others: the sight of Olaf always brought back the memory of his humiliation.

Max looked into the room, shuddering. As usual, Ginger was making the most noise. He was trying to convey information to a newly arrived friend, deep in talk with somebody at the other end of the room. "Hawke!" he was bawling. "Hawke! Heard the ghastly news?"

"No, what is it?" Hawke roared back.

He means to tell Hawke that I am to be sent to his

home, Max thought. Now Hawke will laugh. He will say he is sorry for the family. They will both say things they think are funny. He clenched his hands, bracing himself to endure.

"Did you ever hear," Ginger shouted, "that I had a small brother who was kidnapped when he was a baby?"

"No, I didn't," Hawke roared back. "If he was like you, he wasn't much loss. Has he turned up again?"

"Yes! Little Hitler's him!"

Max did not move when the bomb fell. The blood drummed in his head, a mist gathered before his eyes, and his knees sagged under him; but he stood where he was, gripping the colored pencils with all his might. He heard Hawke say coolly, "Rough on Little Hitler, that! Poor beggar, he has my sympathy. How d'you know?"

"Dym recognized him this morning, from a photograph. No, there's no positive proof—but you don't catch Dym making mistakes. It's Tony, right enough."

"Funny you didn't know him yourself," said Hawke.

"Little Hitler!" said Ginger. "Is it likely I'd guess? I do draw the line somewhere, though you mayn't think so."

"Glad to hear it," said Hawke. "What are you going to do with him?"

"Dym's taking him home."

"Gallant fellow, Dym. Deserves the V.C."

"Oh, shut up!" said Lance.

A sidelong jerk of his head sent all eyes doorward. Max had never known a silence so profound as that which followed. He heard his own voice, strangely shrill, breaking the dreadful hush. "It's a lie," he was saying, "a lie, all lies! I am not—" For a long moment he could not go on. "Not English," he ended, gasping as if he had been flung down and half drowned by a great sea wave. Then, speech failing him entirely, he had no power to do more than walk blindly to his old place on the padded bench under the scuttles, where he crouched with his world in ruins at his feet.

Someone came and sat down by him and talked in a language that was neither English nor German but a succession of sounds without meaning. At first he did not know who the speaker was but, after a time, the sight of the single gold stripe on the other's sleeve told Max that he was Archer, Sub-Lieutenant of the gun room, a stern ruler whom even Ginger obeyed with alacrity. Archer wasn't giving curt orders now; he was talking nonsense in a kind, sorry way that made him seem like the faint, far-off echo and shadow of someone else who had been kind a long time ago, as long ago as the distant middle of the morning.

Then, unexpectedly, he found himself able to understand what Archer was saying. He had been talking in English after all; at any rate, he was speaking English now, over his shoulder to somebody who was standing by the bookcase. "You'd better take over, Ingleford. I can't do anything with him, poor kid. A pretty kettle of fish!"

As Ginger came forward, the other occupants of the gun room melted away like fog wreaths. Within a minute the Ingleford brothers were alone.

"Look here, Tony," Ginger began awkwardly, "I'm terribly sorry. I honestly didn't mean you to hear. Hawke wasn't there when I told the others. I ought to have remembered you might be coming in at any moment, but I forgot."

"I am not Tony."

"Yes, I know it's an awful shock. They weren't going to tell you till you had got used to us all. I've messed up Dym's plans abominably by my carelessness; I'm sorry, Tony, really I am."

That hateful name again! Max shook off the hand Ginger had put on his arm. "Get out! I tell you I am not Tony. I am Eckermann, Max Eckermann."

Ginger drew back, rebuffed. He was all red now, Max noticed, red hair, red face, red ears. "I'd better tell you the rest, since I've let out the worst," he said uncomfortably. "You might as well know it. Mother had a German school-mate who married but had no children. She saw you when you were small, and wanted Mother to give you to her. I suppose she thought Mother could spare one out of such a lot. Mother wouldn't, of course. So she stole you."

"It is a lie, a wicked lie. I was never stolen."

"The Skipper thinks there's proof enough to justify him in sending you home with Dym." He paused, uncertain how far Max had followed his words.

The boy had turned away, hiding his face. A muffled voice said, "It is absurd—it is a mistake—" Two blue-gray eyes gleamed out of his tangled hair. "Go away, can't you? Go to your Captain. He sent a message that you were to come at once."

Ginger sprang to his feet in dismay. "You little bounder, why didn't you tell me before?"

In the midst of his misery Max felt a certain grim satisfaction. "To pay you out, of course. I hope you get into"—he sought for the most emphatic words at his command—"a very thundering row!"

4

The End of the Old Life

THE NEXT HOUR went by like an evil dream. Lights glittered, feet tramped, voices talked and laughed, cups and saucers began to clatter on the long tables. A hand put a cup of tea and some bread and butter before Max. He drank the tea thirstily, but pushed away the plate. Another hand—Lance's, he thought—wound up the gramophone. Max pressed his fingers against his ears to shut out the music; it was one of Beethoven's sonatas that Mutti had taught him long ago. Through the dull blaring came Ginger's voice. It sounded cross. Max had no means of knowing that it was apprehensive.

"I'm going to take you ashore now, Tony."

He opened his mouth to say "I will not go," but the words died away as a sense of his helplessness swept over him. What could he do, alone among a thousand men? For the moment he must submit.

"You'd better change before you say good-bye to the Skipper."

He shook his head. Here at least he could resist with some hope of success. Had he not for days past rejected the offers of warm clothing made by sundry members of the gun room, and had he not withstood Ginger only that morning when they went shopping? He would fight again.

"Oh, come on, Tony! Drop that nonsense! You put on

30

your coat this morning when Dym told you to. Why on earth make a fuss now?"

Dym hadn't given any command, Max remembered. He had said, "Here's your coat, Max," and had helped him into it without giving him time to protest. Then, somehow, he had been afraid that the airman with the quiet voice would think him silly if he took it off again. He had not wanted Dym to think him silly, but Ginger's thoughts did not count. Dym and this clumsy Ginger were miles apart. "No," he said curtly, "I will not wear the overcoat."

"You'll wear every blessed thing we bought for you," Ginger answered. "Do you think you can cross the harbor in a picket boat at this hour in next to nothing? Come and change at once."

"I won't."

"Oh, very well then. It's your own fault." He glanced over his shoulder. Lance, Hawke and another boy came forward. There was a short, furious struggle. Fighting to the last, Max was pinned down, stripped of his uniform, and thrust into the hated English clothes. "What'll we do with these?" Lance asked, holding up the tattered remnants of the *Jungvolk* brown and black.

"Oh, pitch them into the waste-paper basket," Ginger began impatiently. "No, give 'em to me. I'll send them home by Dym. Euphemia'll mend them, I daresay. Here's your knife, Tony. Just see if he's left anything else in his pockets, you two."

Breathless, trembling with rage, Max put the knife into its strange new home. Lance and Hawke emptied the other pockets, fumblingly. Then one of them came forward and, without looking at him, dropped a pencil sharpener, shaped like a tiny model of Cologne Cathedral, into his hand, while the other thrust a handful of German coins into his pocket. They felt queerly heavy, he thought, as if they had been turned into lumps of lead.

With the black-and-brown bundle under his arm, Ginger propelled his captive to the door. At the last moment Olaf Eriksen came forward, white but determined. "Good-bye, Max," he said in his halting English. "Good-bye and good luck. Of the best."

Max flung round. "When we invade Britain it will be my turn. That will be the end of you!"

Olaf's ear told him only that Max had not answered in German. He looked inquiringly at Ginger, who flushed, then smiled at the young Norwegian. "Thanks, Olaf," he said.

No one else spoke. When Max could again think clearly, he was once more in the cabin where he had spent his pleasant half hour. There he made his last protest. "It is a mistake. I am not British, not English. I am a German prisoner of war. I demand to be treated as a prisoner of war. You have no right to—"

"To what?" the Captain asked, very gently.

"To turn me into an Englishman—" He could make no further sound; the sentence quivered into nothing.

"We aren't going to do that unfairly. You are going to the *White Priory* until full inquiries have been made. If we find out that you are German, after all, you will certainly not be left there. That is a promise."

The words were comforting, but the comfort was short-lived. Almost as they were spoken Max saw the deep, steady eyes of the airman and heard again the two terrible words: "It's Tony." He cried out, in anger and despair, "Flying Officer Ingleford will make everybody believe what he pleases. I hate him. I hate England."

"Oh, you'll find that England isn't too bad," said the Captain.

"I shall at least be here to watch her defeat. When we invade her I shall be here to rejoice."

Then he held his breath and waited for the sky to fall. But the Captain still smiled. Laying his hand on the captive's shoulder, he said, "I've made you a promise, Max. Now I want you to make me one."

The use of the familiar name softened Max. His eyes asked a question.

"If you ever change your mind about England, will you write to tell me so?"

"I can easily promise that," said Max, "for I shall never change."

Ginger in oilskins at the wheel of the picket boat was not the noisy cheerful oaf that Max had known. His irresponsibility had disappeared; the young man who gave his orders to the crew was startlingly like Dym, grave, alert, intent. But when the two of them had passed beyond the guarded dockyard gates, Max felt that the young man was Ginger again, cheerful and thoughtless.

"We're going to pick Dym up at the hotel," Ginger said, steering his charge swiftly and deftly through the darkened streets. "Then I'm coming to the station to see you off."

Max said nothing. He had not spoken since his climb down the accommodation ladder; there was nothing to say. An east wind swept blindingly, bitingly down the narrow alleys that opened into the streets, piercing the blanket of fog. Here and there a bluish gleam of light showed under a hooded lamp; everywhere else blackness and silence reigned, save when sea birds cried or an army lorry rattled past.

Max shivered and dug crimson-cold hands into the pockets of the new coat. The British black-out was good on the whole, he thought. Not a glimmer of light showed in the windows of the shuttered and curtained houses. He would have a fair chance of escape in this darkness, if he could contrive to shake off a grip that was not so firm as Dym's. He had stumbled in the fog that morning, but Dym's arm had shot out to save him from a fall under the wheels of a car.

Dym had a grip that would never let go. But Ginger, careless as usual, was holding his arm lightly, apparently assured that his prisoner had given up all thoughts of escaping. A twist might do it. Ah, he was free!

He ran blindly down the street, bumping again and again into dusky shapes whose wrathful exclamations served to guide Ginger in pursuit. Try as he might, Max could not get very far ahead of Ginger, whose long legs covered the ground at an astonishing rate. Once he thought that he had baffled the pursuit, but his triumph was momentary. Ginger, pausing to open a door and shout a summons, resumed the chase with an abler ally at his side.

When Max heard shouted explanations behind him, he knew to whom those other light, swift steps belonged: Dym was hard on his track. Turning, he darted down a dark cobbled alley or wynd. Ginger blundered on down the main street, but Dym was not deceived. On came the relentless feet. Max, running with all his might, felt himself seized and pinioned. He kicked, struggled, and, in a transport of rage, bit the hand that held him.

The last frenzied action sobered him. His rage cooled as though a bucket of water had been thrown over him. Releasing the injured hand, he stood waiting.

Dym had not spoken throughout the encounter. Now, still holding the runaway, he got out a handkerchief, twisted it about his hand, and said in matter-of-fact tones, "You couldn't have gone much farther, Max; you were running into a dead end. There's the wall—not particularly nice to crash into—Lucky we stopped when we did, wasn't it? Now we'll go and find Ginger."

When they came back to the main street Ginger was not in sight. Dym paused outside a chemist's shop. "I'm going in for some plaster," he said in German. "Pull yourself together, Max, and don't look like that! You don't want the chemist to guess that you did it."

The chemist's shop was small and dark and crowded with goods. In the windows were three huge glass flagons filled with colored liquids, green, purple and red; they looked like vessels that might have come out of a giant's wine cellar. A large printed card, prominently displayed, said NO SACCHARINS TODAY. Behind the counter shelves ran from floor to ceiling, bearing line after line of white fat jars and stoppered bottles, labeled *aqua rosæ* and *tinct. sulph.* and *nux vom.* and a hundred other names. Glass-fronted cupboards hid the other walls; they were filled with patent foods and medicines and yellow sponges and boxes of pink and rose and lavender soaps that danced like balloons in front of Max's eyes. He stood passive, leaning against a counter.

All the fight had gone out of him; he felt very tired and his knees were trembling. Through a mist of frightened tears, he saw Dym open the little flat case, peel off the protective gauze squares and apply the sticky-edged strip of plaster to the ugly wound.

"Dear, dear," said the old bald-headed chemist, "that

looks bad. Knocked against something sharp in the black-out, I suppose?"

"Yes," said Dym. "I was unlucky, wasn't I, Max?"

He slipped the case into his pocket, smiling. Max looked down at the floor, which was moving about as the ship had moved. Above his head he heard Dym's quiet voice again, "My brother is rather done up tonight. He's had one long journey, there's another to come and he isn't a good traveler. Can you give him something to pull him through?"

"M'mphm!" said the chemist.

A second later the rim of a glass touched Max's lips. The liquid put new life into him. Instead of swimming up and down, the letters on the big card that said NO SACCHA-RINS TODAY stayed quite still.

Outside the shop they met Ginger, tearing up and down the road with the air of a distracted hen that had lost its only chick. He halted in amazement. Max shrank back, dreading to hear the story told. There would be one more black cross against his name when it went back with Ginger to the gun room that night. It wasn't fair, he told himself desperately. He hadn't been in the habit of biting people; he had never done it before. Then in the darkness he felt Dym's other hand shut tightly round his, as if to reassure him. All at once he knew that never so long as they both lived would Dym let anyone know what had happened in the dark wynd.

"Oh, it's you, is it?" said Ginger, panting. "What on earth did you want in there? I thought I'd lost the two of you."

"Max felt shaky," Dym explained gravely. "I asked for some revivifying mixture. What did he give you, Max? Sal volatile?"

Max made a great effort to speak. "I don't know."

"Sal volatile!" Ginger complained bitterly. "If anybody needs sal volatile, it's me. About a gallon of it, too. We'd better get your case from the hotel, Dym. We've not too much time before the train."

Nobody said another word about the flight that had ended so soon. Ten minutes later they were in a station, with twisted iron girders supporting what had once been a glass roof. Looking up, Max could see the stars twinkling down. There was no waiting-room either; it was a pile of rubble, planks, glass and bricks. Bombed! thought Max, a queer little thrill running through him. "Bit of a mess, eh?" he heard Ginger say to Dym. "Noisy time last night," Dym answered.

They threaded their way among little groups of people whose faces shone ghostlike under the shaded blue lights. Behind the pile of fallen masonry there were sounds of scraping and shoveling. Workmen's voices were singing a comic song that went on and on and never seemed to come to any particular end:

> *"It ain't a-goin' to rain no more, no more,*
> *It ain't a-goin' to rain no more,*
> *Oh, it ain't a-goin' to rain no more, no more,*
> *It ain't a-goin' to rain no more."*

Now Dym and Max were in the narrow compartment of a railway train. Ginger stood on the platform, talking through the open window. Dym was leaning out to answer. Max heard what they said, but the meaning of it floated away from him. Names caught his ear now and then: "Thomas— Euphemia—Richard." Then came the guard's whistle. As he waved his green flag, Ginger's red head poked itself through the oblong opening. " 'Bye for the present, Tony. Cheerio."

Max stared down at the empty cup and saucer somebody had left under the opposite seat. He would not reply.

"So long, Dym."

"So long, old boy."

They gripped hands. "Cheerio."

The train rumbled out. An old life was over; a new life had begun. Max Eckermann had become Anthony Victor Ingleford.

5

Night Express

CLOSE-FITTING black-out blinds blocked the small windows. In the roof a masked lamp shed ghostly blue light on the brothers. Huddled in his corner by the window, Tony waited for Dym to speak; but Dym said nothing for a long time. Tony was glad of that silence; it gave him time to recover from the wild chase through the streets. After some minutes he looked under his eyelashes at his new guardian who seemed to be asleep. He had been asleep early that morning, Tony remembered, all curled up in a big chair, tired out, on the other side of the glass door. Lazy, no doubt, like all the English. Hermann had said that they were weaklings, used to soft living and easy ways. It was certainly true that Hermann would have made two of the slightly built young Englishman. Tony shut his eyes the better to picture the German cousins he had left behind, splendid fair-haired giants every one of them from Wilhelm down to Fritz.

Then he made another survey of his captor. His eyes rested first on Dym's hands, slender but with a look of strength in repose about them. A feeling of respect crept into his heart as he remembered the iron grasp in which he had found himself for the second time imprisoned. "He held me as if he would never let me go," said Tony to himself. The thought of their struggle in the wynd brought with it a tingling of shame. What in the world would Geoffrey and Michael and David think of him if they should ever hear what he had done? He pushed the remembrance of the English boys away. They were not his friends now; they would never be his friends any more. What did their opinions matter to him?

But his eyes, drawn unwillingly again and again to that little strip of plaster, could not help seeing that there were other marks on the airman's hands—jagged scars of shrapnel wounds. Cousin Ludwig of the *Luftwaffe* had scars like these, Ludwig who had fought in the Battle of Britain. Had this feather-weight of a man really dared to match himself with such as Ludwig?

Tony looked once more at the quiet hands, and from them his eyes traveled slowly over the slumbering figure. He realized that it was not as inert as it looked. Dym's air of soft indolence was deceptive; every inch of him was ready to spring when need called. He might not be tall and fair, a son of the gods, but he was certainly fashioned after the Führer's ideal, "slim and strong, as swift as a greyhound, as tough as leather, and as hard as Krupp steel."

Tante Bettina had made him learn those words by heart, years ago. "That's what you've got to be, Max," she had said. "That's what my sons are." And so they were, and her daughters too. But not Onkel Dietrich, poor Onkel Dietrich. He was bald on top like the chemist, round-shouldered, with glasses and a pipe. Funny that Onkel Dietrich had married Tante Bettina. Mutti was afraid of Tante Bettina; most people were. Mutti always agreed with everything Tante Bettina said. Yes, Dym fulfilled the Führer's requirements, though in a way of his own that was not the German way. Something added or subtracted had made him different.

He looked last at Dym's face, hoping to find there the solution of the mystery. But it was not a fighting face at all; it was just one of those cold, reserved English faces that Tante Bettina had always disliked so bitterly. The English, she had said, were carved out of ice, and the more you thought you understood them the more you found you had to learn, you never could tell what they were thinking about. Camouflage! She doubted whether they knew what their own selves were like.

He hadn't understood Tante Bettina's harangue about camouflage; it had been easier to follow her when she calmed down and said, more simply, that all the English had faces like flat fish. No, she was wrong there. Dym's face might be cold and unreadable; but it was not a fish face any more than it was a fighting face like Ludwig's. Ludwig was every inch a fighter, with his heavy jaw and those eyes, grim and brooding, that seemed to be always staring down, down, down into darkness or flames. Did Dym's eyes look like that? Tony wondered. But Dym's eyes would tell nothing; English eyes never did. Yet he searched the masklike face again, for Dym had roused from his slumbers and was sitting upright now. It was possible to see. They were deep-set eyes. "The same color as mine," Tony reluctantly admitted to himself. He felt almost resentful when Dym slept again, his face once more impenetrably English.

Would it be possible to escape from this second careless guardian? If the train stopped while Dym still slumbered, could he slip out unseen into the night? But what would become of him, penniless, friendless, alone, and in the dark? No, clearly he must go home with this man to await the results of the promised investigation. To what sort of home, he asked himself. Not very desirable, he feared. The empty air of the compartment suddenly seemed full of red-headed people with Ginger's face, grinning in good-natured contempt.

"But if they do not treat me well, they shall pay for it," Tony told himself. "When we invade, they shall pay dearly. I have said so to Olaf and the Skipper, and I will say so to them." He frowned at the unconscious Dym. "If you succeed in keeping me, you shall pay worst," he threatened silently. "It's your fault that I am here. The Skipper and that stupid Ginger are not so much to blame as you. And you shall pay—oh, you shall pay!"

Dym wasn't asleep, it appeared. A little lazy smile darted out. "Which of the concentration camps are you planning to send me to?" he asked. "Dachau? That's the worst, isn't it?"

Tony flushed. His friends Geoffrey and Michael and David had been like that, he remembered. They too had the terrible English habit of guessing your thoughts and laughing at you and at them. But it wouldn't be a laughing matter for Dym if the threat should ever be carried out. Dym could not know that at home everyone went in awe of Onkel Dietrich and Tante Bettina because their third son was an officer in a concentration camp.

He was afraid of Ernst, though Ernst had always been kind to him. And it was when Ernst had come to Norway that he had told Max it was his duty to spy on the Norwegians. It was strange, but in a way Ernst was responsible for his being in England now. Just a flicker of a smile came to him when he thought of this, but he repressed it immediately and once more looked at Dym. It was only because the English had been born without any sense whatever that they laughed as Dym was laughing. Well, not laughing exactly; it was no more than a mischievous twinkle.

Spoken in German with that smile, Dym's words did not hurt. But before Tony had decided how to answer Dym's question about the concentration camp the train ran into a station. Out of the blue-darkness came a rush of cold air and a succession of lumbering, snow-besprinkled figures: an old, old lady in black, a soldier, a girl in breeches with a green armlet on her coat, a woman in golden-brown furs carrying a striped canvas shopping bag, a thin sandy-haired Scot and his thin sandy-haired wife. They filled the compartment to overflowing.

Tony stiffened, shrank back into his corner, gave the newcomers a hostile look. He had always felt like that in railway carriages. Tante Bettina had scolded him once for scowling so darkly as to annoy the other people. "You'll be mistaken for an Englishman if you're not more careful," she had said. He had never scowled again until this first night on British soil.

Shocked, he realized that he was already beginning to feel as the English were said to feel. That must not be. He looked at Dym. If Dym were frowning, there could be no escape from the logical conclusion of Tante Bettina's argument. But Dym was on his feet, lifting an old lady's heavy suitcase into a rack plainly marked FOR LIGHT ARTICLES ONLY. He'll get into a good old row when he's caught, thought Tony, but no indignant railway official came storming into the carriage. The guard who presently put in his head with a "Where for, please?" did not even notice it. The train ran on through the night.

Dym slept again, waking with a half apology. "My days are upside-down, Max, and the consequence is that I'm always sleepy at the wrong times. I fly by night like— like—"

"Bats and vampires," Tony said, gritting his teeth.

"That's not pretty of you," Dym responded, with another quick smile. "No. Like moths—*the blown flakes of December snows, tinted with amber, violet and rose.*"

It sounded as though he were quoting poetry. Tony was glad that Dym did not try to interest him in the unknown home to which they were going, did not ask him questions about the home he had left, did not put himself out to be companionable. There was something sinister about this take-it-for-granted-you're-mine attitude; nevertheless, it was easier to bear than voluble comfortings and glib assurances would have been. And it gave him time to steady himself in this strange new world.

Only the two Scots were brave enough to speak at last; all the rest sat like statues, gazing gloomily at the tight red cushioning of the opposite side. On and on and on went the train.

"What about a cup of tea?" asked the woman.

"Fine," her husband replied.

The others sat rigidly still, but with the air of persons who had pricked up their ears. When the Scots brought out a flask and a sandwich case, one by one the English began to fumble in cases or handbags. They ate in a self-conscious manner, bleakly silent. The soldier made one attempt to lighten the gloom. "Here is a mustard sandwich," he said in a clear, ringing voice, "and this is Al-var Lid-dell eating it."

Everybody except Tony smiled or gave a slight grunt not

far removed from a laugh. Only the Scot made any comment. "Plenty of mustard in the shops today, but vera little ham," he said, apparently by way of showing that he understood the joke. Tony did not think it a funny joke, nor could he understand why the soldier had called himself Al-var Lid-dell.

Silence again. Dym, wide awake now, had a thermos flask of coffee, some rolls and a packet of crumbly oatcake. "It's all I could buy in the town, Max," he said as he opened his shabby leather case. "How many rolls d'you think you can eat? Hungry?"

"*Nein,*" muttered Tony.

The British faces did not change; but their jaws stopped chewing and they all looked at him. He felt as if he had strayed into a meadow full of mildly inquisitive cattle. A horror of being different from the rest of the world suddenly seized him.

"I—I mean—" he stammered.

"Nine!" said Dym, easily. " 'Fraid you'll have to take it out in cake, old man. There were only seven rolls left in the shop."

Tony felt almost grateful for the readiness with which Dym had succeeded in making him seem exactly like everybody else, though hungrier than most. Sitting hunched in his corner of the compartment, he took the roll and the cup that Dym offered. Coffee twice a day was a luxury that he had not tasted for a long time. Dym produced a packet of saccharins to sweeten the coffee.

It was a solemn meal, eaten in a self-conscious manner by people who appeared to be ashamed of being seen to eat in public. The British don't seem to enjoy their meals as we do, Tony thought drearily. For no particular reason his mind went back to a picnic meal in a train before the war. How everybody had laughed and talked as they opened the great wicker hamper, and took out the crusty rolls and the sausages and the cold pickled meat and the cakes stuffed with cream and dipped in chocolate! He could see the delicate green of the lettuces and the gold-and-white of the hard-boiled eggs; he could hear the popping of the corks—

"Have some more coffee?" Dym asked.

"No, thanks," said Tony.

Dym put the cork into the thermos and replaced the cap. As he did so, a rapid fierce pattering rattled like hail on the carriage roof. Before Tony had grasped what the noise meant, he felt himself seized and drawn swiftly downward and forward across his brother's knees. Dym was bending over him, protecting him with his body.

Tony had never heard machine-gun fire on the roof of a train, but he knew what it must be. Crushed in Dym's hold, he heard bullets spraying above them like drops of molten metal.

"Nah then, nah then!" said the soldier, reprovingly. "Manners, Jerry my boy, manners! Didn't Ma learn you not to knock at the door like that?"

No one else spoke. There was a swishing sound, a tinkle of glass. Then from a distance came rumbling roars as of a lion disturbed in sleep. The metal rattle stopped.

"Good I didn't drop the thermos," said Dym.

He spoke to Tony, but he was answered by grunts of approval from the Scot and his wife. The rumble of anti-aircraft guns died away in the distance.

"Plenty of ack-ack," said the soldier, approvingly. "They gave him some hot stuff."

"Wonder where the bullet went," said the land girl.

"Look, it came right through the window. Must be some-where. Daresay the little boy'd like it for a souvenir."

And with that all the people in the compartment began to search for the bullet. Back in his corner, Tony gazed at them in amazement. Their stiffness had vanished; they were now like friends of long years' standing. When the bullet was tracked to its billet, four of them tried to dig it out with penknives and a corkscrew, refusing to stop until it became plain that the whole compartment would have to be taken to pieces before the bullet could be reached. Then a guard came down the corridor, shouting, "Any complaints? Any complaints? Any passenger got complaints to make?" A friend of the soldier came in. "Driver's hit, but he's carrying on," he said. "He'll get a relief at the next stop."

"That's where I'm getting out!" said the woman in the fur coat. "I'll be glad to get home, too."

"I'd like something more to eat," said the land girl. She took an apple out of her pocket and gnawed it with strong white teeth. The soldier ate another mustard sandwich with relish, and the Scot and his wife handed round a bag of black-and-white striped peppermints. The wife said to Tony, "Well now, you had a wise big brother to take care of you, laddie. And are you going into the Air Force too, when you're old enough?"

Tony raised his face proudly. "No, I'm going into the *Luftwaffe*," he said.

He was astonished to hear good-natured laughter. After the first shock, he realized that his companions were trying to show their appreciation of the joke he was supposed to have made. Before he could decide how best to undeceive them, the Scot was saying to Dym, "Ye'll not have seen service in France?"

"Yes," Dym answered.

"M'mphm. The R.A.F. put up a good show."

"I'm glad you think so, sir," Dym answered.

"It's surprising to me," said the Scottish woman, "that the Germans should have broken out like this. To look at them, you'd think they were douce, respectable folk. I was in Germany myself once; I stayed in Cologne. Quite near the railway station I was, at a little hotel that was very reasonable in its prices. I was young then and didn't heed the hooting and shunting of the trains in the *bahnhoff.* *Bahnhoff's* German for station, laddie," she explained for Tony's benefit. "Germany's ever such a funny place, laddie. You don't get a good breakfast with porridge and eggs and bacon; you get a jug of coffee and a basket of rolls and slices of brown bread. And in the streets you see stands to hold the workmen's bicycles. They're strung up in the air to preserve their tires, with mackintosh hoods over them to keep off the rain. A thrifty plan, I thought it. I bought a musical water jug one day for my Aunt Eliza. A nice foreign-sounding tune it played when it was lifted off the table. But the young lady in the shop packed up the wrong jug by mistake, and home I came with *D'You Ken John Peel* packed in ma trunk. Just think of the waste o't, me fetching *John Peel* all the way from Germany when I could have bought him in any of the big china shops at home. And Aunt Eliza wouldna give me a thank-you for the jug, either. She disapproved of hunting, you see. So I had ma trouble for ma pains."

"Hard luck!" said Dym.

"A proper wash-out!" said the soldier.

"Germany's a vera strict sort of a country," said the traveler. "Everything's *verboten*. *Verboten* means forbidden, laddie. You mayn't do this, and you mustn't do that. My German phrase book had a sentence in it. I don't mind the German words just now, but the English of them was '*Verboten* is a very important word in Germany.' And that was true!"

The very old lady in black looked up at a notice over the window:

TO STOP THE TRAIN PULL DOWN THE CHAIN
PENALTY FOR IMPROPER USE, FIVE POUNDS

She smiled the gentlest, sweetest smile. "All my life I have been afraid that one day the temptation would prove too much for me," she said.

"Don't suppose there's anyone who doesn't feel like that, ma'am," said the soldier, grinning.

Tony thought contemptuously that here was another proof that the English were mad. Tante Bettina had always said that they hated submitting to any rule or regulation, and here before him was an old lady, ninety at the least, who was not ashamed to confess that she was as mad as the rest. He was glad he wasn't English. Nevertheless, there was something fascinating in the thought of stopping a train, a whole long curving serpent of a train. He glanced upward, thoughtfully.

"No, you don't, Max," said Dym, laughing. "Not this trip. I can't afford five pounds for your fine."

And they all laughed again. Then the fur-coated woman took down her striped canvas shopping bag and gave each of her new friends three large onions in their pale-brown crinkly skins as a memento of their escape that night. The passengers accepted them with joy.

"My word!" said the soldier. "My missus wrote me she

hadn't even seen an onion for the last six months. I'm going home on leave, I am; but it's a toss-up if she won't be better pleased to see them than me!"

"Onions and lemons, they're a sore miss, both of them."

"And oranges and bananas," said the land girl.

"If we're going to grumble, I could do with a spot more meat."

"Eggs," said the old lady.

"Sugar," said the soldier, "according to our kids."

Tony nearly said "Coffee," but saved himself in time. The English weren't short of coffee; they must not know that it was scarce on the other side of the gray, tumbling sea.

"We're pretty well off, I think," said Dym. "There's always something to eat, and if there isn't something there's always something else. And when there's nothing you can generally make something out of that."

They began to discuss ways of making something out of nothing. Tony, listening, thought of a turnip pudding he disliked with all his heart and soul. Tante Bettina and her cook now did all the cooking for both households in order to save food and fuel, and were perpetually serving that turnip pudding. He hoped that the English did not feed on turnip pudding. To his relief, nobody mentioned it.

The furry lady was telling the company how to make date jam without sugar. Quite simple. They'd better remember that recipe because it would be valuable if ever jam should be rationed like tea and butter and sugar and the rest. She had an idea that jam would be rationed; they might depend on it, before very long. "And lucky if we get half a pound a month," she prophesied as the train drew up and she vanished into the dark.

Her parting words cast a gloom over those she had left behind. Tony wondered how much jam there was in half a pound, and felt that he had come to England at an unhappy time. The land girl said, "Jam rationing would be hard on the people who've got evacuées. Evacuées eat a frightful lot of jam."

Tony had never heard the word evacuées before; it was not a word that Geoffrey and Michael and David had ever used. But he soon made out that it meant the children sent out of the big cities by the British Government, to save them from bombing raids. They were put into other people's houses in much the same way as in Germany and the owners of the houses were obliged to take care of them. Sometimes their mothers or grandmothers came with them. "Evacuated mothers," the land girl called them. He wondered how the English, who did not like sharing a railway compartment, enjoyed being made to share their homes with strangers. There had been fierce quarrels in his home town because families, living in blocks of flats, had been ordered to save fuel by sharing sitting rooms. But whether or not the English enjoyed sharing, they evidently made themselves do it. It appeared that six evacuated secondary schoolboys and their master were quartered in Dym's house, and an evacuated mother and her three babies in two rooms over the garage. The Scot and his wife groaned when they heard the number.

"We had one mother and one baby," said the woman, "but she didna stop with us long, she didna like living in a small town after Glasgow. I'm sorry for you, young man. You don't get much peace and quiet when you go home on leave, do you? It must be as bad as living in a boarding school or an orphanage."

"It is," said Dym, "but I'm not often on leave, except for a few hours at a time. My eldest sister has to bear the brunt of it. We're a household of eleven in peacetime, though of course we're not all always at home. Now we're housing three old aunts whose house has been requisitioned by the War Office, and we're taking charge of three young cousins, whose parents are in India, and all our evacuées as well."

"I shouldn't have thought," said the Scot, "that with such a big family and a host of refugee relations you'd have been obliged to take evacuées."

"We weren't compelled to do it," said Dym, "but my brother happens to be billeting officer for the district. He couldn't very well billet children in other people's houses but not in his own!"

"He didna consider your poor sister over much, I'm thinking. But perhaps she has plenty of domestic help? She'll need it."

"She has one general maid and an occasional charlady," said Dym. "But everyone lends a hand."

The woman gasped. "Your sister must be a wonderful woman. And how does the laddie like sharing his home with all these strange folk?"

Tony did not know how to answer the question. It did not matter much to him, he thought, whether he shared the *White Priory* with one person or with forty. So he looked dismal and said nothing, whereupon the other travelers looked at one another and smiled as if they understood and shared his feelings.

He was growing sleepy now. When the soldier began to tell of his escape from Dunkirk in a nutshell of a river motorboat, he listened in a dreamy way, sometimes hearing and sometimes not. As the tale went on and on, everything slipped from him. He hardly knew what was happening when the train stopped again and dark figures left the compartment as mysteriously as they had entered it. A voice from very far away bade him lie down and go to sleep. Later, he had wakened, shivering. "*Es ist mir kalt, Mutti,*" he had murmured, thinking himself back in the air-raid shelter at home.

Mutti did not reply in words, but a moment later something soft and warm was tucked round him. "Kiss me, Mutti," he whispered, and held up his face. There was a little pause. For a few seconds he was afraid that Mutti could not be in the shelter after all, for she did not throw her arms round him as she had always done. But she bent down and kissed him, and he slept.

6

Journey's End

AS THE LONG steady note of the *Raiders Passed* signal
died away in its final howl of defiance, Tony raised
himself on his elbow, bewildered. Where was he? Not in
the air-raid shelter at home, nor in the Eriksens' house in
Norway, nor in the motorboat, nor in the battleship, but in
the narrow compartment of a stationary railway train in the
winter dawn. The masked blue lamp was out, the black-out
blinds were up, and through the nearest black-bordered
window a red ball of fire showed bright over the rim of a
snowy world.

He and Dym were alone; all the other people had vanished like spirits of the night. Looking down, he saw that
he was comfortably covered with Dym's blue-gray overcoat. Its rightful owner, pale in the uncertain light, was
smiling at him.

"That was the *All Clear*. Woke you up, didn't it?"

Tony did not answer; he was struggling with the first
pangs of bitter disappointment. All through the night he
had been at home again, the home of pre-war days when
there were wild-strawberry gatherings in the woods, sailing
parties on the lake, holidays in the mountains or among
flowery Salzburg valleys. Hours of sleep separated him
from the Tony who had clung to his captor while machine-
gun bullets rattled down. Dym was once more the stranger

with the masklike face who meant to rob him of his very name. Flinging aside the coat, he sat with his head turned away.

"Ready for breakfast?" Dym asked.

There did not seem much sense in starving. Tony answered by a nod.

"Couldn't have a meal here last night," said Dym, "it would have cost too much. But breakfast's cheaper than dinner, luckily for us. They'll be serving it in about ten minutes. Ah, that's better," as the train began to move. "You didn't know we'd been standing still for a long time, did you? The line has been blocked for the last two hours—snowdrift, crashed aircraft or time bomb, perhaps."

The commonplace words helped Tony recover himself. With a murmured word of thanks for the loan of the overcoat, he fell to wondering what he would find to eat in the restaurant car. For some months before he went to Norway, Tante Bettina had allowed him nothing but a bowl of bread and milk and an apple for breakfast. When he complained that it wasn't enough, she had said he deserved to go hungry like the English civilians, who would soon be reduced to eating frogs.

But there were no frogs in the dining car, where coffee, cornflakes, sausage, toast and honey awaited him. Another airman looked up at their entrance, hailed Dym, and beckoned them both to his table.

"This is Max," said Dym as they sat down. "You haven't met him before, Kitteridge."

The strange flying officer turned a pair of tired eyes on the boy. "Oh, haven't I?" he said indifferently. "Your place is always swarming with brothers and cousins and evacuées, I never know t'other from which. This one's like you."

Tony did not try to enter into explanations with a passing stranger who was manifestly uninterested in people of
about twelve years old. He slid into his place and remained
silent, listening hard. The other two did not speak of the
war. Instead, they talked about a friend's marriage, the
chances of skating, and the kind of cereal they liked best for
breakfast. Kitteridge said that there was nothing better
than oatmeal porridge; but Dym preferred funny little cream-
colored grains that went snap-crackle-pop when milk was
poured over them.

They made Tony remember more of Tante Bettina's
views on the English. "They are never in earnest, except
over trifles," she had said. "They sport with a straw because
their empty heads can take in only what is silly, frivolous,
irrelevant. Great matters have no meaning for them." Tony,
doing his best to make a little pat of butter serve a large
roll, thought that this was very true.

However, Dym and his friend became more serious
when breakfast was over. They talked then about Mr.
Churchill, a name familiar enough in Tony's lost home. Mr.
Churchill was the plump man with the cigar who made the
Führer and Tante Bettina so dreadfully angry. Dym and
Kitteridge did not talk about him in the way Carl talked
about the Führer. Carl was the fourth of Tante Bettina's
sons, and the quietest—the most like Dym, thought Tony.
When Carl spoke the Führer's name, his face lighted up and
he looked like the picture of an Early Christian Martyr in
one of Mutti's books. As if a white-hot fire burnt inside him,
that was the way Carl looked. But Dym and Kitteridge
discussed their leaders gravely, with masklike cold English
faces. They only laughed once, when Dym said that Mr.
Churchill had in him *A dash of Ariel, a streak of Puck.*

"What?" said Kitteridge. "How about *And something of the Shorter Catechist?*"

"It's there too," said Dym, "when we need it."

Tony could not make head or tail of what they meant. He wished that Kitteridge would take himself off, for Dym, left alone, did not talk in a way that was hard to understand. But Kitteridge did not go back to his own compartment when breakfast was over. He produced a book of crossword puzzles and invited Dym to join him in solving one. Tony's help was not required; plainly, Kitteridge did not think that it would be of any use. "There's a picture paper for you," Kitteridge said, jerking it across the table.

It was a very thin paper indeed, half the size of the stout *Berliner Illustrierte Zeitung* that had whiled away the journeys of old. When he had scanned its few pages, he put it down and sat staring through the window at this wicked England that now held him prisoner. He wanted to think it ugly, but he could not. It was like a fairy country in its spotless white robe. And, like all fairy countries, it changed from hour to hour and moment to moment: mountains, hills, marshes and water meadows through which gray-silver rivers crawled between snowy banks, fields marked by white hedges, lakes or pools ringed by rushes stiff as swords of ice, Christmas-card villages with red walls and snowy roofs clustered about a church tower, miles on miles of snow-clad moorland with birds wheeling dark above. Now he could have thought himself in Switzerland, now in Holland, now in Germany, now in France—and now in no country he had ever seen before. And always he was convinced that the sea was not far off. He looked for it behind every swelling ridge of meadow or broken chain of hills or far stretch of level land; nor had continual disappointments power to make him abandon his search for the triumphant sea.

Triumphant sea! Where had he heard those words? Oh, yes, Michael Cavendish had once learnt a page of Shakespeare for his holiday tutor, lines that told of *England bound in with the triumphant sea.* There was no way of escape from this sea-girt fairy island till the Führer gave the word to invade. When would that be? Nobody could tell. Only one fact was dismally certain: that it would not take place now in bitter cold, amid high seas and drifting snows. He must wait, wait, wait.

A wave of homesickness rushed over him. He wanted Mutti, yes, and Vater too, though Vater wasn't an affectionate father to him as Onkel Dietrich was to his children, who still called him Vati, though most of them were grown up and old, older than this Dym. Vater smoked and read the newspapers with a furrow on his forehead, and now and then he said, "Ach, Max, not so much noise if you please. You are like a whirlwind in the house." Would they say that to him at the *White Priory?* He would have no Mutti now to laugh and hold out her arms with a joyous, "Max, *mein liebling!* My darling whirlwind!" He clutched the edge of the table with all his might. He could not cry in front of these English fools, absorbed in their silly crossword puzzle. He could not cry! But the big window had become a misty square, and all the brown English heads at the further tables seemed swimming about like chestnuts newly dropped into a pan of water.

"Tired, Max?" asked Dym, without turning his head. "This is boring for you, isn't it? We shall change into another train soon. Think you can find your way back to our carriage? I'll come when I've finished this."

Tony rose and fled. As he stumbled from carriage to carriage of the swaying train, he made the poor beginnings of a plan to hide in the wrong compartment and escape as soon as they reached the next stop; but he dismissed it on remembering that, without a ticket, he could not pass the station barrier. I can't get past the—whatever it is in English, he thought. Dym knows I can't get away; if he hadn't felt quite sure of it, he wouldn't have let me come back here alone.

Huddled in his old corner, he cried himself quiet. When he had fought himself back to calm he had time to feel injured by Dym's continued absence. He did not want Dym's company; but he resented being treated as of less importance than a crossword puzzle. This self-styled brother of his might well have been kinder. Yes, Tante Bettina had known what she was talking about when she declared that the English had no hearts; they were a set of ice-blocks dressed up in clothes. But at least Dym should not have the satisfaction of knowing that a German had cried. He pulled out Ginger's last clean handkerchief and rubbed his face hard, hoping that Dym wouldn't choose that moment to appear. His involuntary glance into the corridor made him turn hot all over, for there, leaning against the outer window with its back to him, was a slight blue-gray figure apparently deep in contemplation of the scenery.

But when Dym came into the compartment, no one could have guessed whether or not he knew anything of the tempest that had been raging within a few feet of him. He entered, with a casual, "We're late, you know. I'm afraid we'll miss our connection. But there'll be another train after lunch. It's a long way across the town to the other line. Shall we take a taxi or would you rather walk?"

"Walk," said Tony because it was the shortest thing to say.

"So would I. We've had enough of sitting still, haven't we?"

The train was running into a city. It slackened speed and stopped, and they were on a platform crowded with men and women in khaki. Kitteridge's face showed for a moment over somebody's shoulder, then vanished. They were in the station square now, turning into what had once been a street with shops on either side. But it was no longer a shopping street. It wasn't any kind of street. Huge holes in the roadway were blocked off by rope and red flags; the pavements were a sea of plaster, bricks and broken glass. Behind them the shops and offices lay roofless and windowless, shattered into shapeless heaps. The snow was trampled into gray slush; the air smelt of burning. Grimy and tattered, a rescue party went by, carrying on a stretcher a man who had been dug out of the ruins. Tony shuddered and looked away.

They turned into another street. The wind was very cold; snow was falling lightly. People passed in unending streams, their faces pale, their clothes dark. Soon they came to a maze of small back streets. These too had been bombed. Some of the houses had lost the whole of their front walls, but the furniture was still in the rooms from attic to kitchen. Cousin Margarete's doll's house had looked rather like that, Tony remembered. Other houses were masses of fallen bricks, with planks and beams sticking out of them like the ribs of a ship stranded on the beach. Men and women, their faces streaked with dirt, were coming away from the ruins. Some carried bundles of clothes; others were pushing baby carriages or wooden handcarts or wheelbarrows loaded with blankets and odd bits of furniture. The same bitter smell of burning was in the air, and every now and then dense clouds of brown smoke swept across the strip of sky between the roofs. Firemen in dark blue dashed past with a clatter and clang.

Once they stopped to watch a man rescuing a kitten from the top of a pile of bricks and jagged iron girders that had once been a home. He was risking his life to save the kitten, but the kitten was not grateful for his pains. It snarled and scratched, spat and bit all the way down the ladder. But the man brought the little frightened wild creature safely to earth and held it high in the air, shouting, "Hoi! Hoi! Who wants a kitten? Home wanted for a nice-behaved kitten!"

Everybody stood still to see what would become of the kitten. The weary men and women brought their carts to rest, peering at it through red-rimmed eyes. Faces appeared in blown-out windows. Then a fat, motherly woman opened her shopping bag. "I'll take the kitty, lad," said she. "Shove it in."

Down went the kitten among bundles of firewood, tins of fruit and packets of rice and oatmeal. Its little angry black head stuck out, but the rest of it stayed inside. It can't get away, thought Tony, it's just like me.

Suddenly he felt that he did not want to walk any more. He looked up dumbly and found that Dym understood. "Like a rest, wouldn't you?" he heard Dym saying. "Come along, then. You can sit at this table while I'm telephoning."

And then Tony saw that they had left the road and were in a large post office with a floor tiled in black and white. It was good to be apart from the noise and the brown smoke and the smashed houses, although it was alarming to have no remembrance of how he came to be there. He sank gratefully into a chair by the letter-writing table, and shut his eyes the better to think of nothing. When he felt better, he looked about and saw Dym in a telephone booth not far off. Presently Dym came to the table. "I can't get through to the *White Priory*," he said, "the line's out of order. I tried and failed yesterday, too. Bombs, probably. I want to tell them we're coming."

"Send a telegram," said Tony.

"I sent one yesterday, but I'm afraid it mayn't have been delivered yet. They're so slow in wartime. Now, let's get something to eat. There's a place quite near."

They lunched in a restaurant that had had its windows blown out in an air raid. The waitress did not ask them what they would like. "It's fried fish or hot-pot," she said. "Tapioca pudding."

"Any lemonade?" Dym asked.

"No, sir," said the waitress, "there isn't. There wasn't even a glass of water, first thing this morning. A bomb hit the mains last night and messed things up a bit. It's all right now, though."

The broken windows were covered with plywood shutters and tarpaulin sheets; electric light took the place of daylight. Tony could not eat for the hot glare and the rattle of plates. He was glad to be out in the air again, tramping through the muddy snow to the station.

They stopped at a bookstall with a few papers and magazines on it, all of them thin like the paper he had seen that morning. "We're badly off for paper now," Dym explained as they went down the platform to the train. "A lot of our paper pulp comes from Sweden. It can't come now."

"I know," said Tony.

"Fond of reading?"

"Yes."

"So am I. Have you read many English books?"

Tony hesitated, wondering whether it would be wise to tell Dym that he had read every book that Geoffrey and Michael and David Cavendish possessed. There was a hidden cupboard crammed with English books in his home at that very moment; it held gifts inscribed *Max from Geoff, Max from Mike, Max from David,* as well as all the books they had not been able to take home with them when they went back to England. "Yes, I've read some English books," he answered cautiously. "It is a good way to learn another language."

They got into the train, which was very crowded. Tony's head was aching so badly that he did not trouble to look at the new people; they were merely faces and bodies that flitted in and out from station to station. For politeness' sake he opened the illustrated paper that Dym gave him, but it lay on his knee unread. Dym, opposite, read closely. Once he wrinkled his forehead as if he had found something that displeased him. He tore out a paragraph and put it into his pocket, then held out his hand. "May I have your paper for a minute, Max?"

Tony pushed it over. Dym scanned the columns, frowned again, and tore off a corner before giving the rest back. Tony wondered listlessly what there could be in an English newspaper that Dym did not want him to read. Dym was not frowning now, but the lines of his face were stern. Tony shut his eyes; he did not like to see Dym look stern. When he opened them again, the other occupants of the carriage were hurrying down the corridor. The train itself was standing still.

"It's all right," said Dym. "There's another delayed-action bomb on the line, that's all. We've got to stay put till it's been dealt with or till it goes off, whichever happens first. The guard came while you were asleep. He says we're safe here, but the other people thought they'd prefer to have a few extra yards between themselves and brother bomb."

"I am not afraid," said Tony proudly.

"Good for you. We wouldn't be popular if we tried to squeeze into the far end of the train; it was packed tight before we started, wasn't it? And it's an ill wind that blows nobody any good, for we have the compartment to ourselves at last. I wish we'd had the luck to stop at a station, though, for there's no tea on the train. I'm afraid we're booked for a long wait, too."

Evening found them still waiting. The red glow of a winter sunset had died, leaving them in a solemn white world. With the chill of oncoming night, queer fancies played in Tony's head. This unknown family—it was unlikely that they really wanted to find a brother. No, what they were looking for was a boy slave who would work for them on their farm as that Polish prisoner worked at the farm where Mutti and he had spent a day last summer. Now the tables were turned, now an English family had hold of a German boy. Dym was perhaps less terrible than the rest of them, certainly less hateful than clumsy, grinning Ginger. Better, far better, to be set free to wander in the snow! He would make one last desperate appeal.

"Flying Officer Ingleford—"

The twinkle showed again. "You needn't call me that."

"Herr Ingleford—"

"No, nor yet Herr Ingleford. If anyone is Herr Ingleford, it's Thomas; he's the eldest. I'm only Dym for common and George for state occasions. Call me Dym, please."

"Herr Dym, let me go."

"What, now this minute?"

"Yes."

"You'd be lost in the snow."

"That would be better than—"

"Going home with me? No, it wouldn't, Max. You're tired out and cold and very miserable, but things won't look so black when you find yourself by a fire again."

"I want to be sent to my countrymen."

"You must come with me for the present. The Government will soon make inquiries."

"So I have been told, many times. But I do not want to wait for the inquiries."

"Why not?"

Tony's mouth quivered. "The inquiries will turn the way you want. You get your own way, always. The British Government will say I am your brother, though I am not. Let me go."

"I can't do that."

"There is no reason why you should want me for a brother. I am German, I shall always be German. You do not like how I behave. Your brother, Midshipman Ginger, called me by names of contempt. Let me go, Herr Dym; let me go."

Through the gloom he saw the Englishman's eyes looking at him, resolute and grave. "Anthony," said Dym quietly, "it is just because you are my brother that I cannot let you go."

Tony's last hope had failed. He did not well know what

happened next. In after days he could only remember darkness creeping over the white meadows and blotting out the
larch trees that stood holding out their long snowy arms to
him from a wood close to the line. They seemed to be
inviting him to come to them, those trees, but he was
powerless to answer their call. Then there were drawn
blinds and blue lights, a sudden jerk as the train shook itself
and went its way, a relentless sound of wheels drumming
and drumming and drumming—then a sudden startled
discovery that he wasn't in the train any longer but on the
platform of a country station—then more darkness and
swirling snow and a voice that spoke steadily and cheerfully.

"We shall have to walk, Max, but it isn't very far. My
telegram can't have reached them; they'd have sent the car
if it had. Hold my hand tight; don't let go or you'll slip into
a drift. No, no, you needn't be frightened. I know the way,
and I can see in the dark like a cat. Come along."

Earth and air and sky were blended together in a dancing, eddying whiteness as Tony was led from the shelter of
the station into the night beyond. Stumbling and swaying,
he went forward. At first he held Dym's hand as he had
been bidden, but, after a time, he felt Dym's arm about his
shoulders, supporting him.

"Are we nearly there?" he asked.

"Very nearly there," Dym answered. "This is the gate."

It was a tall iron gate between square pillars surmounted
by stone balls, and it gave entrance to a drive bordered by
trees. The snow did not beat down so fiercely here; the
bitter wind could not reach them. Now a house loomed
above them, no gleam of light showing in any of its darkened windows. Dym opened a door and drew his charge

into deeper darkness. Tony stretched out a hand, gropingly; it met a screen of plywood and curtains.

"Stand still for a minute," said Dym. "I must shut the door before putting on the light. There, now we're safe." He fumbled for the switch. As he touched it, a door opened within the house and faces, many faces, showed in the square hall where the travelers stood.

Voices cried, "Oh, it's Dym! Hullo, Dym!"

"Didn't you get my telegram?" Dym asked.

"Telegram? We've had no telegram," said a woman's voice. "You shouldn't be so extravagant, Dym. The idea of sending telegrams in wartime when you know they often take two days to arrive! It's sheer waste."

The voice was brisk and high; it hurt Tony's ears. A small shrill voice added, "There's a boy with Dym, a strange boy. Who is he?"

"Tony," Dym answered.

Tony tried to say, "I'm not; I'm Max," but the words never left his lips. There was a buzzing in his head; it rose to a roar and died down into great quiet blackness.

7

After the Crash Landing

"HERE IS the eight o'clock news," said a clear, measured voice, "and this is Alvar Liddell reading it."

Bewildered, Tony opened his eyes and stared about him, half expecting to see a khaki-clad figure holding a sandwich that had more mustard than ham in it. But he was alone in a large attic with a blacked-out skylight and windows perched crookedly in the eaves. Three empty, unmade beds were to be seen. A fire was burning. The door stood open, behind black-out curtains the windows were open too, for a frosty breeze was dancing through the room. Tony pulled the blankets round him to shut out the noise of the loud-speaker; he did not want to hear what the British announcer had to say. These precious moments of solitude must be spent in hard thought.

First he tried to remember how he came to be in an attic that looked like the pictures of the old-fashioned dormitory in Michael's copy of *Tom Brown's Schooldays*. Last night there had been lights and whispers and hurrying feet. Then strong arms had carried him upstairs into quiet. Someone had undressed him and put him into a bed with sheets that smelt of lavender. He thought he had seen a tall, thin woman kneeling, bellows in hand, by a newly kindled fire. She had given him a hot-water bottle—yes, it was still there, limp and lukewarm in its red cover. They had given

68

him something hot to drink, and then he had heard a little shrill voice in the hall. "Simon and I want to kiss Tony just once," it was saying. "May we?" And Dym's voice had answered, "Yes, just once, Judy, if he doesn't mind. Will you let Simon and Judy kiss you, Max?"

If his life had depended on it, he could not have spoken. He had accepted two funny solemn kisses without seeing who gave them. After that, other people had kissed him without asking permission. Then everything had slipped back into darkness.

There had been a faraway consciousness that he was not alone, but he had not known how many others were in the room. Once he had fancied he saw Ginger, sitting in front of the fire in his pyjamas, his arms clasped round his knees, but, looking again, he had seen that the face under the sandy hair was younger and thinner and a little like Dym's.

"Are you Ginger?" Tony had asked feebly, anxious to make sure.

"No, Jim," the red-haired boy had answered, smiling.

"Dym?" Tony had asked, frightened and puzzled.

"No, James. Jim's short for James. There's Dym, close beside you in that chair."

When he looked, he had met Dym's slight, reassuring smile close by. He thought that Dym must have spent the whole night in the armchair, for, as often as he woke, gasping, from another horrid dream, there had always been a steadying hand to clutch and a steadying voice to hear.

Tony turned his head painfully, half expecting to see Dym by his side still. But the shabby leather chair held no tireless watcher. Dym and his family were no doubt at breakfast and listening to Alvar Liddell's eight o'clock news bulletin at the same time. They thought their prisoner fast asleep—more fools they! Long before anyone came to make those tumbled beds, he would be gone.

Swaying giddily, he scrambled out of bed and looked round for his clothes. On a chest of drawers his pullover made a spot of dark crimson. He staggered across, leant against the chest for a minute to rest himself, then dressed as fast as his trembling fingers would let him.

The stairs—there were two flights—creaked hideously. They brought him into a square, galleried, red-flagged hall with many doors, behind one of which Alvar Liddell was still booming away unseen. Under cover of the ringing voice, Tony wrestled with unfamiliar fastenings and fled.

It was a pitiful attempt at escape, and it ended ignominiously by the entrance gate, to which he was clinging when Dym tracked his footprints in the snow. Too weary even to feel afraid, he looked up to find out whether Dym was angry. Dym, however, did not appear to have the least suspicion that his prisoner was running away. "So you thought you'd like an early walk, did you?" he said, with a supporting arm round Tony's shoulders. "You're not fit to go exploring yet, truly you aren't. Head's still splitting, isn't it? Come back to bed. We're going to keep you there till you feel better."

Tony said nothing because he had nothing to say. Dym led him back to the house, tucked him up in bed again, and refilled the hot-water bottle. Then the tall thin woman came in, bringing breakfast that he could not eat. He saw her shake her head as she turned to Dym.

"I wish you weren't going away, Dym. He's ill."

Tony had forgotten that Dym's leave was up. He did not love Dym, but for two days Dym had been like a rock in a

wild sea, something that stayed in its place when everything else heaved and swayed about him. He said unstead-
ily, "Herr Dym."

Faint as they were, Dym caught the whispered words.
He bent over the bed, and one pair of blue-gray eyes met
the other. "What is it, old man?"

"Don't go away, Herr Dym."

"I must. Euphemia will take care of you, and so will
Thomas. You saw him last night. He's bigger than I am; he
carried you upstairs. Thomas will be kind; won't he, Euphemia?"

"Of course," said Euphemia. "Thomas is always kind.
We'll take care of you, dear."

Tony was not in the least grateful for the promise. He
pressed his face into the pillow and drew the clothes over
his head again.

After Dym had gone the house seemed empty, though
Tony knew there must be about twenty people in it. Hours
went by in feverish dreams. He was cold and aching from
head to foot; the room moved up and down, up and down,
as if he were on board ship. Through a mist he caught
glimpses of Euphemia whisking to and fro, brushing, dust-
ing, tidying. Then the red-haired James came in softly,
curled himself up in Dym's chair and pretended to read. By
and by it seemed to Tony that there were two of James, two
thin faces with untidy red hair and sparkling green eyes.
They were looking at him, though they still pretended to
be reading. The second James, he discovered, wore a skirt.
It was a girl. He heard James call her Sally. In the afternoon
the doctor came to see him.

"You're not ill," the doctor told him. "But you'd best stay

in bed because you've made what our friend Dym would call a crash landing in England. Bad, these crash landings. Always mean an ambulance party. You'll feel better soon."

Then he turned to Euphemia and said, "The boy understands English, doesn't he?"

"I don't believe he understands it half as well as Dym thinks he does," said Euphemia. "Anyhow he's too dazed and confused to understand anything today."

"There's nothing wrong but shock and exhaustion," said the doctor. "Keep him warm and quiet; that's all you can do for him at present."

"Quiet!" Euphemia exclaimed. "Quiet! Why, I can't even give the poor child a room to himself! He must sleep here with James and Porgy and Simon. As you know, we're crowded like sardines in a tin."

"I know," said the doctor.

Euphemia counted on her fingers. "Two evacuées in Margaret's old room, two more in Mortimer's room, two more in the second attic, Mr. Bland in Richard's room, Thomas in the study because Aunt Addie and Aunt Penelope have his room, an evacuated mother and her three babies in the two rooms over the garage, Mary and Mousie in Ginger's room—"

Tony's head began to spin.

"Aunt Desdemona's sleeping in the drawing room, so he can't even have that. And he can't share with Thomas because the study is a billeting office as well as a bedroom. I might put him in with Mortimer, of course. Mortimer is in Dym's room now; they share it when Dym comes home on leave. I didn't dare put any of the evacuées into Dym's room because he has one or two really good pieces of furniture that belonged to his mother. You never know what may happen with strange children, do you? They might hack at the carvings on his bookcase, or cut their names on his beautiful old desk. So Mortimer moved in, and brought his own possessions with him. Yes, I might put Tony with Mortimer—but it doesn't seem quite fair to Mortimer. He's working desperately hard—fire-fighting, Home Guard, Scouts, and full-time teaching. It's a seventeen-hour day at the least, and that for a man who was turned down as physically unfit for the Army! I don't think he ought to have his night's rest disturbed by the presence of a sick child; it would be cruel. Besides, Mortimer isn't really much good with children—"

"Ought to be," said the doctor. "He teaches."

"That's just it," said Euphemia. "He's all right in the classroom, but otherwise he's helpless. The one we really want is Dym. He was wonderful last night with poor little Tony. I wish you could have seen him. As for me, I feel just as awkward as Mortimer. I've no notion how to deal with the child."

The doctor said, "Don't ask him questions or talk to him too much. And don't overdo kindness. What he chiefly needs is a feeling of security; somebody or something hard and firm to cling to in a world that has turned upside-down in a moment. He doesn't want fussy affection showered on him, probably won't want it for a long time to come. Don't be surprised if he rewards your care with indifference, flat ingratitude, defiance. Don't be surprised at anything. And, above all, don't think too seriously about the reason for his coming here. You needn't regard his bullying of the little Norwegians as an indelible family disgrace! Make yourself and the others see that the fault lay not so much in the child himself as in the way he has been trained."

"That's what Dym says. But I can't help wishing Tony had reached England in some more creditable way. It is disgraceful, look at it how you will. And it can't be hidden, now that the newspapers have told the story of the little Nazi bully. Dym's awfully upset about that. It must have got out through one of the ship's company. You saw it, didn't you?"

"Yes. But remember, Euphemia, the papers didn't give Tony's name, either in German or English."

"They might just as well," said Euphemia. "Of course all the people who know us have read how Tony came back to us. The rest of the world doesn't matter."

It was easy to guess why Dym, frowning, had torn a paragraph out of the newspapers. "He forgot that I shouldn't think it a disgrace," Tony told himself proudly. "I did nothing of which I need be ashamed. Ernst instructed me in what to do." Nevertheless, he listened eagerly to Euphemia's next words, anxious to find out whether these new people were always going to look at him as Ginger had when he insulted Olaf. In Dym's company he had nearly forgotten about Olaf and Nils and Inger. Nothing in Dym's manner had made him think of them.

"The people who know you will understand," said the doctor. "They'll make allowances."

"Dym thinks they will. He says we shall make a fatal mistake if we ever let Tony feel we're ashamed of him. We mustn't be ashamed, he says. That's not too easy. I feel hot all over when I remember those poor little Norwegians."

A sudden blind longing for Dym's company swept over Tony. He moved restlessly. Euphemia looked down. "What is it, dear?" she asked slowly. "What do you want?"

He could not tell her that he wanted Dym because

Dym alone in all the world found it easy not to be ashamed of him. "I would be glad for you to stop talking," he said. "The noise of your much speaking makes my head ache." He spoke haltingly and clumsily so Euphemia and the doctor might not suspect that he had understood them. Euphemia did not guess. She laid her finger on her lip and nodded, smiling, to show him that she did not mean to talk any more. "Go to sleep, Tony dear," she said, shutting her bright blue eyes vigorously three or four times to show what she meant. "You will be well when you wake up."

He went to sleep obediently, but he was not well when he woke. For two or three days life was a strange, shifting pattern of darkness and light. Unknown voices hailed him; unknown faces peered at him. Then, little by little, the earth whirled slower and slower until it went round at a pace that made it possible to sort people out and remember their names. About Euphemia there had never been any doubt. Even in the hours when he wasn't sure whether he was on board the battleship again or huddled in the motor-boat, the sight of Euphemia steadied him. Sometimes in the morning she tied up her hair in a green scarf twisted about her head. Tony knew that green scarf when every other object seemed misty and unreal. And, though he had been told that the British were not to be trusted, he couldn't help trusting Euphemia when she assured him over and over again that she would not keep him at the *White Priory* if he could prove his German nationality.

"You promise, Phemie? You promise faithfully?"

He called her Fräulein Ingleford when he felt well enough to make the effort, but at other times he called her Phemie, the name he had heard Dym use when he said good-bye. Euphemia, he noticed, liked being called Phemie.

It was generally at bedtime that he asked his question, with Euphemia's arms round him as she kissed him good night. Her way of saying good night to Tony differed not at all from her good night to little Simon in the corner bed. He thought she could not be very good at remembering to feel ashamed of him, for she gave him a comfortable nightly hug.

"I promise faithfully, Tony. If you turn out to be a German boy, after all, I won't keep you here one minute after the Government has found a proper home for you. Of course not."

"And you will not allow Herr Dym to keep me here, either?"

"I can't make any promises for Dym, dear. But he wouldn't be allowed to keep you. The Government would take you away."

"Herr Dym will not obey what the Government tells him. You British don't."

"When we have to, we do, Tony. You don't suppose Dym would obey me if he wouldn't obey the Government?"

"N-no. But you will try to make him, Phemie? Please, you will try?"

"I'll try hard. Now you lie down and go to sleep. Good night, old man."

In his way, Thomas was as comforting as Euphemia. Every morning and every evening he mounted the two flights of stairs. Tony, flat among the pillows, could hear steps coming up slowly and heavily. Then a slow, kind voice, that never changed, said, "Well, Tony? Any better?"

Thomas was the largest man Tony had ever seen, a sturdy giant with a kindly face and hair that was going thin on top. When Thomas stood by the bed, looking down, Tony felt as if he were under the shadow of a great protecting oak tree. There was comfort also in the knowledge that Thomas, like Euphemia, would not make a fight to keep him at the *White Priory* against his will. It was only Dym who was resolved to keep him at any cost, Dym who would never be convinced that he was really Max Eckermann, Dym whose steely hands would never let go.

Margaret didn't often clamber up the two flights of stairs to visit him. He was glad of that, for he didn't like Margaret much. She had dark hair, with rather angry blue eyes under it; and when he saw her he always found himself remembering Olaf and Nils and Inger. Clearly, she hated what he had done, hated it bitterly. She was very lame. She walked with a limp and a lurch, with teeth set hard on her lower lip as though walking hurt. Whenever he saw her, she held a ball of wool and a navy-blue sock with four needles that flashed and winked as she knitted at lightning speed.

It wasn't till long afterward that Tony learnt there was a soldier brother Richard, fighting in the Middle East. And some days passed before he knew that the tall, thin, silent young man, with the shade over his eyes, was the Mortimer who worked for seventeen hours a day though he wasn't strong enough to join the Forces.

Then came the second half of the family, the half that was supposed to be more particularly his own. It began, he gathered, with Dym and ended with Simon and Judy. Red-haired James came between Midshipman Ginger and Sally. He was fifteen, and Sally, also red-haired, was thirteen and a half. The twins were only ten. They were small and chubby, like Nils and Inger. But Nils and Inger had always looked frightened, while Simon and Judy had, it seemed, never felt frightened in their lives. They were sleek and plump as kittens, round-eyed and staring. They brought him queer little gifts to decorate the table by his bed: plates filled with moss, red leaves, purple-veined ivy, blue pebbles, or bowls of yellow aconites and winter irises. They also lent him their goldfish to amuse him. He liked the flowers, but he did not like the goldfish swimming round and round and round, never getting anywhere. When they were alone, it would look at him in a cold, knowing manner, as much as to say, "You are a prisoner too. I can't get out, neither can you. Neither can you."

At first he supposed that Porgy and Mary and Mousie were more brothers and sisters, but in time he discovered that they were the three cousins of whom Dym had spoken in the train. They were large and pale, with black shining eyes; they were the same age as James and Sally and himself. He did not like them as well as the family that he would not own for his. They were, however, less objectionable than the six boys who were forever stealing up to the attic to peep at him. Once Euphemia caught them at it and sent them away.

One of them said, "We weren't doing any harm. We only wanted to have a look at your German brother."

"Tony is not German," Euphemia had said indignantly. "He is as English as you are. Go away at once." And she came into the room, shut the door behind her, and told Tony that the evacuées knew quite well they had no business to poke and pry. She would see that they did not come again.

"But I am German," Tony protested weakly.

"There, there!" said Euphemia. It was what she always

said to soothe him. Usually she spoilt the effect by putting "Tony" at the end of it. They all called him by that name with maddening persistence. James and Porgy and Simon were forever saying, " 'Night, Tony," or " 'Morning, Tony," or "Hullo, Tony; you all right?" Margaret said, stiffly, "Good morning, Tony." The doctor said, "How's the world today, Tony?" Thomas never forgot to clap it on. Euphemia was nearly as bad. The horrid name stabbed like a pinprick every time he heard it. Herr Dym, he remembered wistfully, had used it as little as he possibly could. Only three times in all, and once it had been changed into a grave "Anthony," which had not hurt nearly so much.

Euphemia went away, but she sent Sally to mount guard in her stead. Sally brought a book with her and sat hunched in the armchair, slender fingers laced round knees, thin young face pale beneath its mop of wild red hair. She was learning something by heart. Tony could see by the short lines that it was poetry. He could hear her muttering about mountains and fountains and rainbow-colored sea spray and singing seas. A face peered round the door. Sally flew after it at once. Tony heard her light steps racing across an uncarpeted landing. Heavy boots fled before her. She cried after the boy, "If you come bothering here again, Euphemia's going to report you to Mr. Bland!"

"Yah!" But the boots did not return. Sally came back, dropped into the armchair and smiled at Tony. "That's settled him!" she said triumphantly. "Mr. Bland is a master from their school, Tony. He came with them, and he's supposed to keep them in order. He's rather fierce; they don't like getting into a row with him. They're horribly nosy, aren't they? But they shan't come staring at you."

Gratitude softened Tony's heart toward the English girl,

who looked, he thought, very like a slim, delicate elf with her green eyes, pointed chin and auburn hair. "Are you doing your—your prep?" he asked, wrinkling his forehead in an effort to remember the word used by his English friends long ago.

"No," said Sally, "the holidays aren't over yet. I am learning some poetry by heart, for a sort of extra."

"Is it the poetry you learn for Herr Dym?"

Her green eyes showed surprise. "Yes. But how did you know about that?"

"He talked to another Air Force officer in the train," said Tony. "He told him he gave his young brothers and sisters a war-savings stamp every time they learnt poetry or—I don't remember the other word—"

"Prose?"

"Yes, that was it. He said that he didn't want them to think of nothing but bombs all through the war; this gave them something else to think about, and it was a kind of war service even a baby could do."

"You heard him say all that?"

"Why not? Yes."

"Euphemia thinks you don't understand much English."

"Sometimes I do and sometimes I don't," said Tony, guardedly. "I understood then."

"You must be very clever," said Sally. "If Dym had said it in French in front of me, I shouldn't have understood."

"Will Herr Dym make me do this war service too?"

"He doesn't make any of us. Of course not. We do it partly because it's for the war, partly because it's for Dym. He's that kind of person, you see. You do what he asks. But he won't ask you. At least, not yet."

"What are you learning?" Tony asked.

"It's called *The Song of England.* There's nothing about the war in it. Shall I read it to you?"

He said "Yes" not because he wished to hear it but because she had been kind in chasing away the schoolboys. But it was harder to follow than Dym's talk in the train, for his head ached so much that the room still swayed like the sea. The poem moved too, tossing up and down like foam eddies or the sun sparkles on the Wendish meres or myriad white blossom-branches wind-swayed against a blue sky. That night it mingled queerly with his dreams. He was riding to rescue a lady imprisoned in a castle in the heart of a ring of purple mountains. He pealed the castle bell, which made a noise like no bell he had ever heard, a long uncanny wail that rose and fell, rose and fell, till it was lost in a succession of ear-splitting crashes as the castle fell down in a heap. He started up in bed. The last notes of the air-raid siren were dying mournfully away. They were swallowed up in a rushing sound and another thunderous crash. "It's all right, Tony," he heard James' voice, out of the darkness. "Only a raid. They haven't got us yet."

"It was pretty close, though," said Porgy, sleepily, from the next bed. "The chap in charge of that air-raid siren ought to be sacked; that's what I think. I don't object to bombs after the siren's sounded, but I do object to bombs before. It's bad for the nerves."

"I wonder," said James, "whether we ought to take Tony down to the cellar." Another whistle and crash interrupted him. "Seems a bit hot," he ended deliberately, when the reverberations had died away.

"Shouldn't bother," said Porgy, more sleepily than ever. "Thomas will call us if he thinks it's bad enough. I don't want to go down to that clammy old cellar if I can help it, all among the frogs. Ugh! Go to sleep, Jim, and don't be an owl. Jerry's gone home now. Can't hear him."

"He's still kicking round," said James.

Tony, listening, recognized the irregular *thrum-thrum-thrum, thrum-thrum* of a German aircraft. Heard in England it had a new, sinister sound.

"Can't hear any of our night-fighters, can you?" said James.

Porgy's answer was lost in another crash. Then the door opened, framing Thomas' big figure. He stooped down and gathered Tony into his arms as easily as if he had been a baby. "This is a bad air raid," he explained, speaking slowly, and very loudly indeed that Tony might understand. "I am going to take you down to the cellar. It is our air-raid shelter. Come along, boys. Bring Tony's mattress and blankets."

A few minutes later Tony was gazing at the world as seen from the cellar floor. A safety-lantern was burning on a box; it cast fantastic shadows on the whitewashed walls and over the faces of the bunchily-dressed shapes in dressing-gowns and clothes thrown on in haste. Thomas and Mortimer went away together in uniform, wearing tin hats and gas masks; but the cellar did not seem the emptier for their going.

People he had never seen before were sitting on chairs and boxes and empty stone wine shelves. A young woman held three small children to her, the eldest a little boy of four with black fingernails and pale yellow curls. Three old ladies were huddled in three deck chairs. Six boys wriggled on a long bench. They seemed to be under the charge of a little man with a keen eye and hair that bristled like Strewel Peter's in the nursery book at home. Mr. Bland, Tony thought.

I'd rather belong to Herr Thomas than to him, if I had to choose. Then he saw Euphemia and smiled at her. Euphemia was as neat as when she came to him in the early morning. Sitting stiffly upright, she knitted away at a khaki sock. Beyond her were Margaret's black eyebrows and ball of dark-blue wool. Tucked in a corner, Sally was writing a letter. James sat on the end of Tony's mattress and said, "It's all right, Tony. There aren't any frogs, you know. Porgy was only talking."

When his eyes were shut Tony could almost have fancied himself back in Tante Bettina's air-raid shelter, with Mutti and Tante Bettina and the two girl-cousins and Fritz, the youngest of the boys. He wondered whether some of them were down there tonight, listening to the British aircraft steadily searching for Vater and Onkel Dietrich's chemical works and the big munitions factory on the other side of the river. Perhaps Herr Dym was over Germany tonight and Ludwig over England.

The English were talking; they even made little jokes between the explosions. The little boy with the limp yellow curls began to cry. "Poor Charlie's tired," said his mother. "There'd be room for him on the mattress, miss, if the other little boy didn't mind."

"Do you mind, Tony?" Euphemia asked. Her eyes begged Tony not to refuse.

"N-no," he said.

The mother put Charlie and one of the other babies on the mattress and tucked them well in with Tony's blankets. But Charlie did not stop crying. "If I had to choose," said Judy, who was leaning against Euphemia's knee, "I'd much rather hear a bomb than that little yowly noise Charlie makes. It's simply horrid."

"I think it's time for air-raid tea," said Euphemia hastily. Margaret growled, "There's a plane still hovering. Better wait till it's gone."

But Euphemia shook her head. James lighted an oil stove under the kettle. Margaret, stabbing the needles into her blue ball, took a loaf and a packet of margarine from a shelf and cut a slice for each of them. Somebody said to Tony, "Do you have air-raid tea, Tony, over there?"

"We have coffee," said Tony, "when we can—" For the second time he pulled himself up, remembering that he mustn't let the English know that coffee wasn't easy to get. He drank his tea, but he did not want the bread and margarine. Porgy and two of the evacuées squabbled over it. A third evacuée snatched it and ate it under the noses of the others. Porgy glared at him. "Look here," he said to Tony, "just you remember that next time you don't want your share of an air-raid feast I've bagged it. That clear? It's bagged, definitely bagged. What's the German for bagged?"

"*Besetzt,*" said Tony.

"Well, it's bagged and *besetzt,*" said Porgy, "and if anybody tries any funny business it'll be disagreeable for them. See?"

The evacuées snorted indignantly in the background. Charlie picked flakes of margarine from his bread and smeared them on Tony's blankets, scattering crumbs everywhere. His mother did not stop him; she put her head on one side and smiled as though he were doing something rather clever. Tony could see Euphemia pressing her lips together hard to keep herself from speaking.

Far away they could still hear distant gunfire, though no aircraft now zoomed overhead. It sounded like the beating of carpets. By and by it stopped. Euphemia looked at Mr. Bland.

"Better wait for the *All Clear*," said Mr. Bland. "Doesn't do to take risks on a really noisy night."

They waited. When the signal sounded, long and steady in the darkness, they stood up, yawned, and trailed in a long procession back to bed. There was no Thomas to carry Tony this time, but James put an arm round him and helped him up the stairs. When they reached the attic, James said suddenly, "Let's look at the sky."

He pulled the black-out curtains aside and stood with his arm still round Tony, staring into the dawn. The snow had melted, and the earth now lay dark-brown and black and purple-streaked under a gray ruffled sky, where faint blues and greens began to be mingled with spreading rose color. Somewhere in the half darkness they could hear the chirp of a wintry bird.

"It's funny," said James, over his shoulder to Porgy, "when you see that, you feel you've been dead and have come alive again."

Porgy grunted. "What rum things you think about, Jim! Let's have a spot of peace and quiet now, for mercy's sake. You don't happen to know whether it's bacon for breakfast tomorrow, do you, or only porridge?"

"I do not," said James. He let the black-out curtains fall into place, straightened them carefully, and switched on the light. " 'Night, for what's left of it, Tony," he said. " 'Fraid you won't feel any the better for being disturbed like this. Might have been worse, though, if they'd mixed a few fire bombs with their H.E.'s. Or oil."

"Oh, it wasn't too bad," said Tony.

8

Among the Mad English

THREE DAYS later Tony woke up tired but clear-headed and ready for a fight. Throughout the morning he pondered his plan of campaign. It did not take him long to decide that he had better stay quietly at the *White Priory* until the promised inquiries had been made. He was even able to smile at his past ineffectual attempts at escape.

Regarded as a temporary shelter, the *White Priory* was as good as could be expected. Better, in fact. A refuge chosen for him by the British Government might place him with people who would treat him exactly as he had treated Olaf, Nils and Inger. These Inglefords were far from doing that; they all plainly meant to be kind. He had no fault to find with them except for their crazy conviction that he was their lost brother. He wasn't, he wasn't, he wasn't!

Sitting up in bed with his arms hugged round his knees, he said so again, aloud, in the stillness of the empty room: "I'm not, I'm not, I'm not!" Then he was quiet, thinking hard. The goldfish swam in its little bowl, the fire crackled, the windows rattled gently. "I'm not," Tony said again, after a lengthy pause. "No, I'm not, I'm not."

A pricking remembrance troubled him. In those days of helplessness he had been too giddy and miserable to insist on his German nationality. He had accepted the Inglefords' gifts and services, had in some measure responded to their advances, and had even allowed himself to be on markedly friendly terms with Euphemia. Perhaps she was already telling Herr Dym over the telephone that he was sinking tamely from Max Eckermann into Tony Ingleford. That must never be said. With eyes on the imprisoned goldfish, he made his plan.

When Euphemia next addressed him as "Tony," he looked at her with blank, hard eyes. "I am Max Eckermann," he said. "I will not answer when you call me Tony and speak to me in English. When you speak to me, you must speak in German and call me by my proper name."

"But I can't do that," protested Euphemia. "Speak German, I mean. You can't come into an English house and order the people in it to speak German. Besides, I don't know any German," she added.

"Then you will have to learn it," said Tony. "All you English will be compelled to speak German when the Führer invades England, so you may as well start now."

Euphemia was not offended. She laughed as she said, "I'll put off learning German till he lands at Dover, Tony; that'll be quite time enough. Here's your medicine. Drink it up quickly."

"I do not understand," said Tony, motioning the glass away. "I understand nothing that is not said in German."

Euphemia met him half way. "I can't speak German, and I'm much too busy to learn. Will it do if I call you Max when we are alone, as Dym does? Thomas doesn't want you called Max in public because it isn't your name."

"*Nein*," Tony answered, with a resolute shake of his head. "*Sprechen Sie deutsch, bitte. Sie dürfen hier nicht englisch sprechen.* That means," he explained kindly, "speak German, please; you are not allowed to speak English here."

Not allowed! Euphemia looked down at the little figure swallowed up in a pair of James' pyjamas, which she had not yet had time to cut down for him. Her lips twitched into a smile.

"Ick kann nick doytch sprich," she said brightly. "Hier ist medicine vrom Herr Doctor. Das ist the best ick kann do, Max. Ick hopen you understandt."

Tony eyed her resentfully for a second; then, greatly to his surprise, he found himself obliged to laugh. "You monkey!" said Euphemia cheerfully. "Now I can believe some of the dreadful stories in Ginger's last letter home."

"What stories?" Tony asked, as he handed back the empty glass.

"Ah!" said Euphemia. "Who caused fearful confusion by tearing up some of the papers on the notice board in the gun room, and by altering the times printed on the others? And who was caught throwing the gun-room's only packet of gramophone needles into the harbor?"

She was amused, he could see. "I was," he said, not without pride.

"But you're not going to treat us in the same way, are you?"

"No," he said, considering. "Not now. Not while I'm a visitor. But if I am made to stay here for good, I shall do everything I can to make you willing to let me go away."

"That's a bargain, then," said Euphemia.

Afterward, when he thought it over, he was not sorry that he had been defeated. He had made his protest, had warned them what to expect if they tried to keep him at the *White Priory;* surely this was as much as a very tired boy could reasonably be expected to do. Tante Bettina herself could have done no more.

When Tony first came downstairs, the holidays were over and the larger part of the family had gone by bicycle or omnibus to their schools in a town three miles away. They would not be at home that day, he learnt, till after four o'clock.

"But some days they come home at lunch time and do extra prep instead of going to afternoon school," Euphemia told him. "James and Porgy and Simon are sharing their school buildings with Chessington Secondary School; it's rather a tight fit, and they have to use some of the classrooms turn and turn about. Sally's and Judy's school is sharing with another girls' school, too. Is it like that in—" She stopped abruptly, as she nearly always did when she asked questions of this kind. Tony almost wished she had gone on to the end. Any mention of his home hurt badly, but he felt much worse when it was not mentioned at all. He flushed and turned his head away.

Euphemia put him on the sofa in a large, shabby sitting room that looked out on a chilly green garden and willowy water meadows. "This room has to serve us for drawing room, dining room, study, workroom, playroom and first-aid post for the neighborhood," she said. "The other rooms are as full as they can be. I'll show you the whole house tomorrow, when you aren't quite so staggery on your legs. Today you will just have to lie still and keep quiet. Would you like a book?"

He said "Yes," though he feared she would choose, as she always did, a book that had plenty of pictures and very little reading. This had not mattered while his head was bad; but today he felt that he wanted to choose for himself from the many shelves that ran round the room. However, this time her choice fell on *Punch's Christmas Almanac*, open at a picture of two British soldiers sitting in a snowy

wood that was bristling with anti-aircraft guns. Side by
side on a log, they were timidly pulling a Christmas cracker
someone had given them. Their heads were turned awry,
their eyes tightly shut, their faces expressive of the liveliest
terror. The more he studied this picture, the more it puzzled him. "It must be a picture painted by a German artist,"
he said to himself at last. "As if the British would make fun
of their own men like that! They couldn't—it is absurd."

He fell asleep, still puzzling, and only roused himself to
take the cup of cocoa and the hot scone that Euphemia
brought him mid-way through the morning. It was baking-
day, and there was a dab of flour on the end of her nose.

After she had gone away he lay looking hungrily at the
radio set, wondering whether he dared venture to tune in to
his home station. It seemed safe enough. Everyone was
busy; Euphemia herself had said that he wouldn't be disturbed again till dinner at one o'clock.

For half an hour he wavered, torn between longing and
terror. Listening to British broadcasts was forbidden in
Germany; it was a serious offence, heavily punished. Even
if you escaped the notice of the police, there were your own
people to be reckoned with. Once, just for fun, he and his
cousin Fritz— No, it was wiser to forget what he and Fritz
had done. If Tante Bettina ever found out, there would be
trouble for both of them. What madness possessed him
that he should want to play the same wicked trick on the
other side of the water where the punishment would no
doubt be quite as severe?

The danger beckoned him ever more insistently. There
were no police about—Thomas and Euphemia weren't as
alarming as Tante Bettina—weren't alarming at all, in fact.
Margaret was safely out of the house, hobbling down the

road to the village. Pooh! He wasn't afraid of Thomas or Euphemia! Now was the time to show it.

Creeping across the room, he experimented with the unfamiliar knobs. A green cross flashed from the central disk and an unmistakably German voice roared through the house. Panic-stricken, he increased the volume instead of switching off. Then a hand came over his shoulder and touched the offending knob. Big and lean and brown, with one finger missing, the hand of Thomas.

Absent, Thomas had seemed harmless and well-meaning; present, he was unexpectedly formidable. Tony's knees sagged under him; his heart thumped against his ribs. "Listening to the wireless, Tony?" said Thomas' voice, slow and unruffled as ever. "Got it rather too loud, haven't you? See, that's about as much volume as you'll need."

At first Tony could not believe that he had heard aright. He waited, still fearful, but Thomas had apparently no more to say. When the heavy steps had crossed to a desk on the other side of the room, Tony ventured to speak. "You do not object? I may—?"

"You may," said Thomas, kindly.

"Hadn't we better turn it lower?" Tony whispered.

"Eh, what? It's quiet enough, I think."

Tony flung a hunted glance at the window. "You have let me listen in to Germany. If the police find out, there will be great trouble—"

"There won't be any trouble at all," said Thomas. "You're in England, remember. You're free to tune in to any station you please."

Left alone, then, Tony listened with a hand on the knob, ready to switch off instantly if any stranger came up the drive. When the maid came in to lay the table for the mid-day meal he started back, still half afraid. But Vera was as friendly as Thomas had been.

"I daresay it feels a bit more homelike, listening to all that," she said. "Fancy you being able to understand it all!"

"Are you well enough to come for a drive with me, Tony?" asked Thomas after lunch.

It had been a solemn meal, eaten in the company of six grownups who all listened, gravely and closely, but without comment, to the news bulletin. Tony was not used to seeing so many of the family at once; it made him feel shy. "Yes, please," he said, glad to get away.

"Anyone else coming?" Thomas asked.

Euphemia, Margaret and the three old aunts refused the invitation. So Thomas and Tony set off together to the garage. Thomas had billeting business, he said, in the county town. His car was not magnificent like Vater's; it was a disgraceful old car, a veritable down-at-heel tramp among cars, large and shabby. But Thomas appeared to be quite satisfied with it. He drove bumpily down the drive and shot out into the main road.

They drove on through the green landscape. Now and then a military lorry or a Bren-gun carrier rattled past. Once, in the fields, they passed a plowman with his team. Sea gulls were wheeling in white flocks about the plow, crying shrilly as they flashed down the red earth and soared again. Thomas pointed them out. "We're having a hard winter," he said. "I've scarcely ever seen them so far inland as this."

"How far are we from the sea?" Tony asked.

"Forty miles," said Thomas. "In England you can't live more than about seventy miles from the sea."

Airplanes were zooming overhead, rising continually from behind a swelling ridge that spoke deludingly of the sea behind it. "Do those aircraft come from Herr Dym's airdrome?" Tony asked, watching.

"No, from—" Thomas stopped short. "No, they don't come from Dym's station." He smiled at his companion. "Sorry," he said. "You're very small, but we don't know yet what decision the authorities will make about you. Mustn't give you any scraps of information that you might carry home to your German friends. See?"

Tony was surprised to find that Thomas could sometimes think quickly. But when they went into the post office in the county town, he saw that the walls were covered with posters warning the British not to talk rashly or give away secrets. Tony felt obliged to walk round the post office to see whether the Führer appeared in any of the pictures. He had not quite finished his survey when Thomas called to him from the doorway.

They walked on, sociably enough. The county town was a sleepy place with not many signs of life. Sunny and clean, quiet and dignified, it reminded Tony of the towns he had known best; he did not feel a stranger in a strange land. The Town Hall was very old; it had been built in Queen Elizabeth's reign, and it straddled half across the main street on carved wooden pillars, worn with time. Thomas disappeared behind a door marked CHIEF BILLETING OFFICER, leaving Tony to wander about the entrance hall alone. For some time the boy stood by the door to watch a workman shoring up the sandbags that protected the wooden pillars from bomb damage. Then he went into the hall and examined the curios set out in glass cases: a collection of

Roman coins, some ancient documents, and a fine model of a Spanish galleon. A printed card met his gaze.

Model by Thomas Ingleford of the *White Priory*, Greltham St. Andrew in this county. Presented by his son, Thomas Ingleford, Esquire, in 1864.

Thomas Ingleford had done his work well. The galleon, carved and gilded, wore the look of a proud, graceful sea bird about to ride the waves. Round the slab on which she stood ran inscriptions in Latin and English: *Non nobis gloria, Domine* and *He blew with His winds and they were scattered.*

Tony had heard of the Spanish Armada that had gone forth to conquer Britain in the days when the Town Hall was newly built. The Cavendish boys had a book about it; their mother had read aloud from it one holiday summer. He and Michael had christened their boat *The Rose* that summer, after the ship in which Amyas Leigh sailed the Spanish Main.

"Looking at the Spanish galleon, Tony?" said Thomas' voice over his head. "Our great-great-grandfather made her. A beauty, isn't she?"

Tony said "Yes," and followed Thomas out of the Town Hall.

Farther down the High Street, Thomas turned into a stationer's. Tony lingered, having just caught sight of three airmen coming up behind them. One was like Herr Dym, he thought. He did not want ever to see him again, he told himself; but there could be no harm in looking at this man who was so like him.

Dym's double said something to his friends, left them

and came forward. It seemed to Tony that the pale winter sunshine brightened as he came. "Hullo, Max! Didn't expect to see you here."

"I came with Herr Ingleford," said Tony. "He is in that shop," he added.

Dym said, "That reminds me, Max, you'll be wanting pocket money now you're on your feet again. You're my responsibility, you know. I'm going to give you what Thomas gives Sally."

Tony drew back. "No, thank you, Herr Dym. To accept money from you would be as good as saying that I belonged to your family."

"Just as you please," Dym answered. "But I shall ask you again in a week or two, for I think you're bound to change your mind. You'll find it awkward to be without cash for more than a few days. At least, I should."

When Dym had passed into the shop in search of Thomas, Tony felt sorry that he had refused the offer of pocket money; it was awkward not to have even a few pence of his own. He looked regretfully at the tempting display in the window, then put his hand into his pocket and sadly fingered his store of useless German coins. He had not had the heart to look at them before; but now he took them out and turned them over on his palm. As he did so, his eyes rounded in amazement. English half-crowns, florins, shillings and sixpences lay mingled with the German marks.

Had Euphemia slipped them into his pocket? Had Dym? On second thought, he decided that they were not the givers. A flash of memory brought back the struggle in the gun room when he had been dressed in English clothes. Once more he saw the midshipmen emptying the pockets of the *Jungvolk* uniform; once more their hands dropped coins into the new pockets.

They weren't as beastly as I thought, he owned to himself. It's quite a lot. If ever I have to run away it will be a great help. When I refused Herr Dym's offer I forgot that I could not get far without any money. But I'd better not let them know I have so much; they might save it for me.

He put his spoil into his pocket and, with one more wistful glance at the alluring window, followed the Ingleford brothers into the shop.

The knowledge of his secret hoard gave him a friendly feeling toward all the world. He stood by the counter and touched Dym's sleeve. "I saw the ship that your great-great-grandfather made, Herr Dym."

"Are you any good at that sort of thing?"

"Not very. Are you?"

"I'm so-so. James is the clever one. Boat building's not his line, though. Makes model aircraft. Sally helps him. Ask him to let you try."

"Would he?"

"Of course. Look, Thomas has been buying something for you."

With a beaming smile, Thomas gave Tony a halma board and a box of men. "There!" he said, in a satisfied voice. "That was quite a find. Now you'll feel at home."

Mystified, Tony thanked him. It was kind of Herr Ingleford to make the gift, certainly, but there seemed no reason why the mere possession of a halma set, similar to "chinese checkers," should set him at his ease. Looking up, he saw that Dym also appeared to be puzzled. He waited, but Dym asked no questions.

They moved to the door, Tony last because he had caught sight of a pile of blue twopenny exercise books with a map of the British Isles inside the cover and tables and weights set out on the back. Dym noted the longing look.

"I've been put in my place once, Max," he said with a twinkle. "Will you crush me again if I venture to offer you one of those?"

"Please, I would like it, Herr Dym."

He went back to the car clutching a halma set and an exercise book. There Dym bade him farewell. "Aren't you coming with us?" Tony asked.

"Can't today," Dym answered. "See you on Sunday, probably. Right away, Tommy!"

It was nearly black-out time. They drove slowly, with dimmed headlights, through the darkening lanes, home to high tea in the room where Tony had spent the morning. The three old aunts were not present; they always had breakfast and tea by themselves in Great-aunt Desdemona's bedroom, which had once been the drawing room. But Mr. Bland and the six schoolboys were there, with all the remaining Inglefords. The big table was not big enough to hold so many: a board on trestles had to be fitted across one end. Tony sat next to Euphemia, who poured out tea from an enormous teapot. After tea, James and Porgy cleared away the tea things and Mary and two of the evacuées helped Vera to wash up. Then those who had prep to do settled down at the table.

From a corner of the sofa Tony watched all that went on. Simon and Judy had no home lessons. They got out their toys and sat on the floor by the machine table at which Euphemia was busily stitching pyjamas for a hospital-supply depot. Margaret knitted her navy socks. Thomas sat on the sofa by Tony, studying a list of houses in which mothers and children could be billeted.

He did not find his task easy. At last he said to Tony, "It's an awful business, this fitting people into other people's homes!"

"Is it?" said Tony.

"Yes. I put them in, and they don't like their billets and come to me asking to be moved elsewhere. Or the people who've got them don't like them, and then they say I've got to shift 'em sooner than at once. That's what I'm doing now." He bent over his papers, muttering, "Mrs. Atkins, three children, *Rushmere Cottage*—try Mrs. Hearn, 5 Church Lane." It sounded, Tony thought, like a problem that had no answer. Presently Thomas was tired of working in a noisy room. He got up and went off to his cold billeting-office-bedroom to wrestle with his task in peace.

Round the table the six evacuées behaved fairly well till Mr. Bland went off to visit another master who was billeted in the Vicarage. Then they kicked one another under the table, flipped ink-and-paper pills at the girls, and slunk off to play ping pong in the hall.

"They haven't done their prep," said Mousie virtuously. "Somebody ought to stop them." She looked at Mortimer.

"It's Mr. Bland's job," said James.

Mortimer took not the slightest notice of the talk or the whirr of the sewing machine or the noise of the evacuées. He sat at Thomas' desk, rapidly correcting exercises with dashes from a red pen. By and by he stood up. It was his turn to cycle four miles to the school where he taught, there to spend the whole night fire-watching. If no air-raid siren sounded he might rest on a couch in the staff room; but the first note of the siren must find him racing out to protect the buildings from incendiary bombs. The masters took turns at fire-watching, two at a time. Mortimer had hurt his eyes in the last raid when he was emptying a bucket of sand on a fire bomb showering sparks. They showed red and inflamed under a dark shade.

Coughing, he went into the hall and came back in a heavy overcoat, with gas mask and tin helmet dangling at his back. "Sandwiches ready?" he asked, from the doorway. His voice was curt and toneless, as if he were almost too tired to speak; there were heavy, dragged-down lines round his mouth, and he put up his hand to keep the light from his eyes. But when Margaret gave him his packet of sand-wiches and thermos flask he summoned up a smile that for a moment made him look like a very old, very tired Dym. The door banged behind him.

"Game o' halma, Tony?" said James suddenly.

Tony said "Yes" for politeness, not because he wished to play. The game was in progress when Thomas returned. He looked pleased. "We'll have a game next, won't we?" he said, smiling down at Tony.

Once again, Tony had to say "Yes." They had two games before Thomas went out on Home Guard duty. As soon as he had gone, Judy popped up her little head. "Will you play with me, Tony?" she asked.

The red and blue men were swimming before Tony's eyes. Euphemia shook her head at Judy. "Tony's tired," she said. "I think you're more than ready for bed, Tony. You've had too long a day."

Tony was not sorry to be alone in the attic, staring at the shadows in the corners behind the three white, empty beds. Some time later Porgy came in with a glass of milk and two buns. "There's a piece of news downstairs," he said as he gave Tony his supper. "Two of the evacuées are going. Their mother has just rung up to say that she's fetching them tomorrow. Her brother wants her to take care of his house in Wales, so now she can have her family with her. Leslie and Gordon Tripp are the two we're losing."

"I don't know them apart yet," said Tony.

"Euphemia's going to beg and implore Thomas not to billet any new ones in their place," said Porgy. "She says she has quite enough to do now you've come home."

Tony was indignant. "I like that! Did I ask to come here? Let her give Herr Dym the blame. Besides, I shall not remain long."

"Oh, keep your hair on!" said Porgy. "You go all German when you get excited. Nobody's blaming you for being the last straw that breaks the camel's back. The camel," explained Porgy carefully, "is Euphemia. After all, she's running her own large houseful, plus three aged aunts, plus three cousins, and all these evacuées. Then you come along. You can't be surprised that Euphemia is ready to snap at a chance of having only four evacs instead of six." He cast an anxious glance at Tony's second bun. "If you're not hungry, don't force yourself to eat that other bun simply because it's wrong to waste food in wartime," he said. "I know of a very good billet for it."

"Why are you telling me all this?" said Tony, who thought Porgy's news a poor exchange for the crisp satin-skinned bun.

"For interest," said Porgy, between bites. "And it's good news for poor old Mortimer. He'll be able to have his own room again after a year and a half in Dym's. He hates Dym's room. It's so noisy, with us and two evacuées on top and Mr. Bland next door. Mortimer likes quiet. Did you know there's supposed to be a secret room on the right-hand side of Dym's room?"

Tony was awake in an instant. "No!"

"It was lost about a hundred years ago. Dym's room is in the oldest part of the house, and this room was a hidey-hole in history-book times. It was rather a jolly little pan-eled room, with a door worked by a secret catch in the panels in Dym's room. We've been trying to get Thomas to have the room opened up, but he won't. He's afraid he might have to do all sorts of interior repairs."

"But how can you get in to find out whether the room is sound?"

"Through the secret entrance—We've got to find the catch in the panels. And Thomas has promised that the one who finds the catch shall have the room."

"For his own?"

"Yes. We've searched every inch of the walls, I can tell you. No go. Old Tommy knew what he was about, the wily bird, when he made that promise. He knew he'd never be called on to fulfil it!"

Tony had always loved stories of secret rooms and sliding panels. And there was something remarkably attractive about a little lost room that could be claimed for one's very own.

"Would you believe it?" said Porgy, swelling with indig-nation, "that evacuée, Sidney Parker, says he's going to search the panels in Dym's room too. Such cheek! He knows that Dym's room is out of bounds for evacuées. As if they had a right to poke about in the bedrooms belonging to the people of the house! But he says he's going to get the little room for himself!"

Tony said nothing aloud. To himself he said, "No, he shan't. I shall!"

9

Discoveries

TONY'S LAST Sunday had been spent in bed. The next Sunday, waking, he had a conviction that something agreeable was going to happen: expectancy was in the air. Then he remembered that Dym was coming home.

He tried to pretend that it was nothing to him whether Dym came or not. But the eager beginning-of-Christmas-Eve feeling went with him to breakfast and lasted all through the day that was so unlike Sunday as he knew it at home. Nobody hurried off to marches and youth rallies and meetings; they all went to church, leaving him to take care of Great-aunt Desdemona.

When Tony carried tea and cake to her, he thought that the long windows and paneled walls made the drawing room look stately and dignified, in spite of its change into a bed-sitting room. Great-aunt herself looked like an old fairy in the snowy shawl that seemed to be woven out of thousands of tiny spider-webs. She smiled at him as she took the cup. "I think you had better eat my cake for me," she said. "I am not hungry this morning."

Tony decided that he liked Great-aunt Desdemona.

"What are you doing, all alone?" she asked.

"Reading," said Tony. He hesitated a little before answering, for he knew that a wise boy would have left books alone when he found himself among people who nodded their heads sagely every time they saw him at the shelves. It wasn't any use reminding them that he could read English because his English play-fellows had made it his second language; they only smiled and persisted in their absurd belief that English had been easy to him because he was English by birth. But Great-aunt Desdemona did not smile or nod. She said, very kindly, "Dym will lend you all the books you want. He is a reader too."

"I know. Herr Dym told me that he loved reading."

"Yes," said the old lady, "his room is full of books."

Afterward, Tony blamed Great-aunt Desdemona for his surreptitious visit to Dym's room. He would never have thought of going there, he told himself, if she hadn't put it into his head. But the thought of that other paneled, book-filled room drew him as by an irresistible spell. A minute later he found himself on the enchanted ground.

He stood at one end of a long, narrow room divided into two unequal parts by a huge black beam that crossed it three feet below the ceiling. The farther part had a window across the whole width of the room, facing the door; the nearer had a window on the right-hand side. Only the farther part was furnished; on Tony's side of the beam there was nothing but a fine old oak chair and cupboard. He walked up to the beam and surveyed Dym's domain.

His eyes went first to the beautiful old flat-topped knee-hole desk, with drawers on either side, standing under the window. Trained to appreciate beauty of every kind, he knew that it was good, very good indeed, no fit match for the hideous chest of drawers, the iron-railed bed, the Victorian tin bath hanging on the wall. There were no ornaments or pictures except a large motto framed in red-edged cellophane. He read the words at the top: *The King's Message to the Empire.* Frowning, he turned his head away. Then he looked again.

And I said to the man who stood at the gate of the year, "Give me a light that I may tread safely into the unknown." And he said, "Go out into the darkness and put your hand into the hand of God. That shall be to you better than light, and safer than a known way."

A strange feeling of awe went through Tony as he read the words again. So that was the King of England's message to his people? He stood looking at the red-edged card for a long time. Then he turned to the massive bookcase, which had shelves above and long cupboards beneath. The cupboard doors showed seventeenth-century carvings of a harvest scene in high relief, and the shelves were decorated with a multitude of grotesque little faces peering out of tangled foliage and fruit clusters. Books were everywhere, most of them well worn, though here and there a new binding shone out glorious in red and gold, or leather-and-gilt marked a school prize.

Tony knelt on a chair to study the shelves. Dym was evidently a wide reader: there were French books, Latin books—yes, and German books too. He was surprised to see German books in an English bookcase.

He looked at the titles, wondering why Dym chose to read a book like *Mein Kampf.* Tony hadn't read it himself; but he had heard bits of it read or quoted now and then; it wasn't, he thought, the kind of book that a British airman would like. Then he saw other books: poetry, history, novels, guidebooks, books on education. He made a face at these last. Tante Bettina lectured to women and girls on education, and she was never tired of telling Mutti how he ought to be brought up.

Dym and Tante Bettina were poles apart; how was it that they both read that kind of book? And again, why did Dym read some of the stories that were on his own shelves at home? He could see Niebuhr's *Heroes*. Yes, and the book of fairy tales that he had known since his baby days, and a couple of Kurt Berkner's books, and *Emil and the Detectives*, which he had always wanted to read. He pulled it out and slid down on the chair.

The clang of the dinner bell brought him back to earth. He was halfway downstairs before he realized that he was still clutching *Emil*. Dropping it into an empty ornamental flower pot on the staircase windowledge, he hurried on.

He had no chance of restoring the borrowed book after dinner, for James claimed his company for a walk.

"If you come quickly and quietly," he said, "we may be able to escape the evacuées. Mr. Bland's sending them out for a walk too."

"Why do you want to escape them?" Tony asked.

James was too wise to say, "Because they like to hear you talk. They think it's funny." He said, "I hate going round with a gang. But if you prefer looking like an orphanage, we'll join forces."

"I don't," said Tony.

"Very well, then; come on," said James.

The day was cold and windy. "There was a fellow once," said James, "who wrote a poem beginning, *Welcome, wild North-Easter*. I'll bet he wrote it by his study fire."

"Why can't we stay at home by the fire too?" Tony asked wistfully.

"Because there isn't any fire for us, this afternoon," said James. "The three aunts have the drawing-room fire. You don't want to be mewed up with three old ladies and Mary

and Mousie, do you? Vera's staying at home with toothache
by the kitchen fire. Mr. Bland's gas fire has gone wrong, so
he said to Euphemia that as she and Margaret and Sally
and the twins would be at church he supposed he could
have the use of the sitting room fire till teatime. That's
three, and all the fires there are! Those evacuated people are
cool, you know. The use of the one and only sitting room
for a cosy undisturbed nap! Thomas and Mortimer didn't
like to protest as they weren't going to be in themselves, but
I heard Mortimer say to Thomas that it was a bad prece-
dent. Thomas is a lot too kind-hearted, you know. If I'd
been in his shoes I wouldn't have allowed a billeted person
to make the people of the house feel morally obliged to
turn out in the cold so that he could snooze by the only
available fire!"

There was snow in the air; it had already begun to
powder the hills on the skyline. Tony shivered.

"I suppose," said James, "that the same sort of thing
happens in Germany? People having to share houses, willy-
nilly, and hating it like poison? Rubbing up against one
another, and each side thinking the other lot beastly selfish
and inconsiderate?"

Once more Tony remembered the quarrels in Berlin
over the fires. He was glad James did not know about them.
James went on, as though thinking aloud, "But if it isn't
easy to share your home with your own countrymen, it
must be absolutely ghastly to be obliged to share with the
fellows who've conquered you and forced their way in,
like—" He stopped abruptly.

"Like what?"

"Like the Nazi's in Poland and Czechoslovakia and France
and Holland and Belgium and Luxembourg," said James,

taking care to leave Norway out, lest he should hurt Tony's feelings. "And they haven't stopped short at taking some of the rooms, either. In some places—Alsace-Lorraine and Poland, for instance—they've flung the people out of their homes neck and crop."

"No, we have not."

Tony's gaze shifted under the direct glance of James' blue eyes. "That's a lie, Tony, and you know it," said James. "You've been told that lies don't matter when they help Germany. But a lie's a dirty weapon, all the same."

"I am not lying."

"You mean you're not a first-class liar," suggested James. "For the credit of the family, I'm glad you're so second-class."

"I am not of your family. I am not English," said Tony, with something like terror in his voice. It silenced James for the moment. "Sorry," he said, gruffly. "Forgot you felt like that about it. Thought you were getting more used to the idea."

They walked on in silence for a few minutes. Then Tony said defiantly, "It is Germany's destiny. Germany has the right to decide where people shall live."

"A lot of those people didn't live," said James. "The Poles didn't. They died. You do, when you're thrown out of your home and sent penniless and robbed and starving in a freezing cattle-truck to the other end of nowhere. I wonder whether you'd go on thinking the Fürher had the right to decide where you should live if you happened to be one of the wretches he decided for. You're none too well-pleased at being turned out of a warm room for an hour on Sunday afternoon!"

"I will not listen to what the English say about my

country. If you do not stop talking, I shall return to the *White Priory* at once."

"H'mph!" said James. "Going to tell Mr. Bland to move on? Exercising Germany's right to decide where people shall live, eh?"

Tony's wrathful glare changed suddenly into a laugh. James grinned too. "I dare you to do it, Tony."

"I will not take your dare. Not now, when I am a guest in your house. What would Herr Dym think of me? He's coming this afternoon, remember."

"See that wood over there?" said James. "On the other side of it is Tamley Market, where we go to school. I wonder whether you'll be sent to Gantry's, or whether they'll think Mortimer's school would be better for you. He teaches at a school run on special lines for delicate kids."

"I'm not a delicate kid!"

"Dym says you're highly strung, whatever that may mean. I heard him telling Phemie so. They say you've had a shock and all undue strain must be avoided. That means, you lucky beggar, that you can wriggle out of doing your prep. Which school d'you think you'd like best? It would be queer to have to say 'sir' to one's own brother."

"I have no brothers. He is only Herr Mortimer."

"Funny name, Gantry's, isn't it? The evacuées say it makes them think of a bird that's lost its tail feathers. Just the sort of comparison that would occur to Chessington Secondary, staffed by a lot of conscientious objectors and old professors."

"You English are very impolite to one another," said Tony.

"Yes, aren't we?" agreed James. "Anyone who heard you two minutes ago might be forgiven for supposing you were one of us. Well, I was on the point of observing that Gantry was the name of the man who built the school somewhere about 1460. Thought he was doing a good deed. Still, it's not a bad school, as schools go. The Chessingtonians ought to think themselves jolly lucky, being allowed to share it with us. They don't, of course. They're always wailing over the huge assembly hall and marvelous science labs and magnificent swimming pool they've had to leave behind them. There's not much gratitude in human nature, you know. That hill's called the Beacon. They used to light fires on it to warn the country that a war had started or an invasion was expected. You've heard of the Spanish Armada?"

"Yes."

"Our old Beacon blazed that night, though it doesn't figure in the list of beacons in the poem everybody learns at school:

"Till twelve fair counties saw the blaze on Malvern's lonely
height,
Till streamed in crimson on the wind the Wrekin's crest of
light,
Till broad and fierce the star came forth on Ely's stately fane,
And tower and hamlet rose in arms o'er all the boundless
plain;
Till Belvoir's lordly terraces the sign to Lincoln sent,
And Lincoln sped the message on o'er the wide vale of Trent;
Till Skiddaw saw the fire that burned on Gaunt's embattled
pile,
And the red glare on Skiddaw roused the burghers of
Carlisle—"

The blood ran faster in Tony's veins. "Go on!" he urged.

"Can't remember any more," said James. "Poor old Beacon! It's a pity we can't signal that way now."

"Why can't you?"

"Use your brains. It would serve as a guide to aircraft."

"I forgot," said Tony. "Yes, it is a pity."

The two boys stood looking at the distant Beacon far off beyond the silvery-green marshlands. Foam curls of traveler's joy were tangled in the bare hedge beside them. James pulled off a bit and twisted it round his fingers. "We'll spend a Saturday at the Beacon when the summer comes," he said. "That is, if Thomas can spare us from the farm. It's a good place for a day's hiking. And that's Prettyman's Folly. Prettyman started to build himself a medieval castle about a hundred years ago, but his money gave out when he'd only built half. Looks mad, doesn't it?"

"Who lives in that lonely house with the trees?" Tony asked, having just caught a glimpse of Porgy skulking in the garden.

"A stranger," James answered, "with his old housekeeper and her husband. He's here to recover from an illness, so Thomas hasn't billeted any evacuées on him—" James stopped, and his eyes went to the lurking figure in the shadows. "*Querns* is supposed to be haunted by a headless man," he said suddenly. "In Edward the Second's reign, it was. His enemies called at his house one evening and beheaded him just like Piers Gaveston and the Black Dog of Warwick in the history books, but I don't suppose you've ever heard of them. When his relations went to bury him, they couldn't find his head. They wrote to the enemies, asking where it was, and the enemies wrote back, quite politely, saying they were sorry they didn't know. So the relations were obliged to bury him without it. He comes back now and then, still looking for his head, at least, so the villagers say. Don't go there in the dark, Tony."

He doesn't want me to go there, thought Tony. He's telling me that story to put me off going. But Porgy's there, and I'm sure he's seen Porgy. I wonder what he would say if I asked why Porgy is prowling about a stranger's garden instead of coming for a walk with us.

James gave him no time for questions, but hurried down the road, talking fast.

"Hullo, there's Dym! Get off, Dym, and come with us. You can't go home yet."

He waved. The cyclist slowed down and dismounted. At once sunshine brightened the gray afternoon. "Stay out till teatime?" said Dym, having heard James' explanation. "Right: let's go round by Shepherd's Lane to see how Mrs. Mercer's getting on."

Shepherd's Lane was muddy; it wound through country as lonely as the fields round *Querns*. James grumbled again at the cold and the dismal sky.

> *"If the grass grow green in Janiveer,*
> *It grow the worse for it all the year,"*

Dym quoted philosophically.

The English never seem to stop talking about the weather, thought Tony. They can't forget it for a moment. It isn't really cold, not properly cold, over here, though it's much wetter. They'll have to buy me a mackintosh like Simon's when I go to school— Then he pulled himself up. I shall not be here long enough to make it worthwhile for me to go to school. Of course not.

They rounded a bend. A thin man, walking with his dog, turned at the sight of them and plunged down a side lane with nervous haste. "That's the fellow from *Querns*," said James to Dym, in an undertone.

Dym nodded. "Thought so," he said.

"Dym knows something about that man also," Tony said to himself, "but he will not say what he knows. Perhaps Dym also thinks that he is a spy."

He wished that he had taken more note of the man's appearance. The thin figure was hurrying away; it was impossible now to see more than the back of coat and hat.

"This is Mrs. Mercer's house, Max," said Dym.

They had stopped before a shattered cottage. An old woman came to the door, smiling. "Come in," she said.

"Is there any in?" asked Dym.

She laughed. "Oh, yes. I've one sitting room, most of the kitchen, and the cupboard space under the stairs still left. Come and see how nice I've made it."

She turned to Tony. "It's a long time since you last came to see me," she said. "You came in your pram, then, pushed by Euphemia. And you gave me the heads of two butter-cups you had picked yourself."

Tony said nothing; he was tired of telling people that they had made a mistake. He followed the others into a passage that had no plaster on the ceiling save a few odd fragments that fell on them as they passed. Under the stairs stood a chair, a rug, a biscuit tin of stores, a gas mask and a suitcase ready packed. The furniture in the room that was both bedroom and sitting room was scratched and bat-tered. The kitchen had no roof. Near the shattered back door stood a basket of broken china: white fluted dinner plates, a yellow earthenware bread platter, flowery teacups and a brown coffeepot.

"I couldn't throw away my dear little teapot with the

cupids holding blue ribbons and baskets of roses," said old Mrs. Mercer. "It had a private funeral in the primrose corner of my garden. Don't laugh!"

Dym did not look like laughing. "I don't think you ought to be here by yourself, Mrs. Mercer. Won't you come to us till you can find another house?"

"Thomas and Phemie have both tried to persuade me, dear boy. But what's left is structurally sound, I'm told, though it does look as if it might collapse at any moment. I shall be quite safe. And I shall do splendidly when the damage to the kitchen has been repaired. Two rooms ought to be enough for an old woman living alone."

When they were once more walking down Shepherd's Lane, Dym said, "Plucky old lady, isn't she?"

"There are plucky old ladies in Germany too," said Tony defiantly, "and you come over to drop bombs on them."

"No, we don't," said James. "If your old ladies live close to a munitions factory or docks or gun and searchlight posts—well, life's bound to be unhealthy! But there's no excuse for bombs on private houses miles from a military objective."

"Steady on, Jimmy," said Dym. "That's enough."

James grunted and was silent, but the corners of his mouth still looked scornfully superior. The sight annoyed Tony, made him anxious to take his revenge. It could not be taken simply by saying that it wasn't done by Germany either. James wasn't likely to believe that. A moment's thought told him a better way of enraging James.

"Oh, that's what you're stuffed with!" he said airily. "You've never seen our side of the water. Herr Dym enjoys smashing little houses too!"

The blaze in James' eyes frightened Tony so much that

he dared not look at Dym. Till the words were fairly out he had not fully understood what a deadly insult they held. There did not appear to be the slightest probability that Dym would laugh and say, "It's war. It's for England." For a terrified moment he wondered whether he had better apologize. Then he set his teeth and prepared to face the storm.

"Think so, Max?" Dym said, pleasantly.

"Yes," Tony forced himself to say. He wasn't used to telling lies even for Germany's sake; it still hurt, for he had been taught to speak the truth at home. Besides, this particular lie was going to stab Dym again, Dym who hadn't been angry, even with just cause.

"Like to come with me and see for yourself?" Dym asked.

Once more he had been spared. "You wouldn't be allowed to take me," Tony objected. "And even if you were, there wouldn't be room."

"It would be a tight fit," agreed Dym. "I shouldn't care to have you as a passenger, either. You'd take care to give us a lively time, wouldn't you?"

"Of course I would." Tony's dawning smile widened as he pictured himself overpowering the British crew, singly and collectively, then flying victoriously home to Germany. He was just considering how he should contrive to avoid the German anti-aircraft fire when, with a leap and a howl, the four evacuées jumped over a stile and precipitated themselves upon Dym, pushing James and Tony ruthlessly out of the way. The biggest wheeled his bicycle for him; the youngest grabbed his hand; the two middle-sized ones hotly disputed the privilege of walking next to him on the other side. James and Tony dropped behind, disgusted.

"Those evacs have no manners," said James severely.

"None whatever," said Tony. He tried to pretend to himself that he was merely annoyed because a sharp elbow had jabbed him in the ribs, but in his heart he was disappointed at the interruption to his walk with Dym. James, he could see, felt much as he did. They looked at each other with a wry grin.

10

I Shall Never Choose Chrysaor

THE INGLEFORD family had one hour in the week when they could count on being free from the perpetual presence of strangers. It was the hour after Sunday tea, at which time Mr. Bland took the evacuées into the kitchen to write their weekly letters home. Curiously enough, Tony felt lonelier then than at any time since his arrival at the *White Priory*. When the evacuées were in the room he could make believe that he was one of them, a boy separated from mother and home for only a little while. But when he was left for the first time in a family circle, complete save for Richard in the Middle East and Ginger on the high seas, pretending wasn't any use.

He looked enviously at the evacuées as they went out, grumbling that they hated writing letters. Then he eyed his family. Thomas and Mortimer and Margaret were talking to Dym, who had Judy on his knee and Simon on the arm of his chair. Euphemia was writing to Richard, and the three cousins were writing to their mother in India. Sally was reading, and James, at an old piano, was trying to play a hymn backward. A minute later Tony spoke softly.

"Herr Dym, may I go into the kitchen to talk to Bill?" Tony liked him better than the other evacuées.

"If Mr. Bland doesn't object, yes. Ask him first."

Once on the other side of the door, Tony changed his

mind. The evacuées didn't sound as though they were writing letters; they were evidently having a hilarious romp with Vera. He was in no mind to join the revels. It would be better to sit on the stairs, alone.

But the sight of the ornamental flowerpot reminded him of the book he had borrowed. He resolved to return it before anyone found out that he had been meddling with Dym's property. There might be time too, he thought, to test the panels for the secret catch.

He was a little disconcerted by the discovery that Mr. Bland had withdrawn to his room, leaving the evacuées to their own devices in the kitchen. Through the half-open door he could be seen, angrily poking at his refractory fire. Tony slipped like a shadow into the room beyond.

A crimson and gold sunset made a sheet of flame behind Dym's western window. By its light Tony restored *Emil and the Detectives* to its place. Then he began a methodical search of the panels, pressing notches and swellings and cracks. The sound of feet in the passage took him by surprise. He had hardly crouched out of sight behind the ancient black chair when the door swung open and the younger half of the family rushed in, made for the other end of the room and swarmed over chest of drawers, desk, bookcase and bed.

It appeared to be some kind of family conclave. Tony felt hot all over. He was not afraid that Dym would be vexed by his intrusion, but he did not want to make a public explanation of his presence. Crouching in his scanty patch of shadow, he stayed where he was.

"Make James and Porgy get off the bed, Dym," said Sally.

"Knock off sparring, you two," said Dym. "Porgy, sit on the desk."

"The desk is too hard," groaned Porgy. "Where's your old black chair, Dym?"

Tony trembled in his hiding-place.

"You can't have it," said Dym, "it's too fragile to bear your weight. Get up at once."

Still groaning, Porgy heaved himself on to the desk and sat swinging his legs, but carefully so as not to scratch it.

"If you're all quite ready," said Dym, "I'd like to talk about Tony. I feel that in a way I'm responsible for him. I'm not forgetting that Thomas is head of the family, but I'm the one who took him out of the life he knew and plunged him into a new world."

"You didn't," said Porgy, Mary and Mousie together. "It was the Norwegians who did it, not you."

"They didn't turn him into an Englishman. He thinks I'm to blame for his present plight, and I'm bound to agree with him. Though I found him by a fluke, I'd been doing everything in my power to hunt him down. And, as you know, I should have found him two years ago but for the war. Makes me morally responsible, doesn't it? Now I'm faced with a job that I can't tackle alone. Going to help me?

"Yes, Dym," from Sally on the chest of drawers. Her eyes glowed out of her red bush of hair; her little pointed face was propped between her two hands.

"Yes, Dym," echoed Simon and Judy. James grunted an assent. Porgy and Mary stared. Mousie said in a patient voice, "I don't know what you mean, Dym. What can't you tackle alone?"

"It's like this," said Dym. "Tony's in a far worse position than other evacuée children. They have been sent to new homes by their fathers and mothers, and if they're not happy they can be moved elsewhere or taken home again.

Tony has been forcibly taken from the people he loved, and all choice of going or staying is taken away from them and from him."

"It was his own fault," said Mousie. "It never could have happened if he'd behaved decently in Norway."

"No good going into past history," said Dym. "We'll leave all that. What we're concerned with is today and tomorrow. I want us to make sure we know what we're up against. Let's look at the ordinary evacuée first. Some children have settled down happily in their billets. Others have behaved badly—they've been aggressive and boastful, destructive and discontented and all the rest of it. There are reasons for their behavior; their lives have been turned upside down, and they're so unhappy that they take their revenge by behaving badly. Most of us are like that; when we're miserable, our worse self wants to make somebody else miserable too."

"But it's very wrong to give way to our worse self," said Mousie. "Porgy and Mary and I try not to, though we feel very sad when we think of our nice home requisitioned by the Army and our father and mother away in India."

"Of course it's wrong. But you might find it harder to be good, Mouse, if you'd been planked down among total strangers instead of among your cousins. I grant you, cousins aren't all they might be; but they're better than nothing. Anyhow, wrong or not so wrong, lots of children haven't behaved too well in the billets the Government has found for them. Tony may settle down easily, as our own six did, or he may be difficult.

"Well, then, we'll just have to remember every minute of the day what Tony has lost. He had a comfortable home with a woman who made him her idol. Now he's fatherless and motherless in a poor home, one of a big, scrambling family who have grown up without him. You can't blame him for not enjoying the change. And there's worse to come. Think how you'd feel, if you were told with brutal suddenness that you were German, not English."

"It seems to me, Dym," said Mousie, "it's a pity you mentioned that you knew who Tony was. He'd have been much happier if you had left him to go on being what he thought he was."

"I couldn't do that," said Dym gravely. "I had more than one reason. There was a promise I had made to my mother long ago when Tony was lost, and even if I hadn't made that promise I should have felt bound to do what I did. Look here, Mouse, suppose I found you drinking poison that looked and tasted like particularly good lemonade—"

The others groaned. "You needn't be so heartless as to mention lemonade," said Sally dismally. "It's months since we last had a chance at it."

"Or ice cream," said Judy. "Pink ice cream."

"Good lemonade," Dym repeated firmly. "You'd be furious with me for snatching the cup out of your hand, wouldn't you? You'd feel inclined to tell me that you would be much happier if I left you to go on drinking it?"

"I shouldn't be so silly as to drink anything that wasn't lemonade," said Mousie. "And Tony wasn't being poisoned, either. I don't understand."

"He was being slowly poisoned. He was getting the poisonous teaching that is given to all Germans under Nazi rule. You've heard about it in school, haven't you? They are being taught that Germany is a master nation with the right to rule the world, trampling down the smaller nations, robbing them, torturing them, turning them into mindless, soulless slaves. They are taught that lies and spying, treachery and cruelty and broken promises don't matter if they are done for the good of Germany. They are taught that they must be mercilessly hard because pity and mercy are only shown by weak fools. That's all poison. It poisons the soul. I couldn't leave Tony to drink it in."

Tony listened, angry and puzzled. All his life he had heard at school and on the air and at the *Jungvolk* meetings that Germany had a divine mission to rule the other nations, forcing the rebellious to submit and punishing those who dared to flout her wise laws; that she must fight and utterly destroy the enemies who tried to hinder her from taking the lands and goods she required; that Germans must be hard, true, loyal men. That wasn't poison; how could it be? Herr Dym had no business to say that it was.

The quiet voice was speaking again. "D'you remember the book of German legends downstairs *Tales from the Nibelungen Lied?* There was a sword in the story, the sword *Balmung,* stolen from the treasure hoard. It was the sword of conquest and, wherever it went, it brought woe and destruction. That's the very sword Germany's using today. She's fighting with the sword *Balmung.* The United Nations are using another sword, *Chrysaor,* the golden sword of Justice.

"There's a rambling old Elizabethan poem about a knight who carried that sword long ago. He fought for justice and cared only to right the wrong. He wasn't always successful. Made a ghastly muddle of his various quests and collected a host of enemies who loathed him because he tried to do justly. We're using the sword *Chrysaor,* like that knight. We're fighting for freedom and justice and the rights of the weak against the strong.

"Tony's been taken out of the country where the sword *Balmung* has been forced into every hand, and he has been brought into a country that fights with the sword *Chrysaor*. Now he's got to choose for himself which sword he's going to use, *Chrysaor* or *Balmung*. It's lucky he's no older. Another year or two might have set his mind so that he couldn't make a choice. But it's a hard choice, all the same."

"It isn't, Dym," said Mousie, severely. "It's an easy choice. Only a very wicked person would choose *Balmung*."

"There's such a thing as blind loyalty," said Dym. "It can make the easiest choice very hard indeed. What we need to remember every minute of the time is that Tony will judge England and her cause by what he sees in this house in the next few months. What he sees outside the house will influence him too, but not so much as what he sees inside it. As far as he is concerned, we are England. He isn't very old, and you can't expect him to read deep books or listen to broadcast speeches by way of finding out for himself whether England's cause is just. He has been told that the British are greedy and treacherous, soft, selfish and arrogant. That means that if we in this house allow ourselves to be impatient, unkind, self-righteous, he won't choose *Chrysaor*. How could he? And what would be the use of keeping his body a prisoner on English soil when his soul belongs to Germany. None. If he chooses *Balmung,* we shall have failed, utterly failed. But we must not fail.

"Think it out for yourselves. For Simon and Judy it means just being friendly, sharing toys and things, and not flying to Thomas or Phemie every time there's a quarrel. The rest of you ought to be able to find the answer to your own problems."

"I shall read some of Mortimer's little paper books about

the war," said Mousie. "He's got heaps of them, all showing why Germany is in the wrong. And then I shall explain the reasons to Tony."

"A fat lot of good you'll do that way," said James. "Tony's primed with reasons on the other side, and he's like all his loving family, as pig-headed as they're made. You'll never get him to admit that Germany could do wrong. It's a waste of time to try. I have."

"I don't think that arguments will help much," said Dym, "but I'm just as likely as anyone else to be mistaken. I'm afraid we shall all make mistakes in our dealings with him, however good our intentions."

"Like me," said Mousie, complacently. "I made an awful mistake the other day, Dym. I found a very pretty Christmassy German gramophone record and I put it on for Tony to hear. Something about frolicks and seligs, I think. Tony cried."

"Oh, drop it, Mouse!" said James.

Tony writhed in the darkness behind the chair. He had been hoping that Herr Dym would never hear what had happened when *O du fröhliche, O du selige* rang out unexpectedly on the quiet evening air. Euphemia had promised that she would never, never tell anyone.

"I think," said Dym hurriedly, "that we've talked long enough. The evacs and Tony ought to be back in the sitting room any minute now. I don't want him to find out about this confab. That's all for the present, thanks."

The meeting was dismissed. It streamed noisily past Tony. Sally alone lingered for a moment. "I liked what you said about the two swords," she said.

"Hope I didn't make England sound too noble and holy," said Dym. "We've made awful mistakes ourselves in our own dealings with other nations. I wasn't forgetting that, but I hadn't time to embark on a regular philosophy of history. Not with Mousie as audience, anyhow. And whatever we've done wrong in the past, there's no doubt that today we're fighting with the sword *Chrysaor*. If I didn't believe that, d'you think I could do what I have to do?"

Sally stared at the red, red sunset. "No, Dym. I wonder which sword Tony will choose; I do hope it will be *Chrysaor*."

"So do I," said Dym.

"It won't," said Tony to himself, between his teeth. "It will be *Balmung*."

They were moving to the door now. Tony remained in hiding till their footsteps had died away, then crept cautiously out. To his dismay, he saw that Sally had not gone downstairs with Dym. She was standing on a chair in her tiny room on the other side of the passage, readjusting the black-paper shade that screened her electric light. "Tony!" she exclaimed.

He stood still, sullenly. She took a flying leap over Judy's bed and came out into the passage. "Oh, Tony! You were there all the time! You listened!"

"I didn't mean to listen. How could I possibly know what you had come to talk about? I went to Herr Dym's room because—" He explained his two reasons. "And then you all came before I could escape, and I did not like to come out before everybody. You need not tell Herr Dym."

"Of course I won't. Did—did you understand what Dym said? All of it?"

"I shall never choose your *Chrysaor*," said Tony, "if that is what you mean. *Balmung* is the sword for me. It is Germany's sword."

There was a pause. "Let's talk about something else," said Sally, as if resolved not to argue. "I'm glad you like old houses with secret rooms. This house is very old in parts. It's built on the site of a monastery, and bits of the monastery are worked into it. Nobody knows how old the cellars are. We're supposed to have an underground passage leading to the church, too, but it's lost like the paneled room. And just come here a minute."

She led him down the passage to a thick black oaken post imbedded in the wall opposite the bedroom shared by Euphemia and Margaret. "See that hole? Now listen."

On a bracket close by stood a jam jar filled with pebbles. Sally took one and dropped it into a hole in the beam large enough to admit her hand. After what seemed a long time they heard a faint sound. "There!" said Sally. "Anything dropped down that hole is gone forever. You'd have to take the house to pieces if you wanted to find it again. Thomas thinks the beam must be directly over an old well about ninety feet deep."

A cold prickly feeling ran down Tony's spine. He backed, hoping that the house was solidly built.

"Simon and Judy are very funny," said Sally. "They won't go past this corner in the dark because they think the hole goes down to Satan's house. Dym says he thought so too when he was little. All sorts of things have been dropped into the well. Pat Jefferson's school report was the last. It was so bad that he didn't want his people to see it."

The loss of the school report horrified Tony. He could not imagine what would have happened to a German boy guilty of such a crime. "What did Herr Jefferson say?" he asked breathlessly.

"Oh, nothing," answered Sally. "When Phemie told him, he laughed and said he'd never had a decent report in his life, so he couldn't blame Pat."

"Never had a decent report in his life!" Tony repeated, hardly able to believe the words. He was thinking, in shocked surprise, that even Tante Bettina did not know how mad the English could be.

Sally turned to lead the way back to the sitting room just as Pat Jefferson and his three friends came charging out of the kitchen. "Now they'll stick to Dym like burrs all the evening," she said. "They always do. He's very good to them because he thinks they're lonely, away from home."

Tony did not compete with the evacuées for a share of Dym's notice, but as he sat in a corner with a book, he told himself jealously that it wasn't fair. Herr Dym needn't have spent so much time in looking at the youngest evacuée's stampbook and in telling the three others all they wanted to know about flying-training schools. There were other people who were lonely too, away from home.

A small voice inside him said mockingly, "The reason why Dym takes no notice of you is that he thinks you are at home."

"I'm not!" Tony answered the small voice. "I'm not! This isn't my home. And I shall never choose *Chrysaor*."

11

Nine Lives

"NOW WE WANT you to tell us about yourself,"
said one of the men on the other side of the sitting
room table.

It would have been easier to answer if Dym hadn't been
there, quiet and self-contained, lips set firmly, eyes intent as
if his hands were on the controls of a machine. Hesitating
sometimes because he could never tell what use Dym might
make of his revelations, Tony told them nearly all he knew.
No, Mutti had no relations; they were all dead. Vater had an
only brother, Onkel Dietrich, his partner in the chemical
works. Onkel Dietrich and Tante Bettina lived next door.

No, he had not been born in Germany but in South
America where Vater was doing research work on dyes. But
when Grandfather died, Vater took Mutti home to Germany, and except for holiday visits to other countries he
had lived in Germany till he left for Norway, six weeks
before he came to the British Isles.

From the way they listened, Tony knew that they had
heard the story before, partly from the Captain, partly from
Dym who had, no doubt, gathered together every stray
scrap of information. He had told Euphemia about himself
when he was ill and lonely. No doubt she had passed her
knowledge on to Dym.

"Have you ever been mistaken for an English boy?"

When that question was asked, Dym looked at him so searchingly that he could not make himself forget words spoken from time to time by Mrs. Cavendish's English friends: "So you have found an English playfellow for your sons?" . . . "Oh, really? I thought he was English."

"Only because I spent most of my playtime with English people," he answered, feeling that Dym's eyes had dragged the truth from him against his will.

"Have you remembered their address?"

"No, I still cannot remember it. And Frau Cavendish could only tell you that I am German, though I have the misfortune to look English."

The English did not press him to try to remember; it appeared that Frau Cavendish's possible evidence was not worth fighting for. The net could be drawn tight enough without it. And they drew it tight, slowly, slowly. By and by they showed him a photograph of a boy of six with *Tony* written on the back. There was a long smear under the *Tony;* but it was possible to pick out the first *a* and *n* of his name. Did he know how the smear came to be made? Had his name been written on the card, and had Frau Eckermann rubbed it out? Or had he?

Before he had made up his mind how to answer, one of the strangers said, suddenly and sharply, "Had you ever any reason to suppose that you were an adopted son?"

Dym looked up quickly. "No, no. That is a question we have no right to ask."

The man who had asked it frowned, but his two companions nodded approval. "You need not answer," Tony was told.

Afterward he realized that he ought not to have let the question pass. But he kept silence, bewildered first by the abruptness with which the words had been flung at him, then by the unexpectedness of Dym's intervention. At the end of a pause, the men went back to the earlier question. Still confused, he decided that here also silence would serve him best.

Then for what seemed endless ages there was talk among his elders, much of it too hard to follow. At last a voice said that the evidence Tony had supplied enabled Mr. Dymory Ingleford to fill in the gaps in the very considerable body of information already in his possession. It was now known that Herr and Frau Eckermann had visited England half way through their stay in South America. Their son's name could not be found in the registers of the town he had always been told was his birthplace, and friends who well-remembered the Eckermanns declared that there had never been a child. After the visit to England Herr and Frau Eckermann had not returned to the town they had been living in, but had gone to a different part of South America before leaving for Japan. There could be no doubt that he was the lost Anthony Victor Ingleford. When the war was over, it would be possible for Herr and Frau Eckermann to come forward to establish a claim to him, but in the meantime he must consider himself a British subject. It was considered wisest to tell him frankly that if such a claim were ever advanced it would be most unlikely to succeed.

Dym had won. The men behind the table were wavery black shapes with pale blank faces. Tony could see nothing clearly save the slight blue-gray figure that was master of his fate.

Then Tony heard his own voice speaking, but it sounded like the voice of a stranger: "I am not English; I am German." The answering silence smothered the words as if in a blanket of fog. "It is you, all you, all your fault!" he cried. "I will never speak to you again, Herr Dym!"

He did not remember what he said next; ever afterward it was hard to tell whether he had really shouted insulting remarks at Dym or whether his angry thoughts, bubbling and beating in his mind, had sounded so much like speech that he could not tell the difference. But he rather thought he had said exactly what he felt, for he did not think he could have imagined the mixed pity and amusement on the English faces opposite him. And he knew beyond all possibility of mistake that he had not imagined the quiet words that came at last: "That is enough, Anthony."

They had made him halt, those words. He had to listen to Herr Dym, just as, once before, he had been obliged to listen to the Captain of the British battleship. Yet the crisp note of command was absent from the airman's soft voice; it might be possible to defy him as he had not ventured to defy the other. He opened his lips, but the check, slight as it was, had done its work. Not a sound left them. Then, to his horror, he knew that if he tried again speech would end in tears. He was silent. There was a confused babel of talk all about him, a moving to and fro, rustlings, the scraping of chairs. Now he was alone. At first he did not think of anything except the queer way the winter sunlight glittered on the windowpane. Then the insides of his hands felt suddenly damp. He wasn't a guest any longer, but a member of the family and a very young member too. If it was true that he had hurled those outrageous insults at Herr Dym, there would be trouble when Herr Dym had finished seeing the strangers to their car.

But when the door opened again it only admitted Thomas, who stood looking at him with the air of one who wanted to say something kind but did not know how to begin. At last Thomas said, "There's half an hour before lunch, Tony. Come and have a game of halma."

Dumbfounded, Tony got out the board. Not until he had set the pieces in array did he realize that Thomas, knowing no German, had not understood his violence. Nor, apparently, had Herr Dym translated it.

"Dym has gone back to the station," said Thomas, taking up a blue man. "He's coming—" A glance at Tony's face made him break off in the middle of the sentence. "Well, well," he added, "let's get on with the game." And not another word was spoken until the dinner bell brought the whole family hurrying into the room.

Tony felt that he could never play halma again as long as he lived. Pushing his way past the people who were coming in, he dashed upstairs and, with no small difficulty, forced a crushed box and doubled-up board through the hole in the beam. The tiny men fell, with a hollow sound.

He would have stayed away from the meal had he not feared that someone would come to fetch him. So he went downstairs again and entered the dining room just in time to hear Euphemia saying, "Now do be careful, all of you, not to tell Tony you're glad. I don't know what will happen if you do."

"I'm more interested to hear," said Porgy, "whether we're having the second of the two plum puddings the food controller allowed you to make. I suggested, you remember, that it would be rather a nice way of marking Tony's entrance into the family—"

Then he caught sight of Tony and stopped, but Euphemia said, "It's coming, Porgy, but you know very well it's only a plum pudding's poor relation. In wartime—"

The four evacuées interrupted her by loud cheers for the poor relation. Under cover of the cheering Tony slipped into his chair, and the whole gathering became unnaturally polite. After the painful half hour was over, Tony sat in the window seat alone. Thomas came up to him and put a big hand on his shoulder. For one horrible moment Tony feared that he was about to propose another game of halma. But the fear was groundless. "Will you come out with me this afternoon, Tony?"

"If you like, Herr Ingleford."

"You mustn't call me that now, Tony."

Tony's mouth went tight. "I can't call you anything else, Herr Ingleford."

"Well, well," said Thomas, "never mind. I'll come for you as soon as I've finished a letter."

"We will amuse Tony till you are ready, Thomas," Mousie promised, with marked emphasis on the Thomas. And as the door shut she asked, "Would you like a game of halma, Tony dear?"

"The halma set is at the bottom of the hole in the beam," said Tony, "and I wish you were too, the whole lot of you."

After a surprised pause someone was heard asking in a dazed way, "Don't you like halma, Tony?"

"I loathe it," said Tony.

There was another pause. James said, "I'm very glad to hear it. Thomas can't stick halma himself, neither can the rest of us. We only played it with you because Thomas read, probably in some schoolbook of forty years ago, that every man, woman and child played it in Germany. A sort of national parlor game, don't you know? Was the book wrong?"

Tony shrugged his shoulders contemptuously.

"I suppose you thought just what we were thinking, that everybody played it all day long over here?"

"Yes," said Tony, "I thought you were a pack of idiots. I think so still."

It was a relief to find himself alone with Thomas in the quiet of lane and meadow, away from staring eyes. Under the cold gray open heaven the load of his unhappiness did not seem so hard to bear: he felt a dull ache now, instead of tearing pain.

They walked a long way to the house of the agent who supplied Thomas with cattlecake when there was any to be had. After Thomas had finished his business with the agent, they crossed water-logged meadows to the cottage of a shepherd who had promised to take three evacuées. Halfway there Tony began to flag. "Tired?" asked Thomas, looking down from his great height.

Tony nodded piteously.

"Like to rest on this stile till I come back?"

"No. It is too cold."

"You couldn't find your way home alone?"

"Yes, I could."

"This billeting must be done today," said Thomas, "so I can't come back with you. Don't try the short cuts across the marshes without me; they're dangerous. Go the long way round by the road."

A runaway's path was made plain before him. Tony had no clear plan in his head as he went down the road. Romantic dreams of a return to Germany in stolen airplane or motor launch melted like thin cold clouds at sight of the February sky. All that could be done was to follow the tamer course of making his way to one of the great cities in the hope of discovering the present whereabouts of some of Vater's German business friends. If he could get to Liverpool, Leeds, Manchester, Birmingham, Sheffield, Bristol or London, there would be German names in the directories in the public libraries. He would go to the addresses printed there and would claim help and protection, assuring his helpers that Mutti would pay after the war. Oh, Mutti would pay anything they chose to ask!

The wind shrilled; the air darkened. A new thought sobered him. What had Ginger said, long ago on board the battleship? Tony wrinkled his forehead, trying to catch at the half-forgotten words. *Ginger told me that he thought all the Germans in Great Britain had been parked on an island where the cats had no tails. I didn't ask him the name of the island because I thought he was making one of his stupid jokes. He went over some of the islands on his fingers: the Hebrides, the Orkneys, the Shetlands, the Isle of Wight, the Scilly Isles, Lundy Isle*—For a minute or two he was tempted to turn back to the *White Priory:* what was the use of searching for friends who were cut off from him by the sundering seas? Other counsels prevailed. He would go to the big towns first, in the hope that some Germans were in hiding there, having escaped the notice of the British Government. If that plan failed, he must make his way somehow to the island.

Once there, he would coax some kind German woman to pass him off as one of her children. She would hide him somehow till after the war. He was good at coaxing. Mutti had been as wax in his hands; he had always had his own way with her. You couldn't coax Tante Bettina, of course, and you didn't try. But Mrs. Cavendish had sometimes said "Yes" to him when she said "No" to her own sons. And now there was Euphemia who always gave him the nice oily tin to scrape out when she made Mortimer sardine sandwiches for his fire-watching nights—Euphemia who wouldn't listen when the evacuées grumbled that it wasn't fair. "No, I'm not spoiling Tony," she had said. "Tony needs more of that kind of food than you do; he hasn't been getting enough fat in Germany." Oh, yes, he had Euphemia under his thumb too. It was almost a pity he had been obliged to leave her.

He walked on, wishing he had made better use of former opportunities of finding his way about. The map on the cover of his blue exercise book could not help him in a tangle of country lanes with never a signpost visible. Why didn't the English have signposts, he wondered. But it was one of the questions to which at present there was no answer.

Passing a solitary wayside cottage, he asked to be directed to the nearest railway station. The boy and girl hanging over the gate had pudgy faces like small hard red wind-bitten apples.

The boy said to the girl, "He's not an evacuée."

Tony wondered how the boy knew. He did not look as though he could know anything.

The girl said, "Don't give information when people you don't know come asking questions. That's what Teacher told us, Billy."

The boy said, "Best ask the policeman, hadn't you? He lives a bit farther down the road."

Tony did not trouble the policeman. An hour later he stumbled upon a town about the size of Tamley Market, a sleepy place in which, hunt as he might, he found no railway station. Afraid to make inquiries, he wandered into the market place, which stretched its cobbled length between the High Street on one side and a church at the other. A small group of people was standing round a lorry in the empty square. Tony looked, then drew back quickly. There were some iron railings near him, and he clutched their cold firmness hard. On the lorry lay a long slender aircraft with a yellow nose and crushed wing tips that had once been square-cut. "It's a Messerschmitt," he heard someone say; "it's being taken along to be broken up."

The people round the lorry gazed solemnly; one old woman said, "Well, there!" to her friend, and the friend answered, "Well, there now!" No one else spoke.

Tony walked on, his head bent, his hand covered with brown stains and flakes of rusty iron. In the main street he saw a stationer's shop. With thoughts still full of the broken Messerschmitt, he went in to make a purchase.

"Can I buy a—a—a map here, please?"

"What sort of a map? School atlas, do you mean? Don't stock them. Could order one, if you like."

He was at a loss for the right word. "A map of these roads, please."

"What do you want a local map for? Been evacuated to these parts?"

"Ye-yes," said Tony.

"Privately, I suppose," said the woman. "You didn't come under the Government scheme."

Tony began to wonder how he could make himself look more like a Government evacuee. They appeared to be recognized and accepted at a glance where other strangers were regarded with suspicion. "No," he admitted reluctantly.

The woman moved to a door at the back of the shop. "I don't know where my husband keeps them," she said. "I'll ask him."

She went into the room behind the door. Though she lowered her voice, Tony caught part of a sentence about spies— He did not wait for more. When the stationer entered his shop, the customer had fled.

Hours later Tony was sitting in a forlorn heap on a frosty grass patch between five roads that went twinkling like white ribbons away into the gloom. The British were disappointingly unlike Tante Bettina's picture of them, after all. She had said that they were so casual and sleepy-headed that they would be taken completely by surprise when the Führer's troops landed on their islands. But all Tony's experiences that afternoon went to prove that the British were not sleepy. There wasn't even a name left on a Church notice board to guide a stranger on his way; children younger than himself were alert and cautious; shop-keepers sold dangerous goods only to those whom they could trust.

Earlier in the afternoon the birds had sung a good deal in such sweet and mellow notes that spring seemed far on its way. Now they were silent; not a solitary twitter disturbed the cold evening peace. The hedges were dark where before he had seen purple bramble sprays and the bare red slender stems of unknown wayside plants. Over them the sky showed great lakes of limpid blue and green, fringed with sunset clouds.

A tiny distant light wavered its way down the lane, and Tony knew it for the masked head lamp of a bicycle. He watched its approach without interest and without fear. Probably the rider's thoughts would be with the ruts and stones in the road; it was unlikely that he would notice a small dark heap on the grassy triangle. But when the bicycle stopped, he knew that the rider was Herr Dym. It seemed to him that he had known all along that it could be no other than Dym.

"Oh, there you are!" said Dym's quiet unmoved English voice. "Frozen, aren't you? Like to ride for a bit? I'll wheel you. This old crock won't carry two."

Tony scrambled on to the bicycle in silence. They wound in and out of the lanes till they reached the town, moon-silvered, dark and shuttered. The lorry with its burden stood stark and grim in the market place. "We'll go this way," said Dym, and swung the bicycle into a side street between half-timbered houses, black and ghostly white. By and by he paused before a window of bulging green bull's-eye glass, over which a shop sign creaked in the wind. Looking up, Tony saw a kettle painted on it.

"This is *Polly's Kettle*," said Dym. "We'll get something to eat before we go home."

Tony had not the strength of mind to turn away. He followed Dym.

Polly's Kettle had been made out of two cottages thrown together. A glowing log fire danced on whitewashed walls, dark furniture, blue curtains and thick yellow-glazed crockery.

"You're very late, sir," said Polly. "I've not much left."

"Anything will do, provided it's hot," said Dym. "We're perishing with cold and we've missed our tea."

"There's about half a fish pie," said Polly. "Only tinned salmon, of course. And blackberry-and-apple tart and buns and tea. I've nothing else."

"That will do splendidly, thanks," said Dym.

They ate their meal by the fire. A little black cat came mewing and pawing for fish. "How many lives has a cat?" Dym asked, tickling her gently under her furry chin.

Tony would not answer.

"Nine," said Dym. "So have you. I mean that if you run away as often as nine times you won't get into trouble when you are caught. But the tenth time you are caught running away there will be a row, a really serious row. Understand?" Tony scowled.

"You've lost three of your lives already. That leaves six, doesn't it?"

There were disadvantages, Tony found, in a vow of eternal silence. For example, one had no power to protest violently against such a flagrant injustice as this. He turned eyes glowing with indignation on Dym.

"You think that's not square, eh?"

But Tony was wrathfully silent. Dym's grave young face broke suddenly into a smile. Though Tony would not have owned it for the world, he liked to see his captor smile.

"Not going to be tricked into speaking to me, are you, Max? I'm afraid I did it on purpose—I wanted to see whether I could make you speak. Very good, then; we'll start from tonight. You have nine lives and no more. Is that fair warning?"

Tony did not answer in words. In his heart he thought it fair enough.

The evacuées were playing ping pong in the hall when Dym and Tony entered. "Oh, so you're back again," said the eldest. "We thought you'd be out all night at least." His voice showed plainly that he thought Tony a poor hand at running away.

"Uncle Thomas and Uncle Mortimer and James and Porgy are out hunting for you," said the smallest evacuée.

Tony did not follow Dym into the sitting room. Feeling shy, he sat down on the corner of an oak chest.

"You're not going to get into a row," said the smallest evacuée kindly.

"I know."

"But you're going to—"

"Shut up, Harold. He isn't to be told tonight."

"I'm going to tell. You're going to school on Monday. Gantry's, with James and Simon."

Tony felt like a fish in a net.

"Auntie Euphemia has been ringing up the Headmaster," said the little Harold. "Uncle Dym asked her to do it. I heard what they said. It's to give you fresh interests to think about."

Tony's shoes were heavy as though weighted with lead. Running away would be a hundred times harder to manage once his days were filled with the claims of school. This, too, he owed to Herr Dym. He sat motionless, staring at the stone floor. When the others came back one by one from their vain search, he hardly noticed their entrance. The flame of anger, partly quenched, was burning again. It rose to a white heat when Dym went back to the airdrome.

Dym looked back from the doorway with a " 'Night, everybody." Tony saw them look up. Their eyes traveled over Dym as if they were trying to remember all they could about someone they might never see again. Thomas said, "So long, old man." Margaret said, "There's a bit of white cotton on your sleeve, Dym. Take it off." The eldest evacuée said, "All the best, Dym. Happy landings!" Dym smiled, making the "thumbs up" sign.

It was hard to remember that Dym was an enemy. But the boy on the chest flung back his head and put his thumbs down. "May you never come back!" he said to himself, just above his breath.

He thought that no one had seen him; but when Dym had gone, Judy said in a frightened squeak, "He said, 'Never come back!' and he put his thumbs down, down! I don't like it."

And she tumbled herself into Euphemia's arms and hid her face. Tony flung Euphemia a mocking smile and went on holding his thumbs down.

"Dym saw. I'm sure Dym saw," sobbed Judy.

"Hope he did. I meant him to see," said Tony.

Euphemia said clearly, "Pagan signs can't help or hurt, Judy darling. Do you think Dym doesn't know that? You needn't be afraid. Dym is safe in God's keeping always."

She shut the sitting room door. Tony continued to sit on the chest, uneasy in his mind. The evacuées seemed restless, too. They whispered to the eldest, "Think he's flying tonight?"

The eldest evacuée put on the look of one who knows. "Oh, not tonight; it's impossible. He'd never have been allowed out of the station if there had been the smallest likelihood of ops tonight. How could he have got leave to be away from the briefing and the bombing-up and all that? Don't you worry. There's nothing to worry about."

Somewhere deep down in his heart Tony wanted to agree.

Upstairs in the attic, James spoke his mind. "I hope you're not going on with this kind of game," he said. "Porgy and I haven't had much of a Saturday holiday today. After helping Thomas on the farm till teatime, we had to set to work hunting an eel in the dark. It wasn't much fun."

"It is Herr Dym's fault," said Tony. "He brought me here and he keeps me here. I hate him."

"What did Dym say, Tony?" Porgy asked.

"I have nine lives. I may run away nine times if I choose."

"And after that?"

"If I am caught the tenth time running away, there will be a row. But there will not be a tenth time. I am not a fool like you English."

"We're not such fools as we look," said James. "And if by any chance you lose your nine lives, you'll be well advised not to try a tenth getaway. Dym's long-suffering, but if there's one thing he's better at than another it's keeping his word. I don't recommend your plunging yourself into a row with Dym. Thomas or Richard or Mortimer or old Ginger if you like—but not Dym!"

"You talk too fast," said Tony. "I do not understand what you say."

"Oh, yes, you do. You understand a lot too well for your own comfort," said James, grinning.

Unable to think of a retort, Tony got into bed. James regarded him disapprovingly. "Look here, it's about time you started saying your prayers. To my certain knowledge you haven't said them since you came. You're not ill now, you know. Two minutes wouldn't kill you."

"I don't say prayers," said Tony scornfully. "Haven't since I was small."

James switched off the light, then groped his way past Tony's bed to his own. On the way he paused. "That's for you," he muttered, thrusting something cold into Tony's hand. "You won't have to muffle it in two layers of tissue paper when you use it out of doors, 'cause the glass is frosted already. I thought perhaps you'd like one."

Tony pressed the catch of the electric torch. For a moment pride struggled with some other feeling. Then he smiled at James over the dimmed yellow circlet. "It will be very useful," he said. "I'll take it with me when I use my next life."

"Oh, go on!" said James, laughing.

He ran a shy, thin hand through Tony's hair, ruffling it wildly. Silence and darkness followed. Tony did not sleep at first. He was thinking of the old life with its round of marches and rallies and processions, its songs and scarlet banners and gay excursions. This English life was so strangely different, so colorless, so austere in its land of gray skies, gray seas, and gray churches in gray-green meadowland beyond the mazy little lanes that ran on and on till you lost yourself and were Max again, listening to the stories that Mutti told. Now Mutti wasn't telling stories. They were in the orchard at home among the peach blossoms, or wandering in the vineyards among the purple ripening grapes under a blue October sky, or saying together the prayer he hadn't said since he was very little:

> *"Guter Vater in Himmel du,*
> *Meine Augen fallen zu;*
> *Will mich in mein Bettchen legen:*
> *Leiber Gott das bitt' ich dich:*
> *Bleib bei mir, hab' Acht auf mich."*

Mutti had taught him that prayer out of the little yellow *Bilder A.B.C. Buch* that was precious because it had belonged to her grandmother, who had colored the three oddly-dressed children on the cover and the bird pictures inside. Sometime he would like to paint pictures with the colored pencils the Captain had given him.

12

The Terrible Fortnight

AFTER IT WAS over, the Inglefords always called it "Tony's terrible fortnight."

It began quietly enough. There was nothing to be gained by refusing to go to church, so to church he went. Sitting between Euphemia and Porgy, he looked about him curiously. The Home Guard had come to Church Parade that morning, with Thomas at their head. The horseman and cowman from the *White Priory* were there, with the grocer, the blacksmith, two roadmen and the owner of *Glardon Hall;* the rest were men he had not seen before. Thomas made a fine figure in his khaki uniform, but some of the others were elderly, bowed, gray-headed. These were the men, Tony knew, who were pledged to defend their country when invasion came.

They will never defeat us; they couldn't, he thought exultantly. And he whispered to Porgy, just to annoy him, "We shall chew you up."

"Oh, all right," said Porgy. "Mind you don't choke on the bones."

"Hush, boys," said Euphemia.

Margaret was playing a voluntary on the harmonium that did duty for an organ. Tony's band had played Handel's *Water Music* at a Winter Help concert; this, he felt, gave him a right to be critical of her playing and her instrument. The voluntary ended, she struck a single chord.

"Stand up," Porgy whispered as he rose. "It's *God Save the King.*"

"Shan't!" Tony answered.

He gripped the edge of the seat hard for fear any zealous person should try to uproot him. Nobody did. He sat still, watching. Though he had often heard the air, he had never heard it wedded to those words. The congregation stood before him, their faces blank and rigid, their eyes staring straight ahead. They look as though they hated everybody in the world and themselves most of all, thought Tony. They look as though they felt perfect fools. They look as though they would die if they caught sight of anyone looking at them.

As the song ended, Margaret's black brows scowled at him. He returned the scowl, wishing he could do something more to show where he stood. But for some time there was no opportunity; it was a service hardly to be distinguished from the services in the English church in his home town. He had attended those services long ago with Auntie Nell and Uncle Laurie and the boys, but he had taken good care not to let the Inglefords know it. They didn't even know that he had called Mr. and Mrs. Cavendish by those affectionate names; he could keep secrets when he chose.

Thinking about the Cavendishes carried him far away from the little church. A whisper from Euphemia brought him suddenly back again. "You needn't kneel, Tony; you won't want to join in the next prayers. Read your hymn book instead."

His own family carefully took no notice of him during

the special prayers for victory and peace; but the evacuées telegraphed marked disapproval from the pews where they sat with their schoolfellows. Gratitude for Euphemia's thoughtfulness kept him from making any return demonstration, though it was not easy to ignore those rolled eyes and pointing fingers. He would take his revenge later, he decided. His chance came sooner than he had expected.

The Vicar gave out the number of a hymn. Wheezing, the harmonium made a response that sent Tony to his feet with a face as white as paper. He had last heard those notes played by full orchestra and sung by many thousand voices amid the tramp of marching men.

> *"Glorious things of Thee are spoken,*
> *Zion, City of our God,"*

sang the congregation—all but one. The exception sang *Deutschland über alles* at the top of his voice. It was plain that only a few people understood what was happening. Margaret was not deceived. She played the harmonium louder and ever louder in an attempt to drown his voice in a storm of roaring and blaring as had never been heard in the peaceful church before. His spirit rose to the challenge. He wasn't going to be defeated, not he! And he was not. The harmonium's unwonted struggles proved too severe a strain on its powers. There was a sudden despairing sound like the squawk of a frightened hen, followed by silence. Tony finished his song unaccompanied and alone.

Thomas was the only Ingleford who listened to the sermon. Tony for his part did not hear a word of it. The excitement over, he had time to wonder how soon the police or the Home Guard would come to arrest him. Arrest! It was an unpleasant word. Though he despised himself for a coward, he could not help feeling that the rows of khaki shoulders in the front pews looked broader than they had less than an hour ago. He laced his fingers in and out; they felt cold and clammy, and his knees were shaking just as they had shaken in the chemist's shop on his first snowy evening, weeks ago.

A shuffling sound startled him. They were getting up and going home; they were in the churchyard; they were on the road. Somehow, he wasn't with Euphemia any longer, but with James and Porgy and four staring evacuées.

He was frightened, desperately frightened, under a show of calm. It was not the *White Priory* people that he feared. There was a fairness about them, the same kind of fairness that he had had from his Cavendish friends. They recognized that enemies were bound to fight, but the police and the Home Guard could not be expected to take the same view. Sooner or later he would be made to answer for his double insult to the British flag. He would get his wish about leaving the *White Priory;* but the manner of his leaving it would not be pleasant.

"I will do it again if I get the chance," he said, suddenly and loudly, the better to assure himself that he wasn't afraid.

"You won't get it from Margaret," said Porgy. "She'll play that tune at your funeral, but not before."

The evacuées sniggered. Tony wished he were alone with James. He wouldn't have minded asking James how soon the police would come and what they would do; but pride forbade him to ask questions before Porgy and the evacuées. He waited, therefore, for something to happen. It did not happen. Soon he found himself at the dinner table. The voice of Aunt Addie woke him out of an uncomfortable daydream. "Anthony, my dear," said Aunt Addie, "it is not usual to join in the singing quite so heartily. You must not sing so loud next Sunday."

Thomas said with his slow, kind smile, "You sang a German hymn that goes to the same tune, didn't you, Tony?"

Nobody cared to enlighten Thomas. At last Margaret said wrathfully, "It wasn't a hymn at all. It was *Deutschland über alles* that he was singing."

There was another, longer pause. Then Thomas said questioningly, "That hymn tune is also the tune of *Deutschland über alles?*"

"Yes," said Margaret, "unfortunately it is."

"Then avoid it for the present," said Thomas, "when Tony is in church. If you explain to the Vicar, he'll understand."

"And in order to avoid other disgraceful scenes," said Mr. Bland, "it might be well, Miss Margaret, to make sure that none of the other German patriotic songs are set to our hymn tunes."

"Your hymn tunes!" exclaimed Tony. "It's Haydn's *Austria*. Yours, indeed!"

"Tony!" said Euphemia.

"I am in the right," said Tony indignantly. "He is entirely ignorant—"

"Now, Tony, don't talk any more," said Euphemia. "Eat your dinner before it gets cold. I'm sorry, Mr. Bland. You must excuse Tony; he's finding the new life difficult."

Tony saw her look at Thomas out of the corner of her eye, and he saw Thomas give her a return glance over his Yorkshire pudding and roast beef. That swift interchange of looks gave Tony the comfortable knowledge that neither

Thomas nor Euphemia approved of a stranger's taking it upon himself to meddle with the affairs of their household; and in some inexplicable way it quieted the fear that the police would soon be vengefully hammering on the front door. He ate his dinner with the conviction that he had served his country well enough for one day.

So the rest of Sunday passed more peacefully than the Inglefords had dared to hope. An unapproachable Tony who buried himself in a book was at least a Tony who gave no trouble. By bedtime they had begun to hope that the outburst in church had, been, as Porgy put it, "the last flare-up of the incendiary bomb."

In the faint morning light Tony looked so pale and hostile that the hope of the night before faded away. His family sat round the breakfast table, fully expecting to hear him declare that nothing would induce him to go to school. But he did not speak. Shrugging one shoulder he went slowly on with his porridge.

Tony went to school and came home again, apparently resigned to his fate. It was considered a good sign that he answered Thomas' "How did you get on, Tony?" with nothing worse than "Thank you, Herr Ingleford. The school was not more beastly than I expected."

"He likes it," said Porgy to the others. "If he can't find anything worse than that to say, you may safely conclude that he doesn't feel too bad. What would be abuse from anyone else is high praise from him."

Further well-meant questions were met by "Yes, No," and "I don't know." Of positive information Tony vouchsafed not a single word.

"How does he really get on?" Euphemia asked James, when another three days had brought no change in Tony's sphinx-like attitude.

"Rather well on the whole," said James. "He never opens his mouth if he can help it; but at least we've had no scenes so far. Everybody's decent to him. The masters seem to think that he's well up to the level of his class in most subjects and oughtn't to have much difficulty in adapting himself to new methods and textbooks."

"I wish he found it as easy to adapt himself to us," sighed Euphemia, looking down the long table to where Tony was sitting apart, busy with his prep. "There's someone at the front door, Jim; will you be an angel and see who it is? Vera's out."

James went. Agitated voices were heard in the hall, a door slammed, footsteps raced upstairs and down. James came back into the sitting room and shut the door on the voices.

"It was the Air-Raid Warden. He wanted Thomas. There was a light showing from our roof."

"Oh, James, how awful! Where? There couldn't be!" cried Euphemia.

"There jolly well could!" James answered. "I rushed upstairs and found it. The Warden's foaming at the mouth. He says he'll make an example of Thomas for the most flagrant breach of the lighting restrictions that he's ever had the misfortune to meet."

"I never heard such nonsense in my life!" cried Euphemia. "It must be a mistake."

"No mistake, worse luck," said James. "Somebody must have deliberately taken down the shutter in the boxroom. The light was streaming out of the window like a neon sign. I saw it myself."

"But the light in the boxroom is only a glimmer from a five-watt globe—"

"The globe's been changed. What I switched off was a seventy-five at the least."

"But who—" began Euphemia, only to stop short as she saw that everybody in the room was looking at Tony. She whispered to James, "It wasn't— It couldn't have been—"

"Must have been," answered James.

"But how could he possibly have moved Ginger's big press in front of the window? How could he have got hold of tools to unfasten a shutter that was nailed in place when the war began? And he doesn't know where we keep the spare electric bulbs, I'm sure he doesn't."

Tony knew what was being said. He drew himself up proudly, expecting to hear a public accusation. "I did it," he meant to say. "I am not ashamed. I don't care what you do to me."

But he had no occasion to make his speech; for he was not accused. The hall door shut, and Thomas, looking worried, came into the sitting room and talked in a low voice to Euphemia. Then he went away again, his face still troubled. "I don't care," Tony said to himself. "I don't care."

Nevertheless he could not keep his mind on his lessons or even on the pirate story that he had borrowed from Sally. He was glad when bedtime took him out of the company of people who went steadily on saying nothing. But even bedtime did not bring the relief he had hoped for. Waking from an uneasy dream, he heard James and Porgy talking softly in the dark.

"How much will the fine be, d'you think?"

"Mortimer says they'll let him off with a pound and a caution. Thomas says it will be five. I think so too."

"Rough luck! Poor old Thomas!"

"Dym's certain to make it good, though. Tony's his responsibility. He'll insist."

"Of course. But that's awkward for Thomas too. He knows Dym can't afford it. Dym's doing a lot for the family already—Sally's school fees, half Ginger's allowance, a contribution to the support of the aunts, and the entire support of Tony. But Thomas won't be able to help himself. Five pounds is five pounds, especially when you've got three practically penniless aunts to house and feed for the rest of their lives."

"Little bounder, to play a trick like that on poor old Thomas! I've no patience with him. If it wasn't for the bother it would cause, I should say that the best thing he could do would be to take himself off again."

"Umph!" said James.

In the morning Tony did not answer repeated calls. James, half dressed, went over to the bed and shook the sleeper's blanketed shoulder. It yielded with pillowy softness to his touch.

Tony had taken Porgy's advice.

13

Six Lives Lost

"WHERE DID YOU go when you ran away, Tony?"
Tony was in bed again, a white-cheeked Tony
propped up with pillows. His travels were over and, in the
course of them, he had lost four lives. Tracked by the police
at the end of the second day, he had been kept in their
charge until Mortimer came to take him home. Mortimer,
short-sighted and unsuspicious, was an easy guardian to
run away from. He had run away from Mortimer three
times, remaining at liberty for a good many hours. The
third time he was caught not by Mortimer but by Herr
Dym, whereupon he gave up the struggle, partly because
the odds were now against him and partly because he had a
pain in his side when he breathed, such a sharp pain that he
had hard work to keep his resolution of never speaking to
Herr Dym again. Telling him wouldn't have made the pain
better; still, he felt it was only right that Herr Dym should
know. But Herr Dym guessed that something was wrong;
and on reaching home he had marched his prisoner upstairs to bed in broad daylight. "This isn't a punishment for
running away," he had explained. "You've caught cold."

It was worse than a cold, much worse. There were days
and nights more feverish and painful than those that had
followed his first coming to the *White Priory*. Porgy told
him, giggling, that there had been one night when he

talked nonsense in mixed English and German for hours on end.

"Where did you go when you ran away, Tony?" Porgy asked again.

But Tony wouldn't tell. Only his diary knew how he had spent the adventurous days. Its pages told of a visit to a city where he had stood with a crowd of cheering people to watch the King and Queen going to inspect a factory that made munitions in the sheds where once it had made gay Christmas crackers. And it told also of the night he had spent in the house of deaf old Jane Grimes, who had taken him for an evacuée when he asked her for a night's lodging. He hadn't undeceived her because he hoped to get a night's lodging free of charge. But it had not been a comfortable night that he had spent in her stuffy cottage with the red geraniums in the window and the black-edged memorial cards of all her deceased friends tacked to the walls. Jane Grimes had done nothing but revile the billeting officer; there had been little food in the larder; and the unaired bed had been clammy and cold. In the morning Tony had been obliged to escape by the back door as soon as she had set off down the road to get her money and his tins of rations from the billeting office.

He kept his diary in a blue exercise book that Simon had exchanged for the pencil sharpener made in the shape of Cologne Cathedral. The exercise book was a counterpart of Dym's gift to him some weeks ago, a gift that he had kept hidden in a hidey-hole ever since. There were many pages of writing in that book too, some of it in a kind of shorthand he had invented, the rest in ordinary German script. But the writing in Dym's book was not diary writing. Those pages showed sketch maps, lists of names, scraps of miscellaneous information meant for his own side. He smiled when he thought how pleased Ernst would be that he had learned his lesson so well. The Ingleford family figured there, from Thomas, Home Guard and Billeting Officer, down to little Simon and Judy, who helped with paper salvage and with the collection of cotton reels and pillboxes and tins. "A very dangerous family," he had called them.

When the right time came, he would make use of those notes, to which he was adding steadily, day by day. He did not know yet how he should dispose of them; but he thought that the stranger at *Querns* would probably welcome any news that he could give. For it had not been hard to discover that James, Porgy and the eldest evacuée were keeping watch on the lonely house. Convinced in their own minds that its owner was a spy, they took regular turns of what they called duty, during which they haunted his footsteps and watched for any mysterious comings and goings and for signals made by lights flashed to enemy aircraft. If they hadn't been on the wrong side, it would have been the greatest fun in the world to join their whispered conferences and secret expeditions. So far they had no positive evidence against their man: it would, therefore, be foolish to approach him yet.

The note taking could be done easily at all times; for the family always supposed him to be writing his diary. They knew that he was keeping a diary to show Mutti when he got back to Germany, and Porgy had stated that it was just as well the diary was being written in German because he himself made a point of reading any diaries he found lying about, just to see whether the writers had said anything about him. "You needn't trouble to learn German in order to read my diary," Tony had said in reply to that. "I don't put you into it. You're not worth troubling about."

"Well," Porgy retorted, "you must think Dym's jolly well worth troubling about, at that rate. I can see his name at least fifteen times on that page."

"Rot!" said Tony, but when Porgy had gone away he looked at the diary and found to his surprise that his worst enemy's name appeared constantly:

Herr Dym brought home chocolate from the canteen today. I ate as much as I could to save it from falling into the hands of the English . . . Herr Dym has the D.F.C. with two bars for his wicked exploits in the Fatherland . . . Herr Dym plays the piano and most of the strings, but he likes the viola and the 'cello better than the fiddle . . . Herr Dym has learnt at last that it is no good speaking to a person who refuses to answer . . . Herr Dym is supposed to be the lucky one of the family because two of his mother's cousins are very fond of him though they don't care much for the others. They are Cousin Basil and Cousin Olive Fairleigh. Sally says they are old and rich and eccentric . . . Herr Dym's friend Paddy spent the evening here; he is in the R.A.F. too, which is surprising as he does not like the English. All through tea he kept saying how he hated their cold manners and smug faces and superior voices and self-righteous attitude and mouse-colored hair. The English seemed interested but not at all annoyed; they said, "Really?" and "Have another piece of cake, Paddy?" So he lost his temper and said, "You are a mouldy lot, you English; it's awfully hard to get up a fight. When I go out to tea at home, I always come back with a black eye." Herr Dym said, "Oh, come off it, Paddy!" and Paddy came off it quite suddenly and sang a whole book of songs called Cautionary Tales. The one I liked best was "The chief defect of Henry King was chewing little bits of string!" . . . Herr Dym has a friend, Jacob, who is a Jew, a musician before the war, but now he is in the R.A.F. When he plays he cannot bear to see Euphemia knitting socks; it upsets him. Once he turned round on the piano stool and roared at her, "Miss Euphemia, put that down!" But she laughed and went on. Herr Dym says he is a genius . . . Herr Dym has lots of friends; they are always turning up and they make themselves quite at home. One is Scotch or Scottish or Scots; I am not quite sure which, neither are the English. They keep on using the wrong word by mistake. But they know that they must never put N.B. for North Britain on a letter going to Scotland; it gives great offence. The Scotch friend likes coming here because there is an iron plate called a griddle in the kitchen; it belonged to the Inglefords' Scotch great-grandmother and it bakes scones in the Scotch way . . . Another friend is Welsh; Herr Dym calls him Taffy. He is teaching me Welsh, which he says is the most important language in the world because it is the language spoken in Heaven . . . At first I thought the Inglefords had a very young uncle named Uncle Sam, but it turns out to be the nickname they have given to Herr Dym's friend in the Eagle squadron . . . Herr Dym and Uncle Sam helped James tonight with his model aircraft. I am making a Dornier with some bits James has given me. I thought they would tell me I wasn't to make a Dornier, but they didn't. Herr Dym . . .

There was plenty of time to write up his diary in bed. Afterward he had too many other things to do. He was not sent back to school at once, but was free to wander about the fields and lanes with Thomas, who was as friendly as ever despite the five pounds' fine. The remembrance of that fine made Tony feel shy sometimes. He told himself that he didn't care in the least for Herr Dym's share in the

misfortune—Herr Dym deserved to be punished! But he
hadn't meant kind Herr Thomas to suffer the indignity of
appearing before the magistrates. And one day when they
two were alone in the gray-green meadows he slid his hand
suddenly into the big hand beside him. It tightened round
his; then Thomas turned and looked down with a slow
smile, saying nothing. And he knew that Thomas understood, without troublesome explanations.

He picked snowdrops in the copse for Euphemia that
afternoon, as well as an armful of the long dark-brown rods
that the Inglefords called "pussy willow." Sally had put
pussy willows in a jar by his bedside when he was ill, that
he might watch their unfolding. First the fat buds had
shrugged off their light-brown hoods and had shown themselves as morsels pale silver-green in color, silky soft to
touch. After that they had puffed themselves into plump
silvery tufts that were presently dusted with pollen gold.
"They really are rather like silver and gold kittens," he had
heard Dym say once, laughing.

Euphemia was pleased with the snowdrops and the new
set of silvery tufts; and Tony himself was pleased to discover that from the hour of that walk he was set free from
the constant watchfulness that had followed him ever since
he had meddled with the light in the roof. Everyone seemed
suddenly to take it for granted that he could be trusted not
to do it again. He could not think how they knew he was
sorry for what he had done, but enlightenment soon came
through Porgy.

"It's funny, isn't it," said Porgy amiably, "that you should
be a bit like Dym in character as well as in your face?"

"I am not like Herr Dym."

"Thomas says you are, and he ought to know. I heard

him telling Phemie that the other day you did just what Dym used to do, years and years ago, when he wanted to show he was sorry for anything that had gone wrong. And Phemie said yes, she thought you were beginning to settle down."

"It is true that I was sorry Herr Thomas was made to suffer for Herr Dym's fault," said Tony defiantly, "but it is not true that I am like Herr Dym or that I am settling down. I am not. I have been ill; that is why I have not run away again. But if you think I am changing my mind, I will soon prove to you that I am not."

So he lost another life that very day.

Running away in haste did not pay, Tony decided, when after a few hours of freedom Herr Dym's hand was once more laid on his shoulder. But the loss of the fifth life had a sequel that Tony had not looked for.

The two of them reached home in the middle of the morning. Euphemia was busy ironing. She put aside her work but asked no questions. The dogs came in at the open kitchen door and rushed to greet Dym. When at last they took notice of Tony they eyed him disapprovingly, evidently thinking that he ought to be at school. Tony ate and drank and pretended that he was alone in the room.

"Max," said Dym, when they had finished.

Tony went on pretending to be alone.

"Max," said Dym again, gravely, "you have some English money. You couldn't have paid railway fares or bought food without it. I want you to let Phemie or me take care of it for the present."

Tony turned to Euphemia whose face said, as plainly as Dym's, that it would be useless to tell a lie. "It's mine," he said. "If you think I stole it, you think wrong. Your brother

Ginger and his friends put it into my pocket with my own money when they made me change my clothes. You can write to him if you don't believe me. It's mine."

He thought he saw a look of relief on both faces. "Yes, it is yours," Dym agreed, "but you can't be allowed to use it for running away. If you will give it to one of us, you can ask for what you want when you go shopping."

Still ignoring Dym, he said to Euphemia, "No!"

"Tony," said Euphemia, "I'm afraid you must."

"I won't!"

"Choose your banker, Max," said Dym. "The sooner it's done the better."

Tony had heard that note of quiet determination before. Tears of anger welled into his eyes as he put down some mixed coinage on the table in front of Euphemia.

"That isn't all," said Dym.

"Yes, it is," but the glib words faltered as he met a keen look from the other side of the table.

"Oh, Tony!" said Euphemia reproachfully.

"I don't care!" said Tony. "I won't give my money up. You and Herr Dym will have to take it by force like the bullies you are. Especially him," he added quickly. It wouldn't do, he thought, to make Euphemia angry. She was a useful kind of person.

"Especially me," Dym agreed cheerfully. "I should hate to search you, Max. If I do it, though, I shall do it thoroughly. But you may be able to hide something if you're willing to turn your pockets out yourself. Which is it to be?"

Tony replied by flinging the contents of the first pocket at his captor. Laughing, Dym caught some of the coins. Euphemia picked the rest up and stacked them neatly on the table. Sobered by the size of the pile, Tony emptied the other pockets slowly, trying his best to smuggle some coins away. But Dym was lynx-eyed: one by one the florins and half-crowns and shillings had to be surrendered until, at last, there was nothing left but one little sixpence pressed tightly between two fingers. He saw Dym looking at the two fingers just where the milled rim of the sixpence peeped forth, but all Dym said was, "Thanks; that will do."

Euphemia made a small brown-paper packet of the money, tied with gay Christmas string from her workbasket. "Over a pound!" she said to Dym. "Those extravagant boys!"

Tony walked sullenly to the fireplace. He heard Dym say good-bye, but he would not look round. The door shut. Euphemia took up her iron. "Don't look like that, Tony dear," she said. "You understand, don't you, that you can spend your money as you like? You've only to tell me what you mean to buy."

"I hate Herr Dym," said Tony moodily. "He is no better than a thief."

For a long time he glowered into the flames. Presently a smile came to his lips. "He took my money," said Tony to himself, "but he didn't take my knife. I know how I can pay him out."

By and by he stole upstairs. Going into Dym's room, he went straight to the desk and took out his heavy clasp knife. Then he bent over the dark shining surface.

"Tony dear," said Euphemia at dinner time, "how did you get such a dreadful blister on your thumb?"

Tony's reply puzzled Euphemia; it was not an answer to her question. "You needn't pretend to be nice to me," he said sullenly. "You've got me a prisoner here. I can't run away without the money that has been stolen from me. But I can still show that I am loyal, and I mean to show it. I shall not turn the lights on again because I don't want to hurt Herr Thomas, who is not to blame. But I shall do everything I can think of to hurt other people, so that in time you will get so tired of keeping me you will give me my money and let me go. It is Herr Dym's fault if I behave as I never should have behaved at home."

Though Euphemia had no means of knowing it, this explanation was intended to prepare her for the shock that awaited her when she next dusted Dym's room. Nor could she tell that Tony's extraordinary behavior during the next two weeks was largely due to her omission of this household duty. He was not angry now; his anger had died during the time spent at Dym's desk. But he was restless, uneasy in mind, and very anxious to convince himself that he was not in the least afraid of the explosion that was bound to follow discovery. "He's turned into a German hedgehog again at a moment's notice," was Porgy's verdict. "He was such a meek lamb when he was ill that I thought his prickles were off for good. It's disappointing."

Tony would have run away more than once in those slow waiting days, if he had not been afraid that the Inglefords would think he had fled out of cowardice. And when he next lost a life, it was lost through a misunderstanding that he could not very well set right.

"You might have chosen a better night for escaping," said Euphemia, as late at night she surveyed a drenched and dripping Tony who had just been deposited on the mat in the back-kitchen by an equally damp Mortimer.

"I wasn't running away," said Tony. "I meant to come back. I went for a ride by myself after school, that was all. And I lost myself in your stupid roads without any sign-posts."

This lame explanation did not satisfy Euphemia any better than it had satisfied Mortimer.

"Oh, Tony, that can't be true! Who would go cycling for pleasure on a wild night like this?"

Tony had no further explanation to offer. He kicked off his shoes, took his tray of supper from Euphemia's hands, and stalked upstairs to bed in dignified silence. Euphemia and Mortimer looked at each other.

"Well, that's over," said Mortimer wearily.

"Did you have much trouble with him?"

"None whatever. I think he was really rather glad to be caught. And oddly he was very insistent that he hadn't run away. I suppose he didn't want to lose another life so easily. He has only three left."

"Mortimer, do go and change. You'll be ill again."

"I'm just going. By the way, did you hear anything of a rumor that Dym had crashed?"

"It seems to be all over the place. Sally heard it at school, poor mite. She even heard the name of the hospital he was supposed to be in."

"I hope the rumor-mongers weren't heartless enough to make it Rond Cross. You remember Sally saying, last year, when he was there, 'I think the Matron is the hardest, savagest woman in the whole world. She's cruel to Dym and those other poor men—they're afraid of her, positively afraid!'"

Euphemia laughed. "The young scamps, they probably had good reason to be! But Sally overdid her championship.

Dym liked the Matron very much, you remember. There must be a heart under the starch and steel."

"Never met anyone but Dym who caught a glimpse of it," said Mortimer, turning away.

But he was mistaken. Upstairs was a boy who had caught a considerable glimpse of it that very night. Now that he was back again in the familiar attic, Tony couldn't be quite sure that he had not been dreaming. Had he or had he not overheard two of the masters saying that Dym was lying seriously injured in Rond Cross Military Hospital? Had he cycled off to Rond Cross to learn the truth for himself? Could it be that he had actually scaled a high wall and crept secretly through the hospital grounds when the sentry at the gates turned him back became he hadn't a pass? Had there ever been a stern-faced woman who caught him stealing down one of the bare white corridors and made him tell his business? Had he actually dared to disbelieve her when she said that Dym was safe, quite safe; it was his friend Kitteridge who had crashed.

He could not answer the questions with any certainty; but the same dream pictures came into his mind every time he asked. Again and again he saw a boy in Matron's sitting room. A mirror on the wall showed him the boy's face, very like his but much whiter, with wet hair all in a tangle and damp clothes stained red and green from wet railings and rain-soaked moss-grown walls. The boy was persistent. He seemed to be half crying as he asked Matron—yes, that was who she was, Matron, evidently a person of importance—whether she was positive-certain-sure it wasn't Herr Dym who was hurt. And then Matron said, in a gentle voice, "Would you like to see for yourself?"

Then they were walking through miles of long corridors. Now there was a door in front of them. Matron was saying, "Not frightened, are you?" The boy was answering "No." The door opened. They were in a bare small clean room with glass and steel furnishings and a white bed. On the bed lay somebody so heavily swathed in bandages that it was hard to see who he really was. The boy's heart seemed to stand still for a moment, then it thumped so hard it nearly choked him. No, this wasn't Herr Dym. This was only Kitteridge, frowning as though he had met with a puzzle he couldn't solve. His eyes were shut; once or twice he moaned sharply in his sleep.

Matron and the boy were back again in the sitting room. They were having some tea, though it was past teatime. The boy wasn't telling her about himself because she said she knew. She was telling him about Herr Dym instead, who had been at Rond Cross in the previous summer, seriously wounded.

"Worse than Herr Kitteridge?"

"Yes."

The boy twisted in his chair, trying to forget the rigid figure, the queer little moans.

"He was very plucky and cheerful," said Matron. "He had a smile for everyone; he never complained."

But the boy still twisted on the chair, unable to forget. Then Matron showed him a laughing photograph. "From your brother," she said.

Across the photograph Dym had written:

All my love to Madam Dragon. Thank you for putting Humpty-Dumpty together again so nicely.

The sight of the photograph made the boy stop feeling as though a tight hand clutched his throat. He smiled a little. "Herr Dym is not very respectful," he remarked.

Matron smiled grimly. "Not always. He and his special friends gave me a lot of trouble when they were getting better. It would have been easier to nurse handfuls of quicksilver."

"You mean, they ragged as they do at the *White Priory?*"

"They did."

The boy breathed freely again: being seriously wounded did not seem so terrible after all. He heard himself asking, "What did they do?"

Madam Dragon looked at him and actually laughed. "I'm not going to tell you about their pranks, young man. How do I know that I may not have you as a patient some fine day?"

But she softened her refusal by telling him about the German prisoner who could speak very little English. Dym, it appeared, had acted as interpreter.

"Herr Dym did not object?"

"No, why should he? He did all he could to help. Are you surprised?"

The boy was offended; he said that he was not in the least surprised. Matron said, "Dym comes to see me sometimes; he doesn't forget old friends. Shall I ask him to bring you over to tea when he gets his leave?"

The boy was taken aback. "No, please! I do not want Herr Dym ever to hear that I came on his account. He must not know. Please not, please!"

Matron nodded understandingly. "If we meet again, we meet for the first time? This visit is not to be mentioned? I see."

And then all the pictures faded into mist and darkness and driving rain and the horrible feeling that he was lost. His adventures would have seemed no more than a fantastic dream if he hadn't had proof of their reality in an illustrated journal hidden under his pillow. Matron had given it to him because there were pictures of Dym in an article entitled *A Visit to a Station of Bomber Command.*

He told himself that he meant to throw the journal down the hole in the beam; it had only been accepted out of courtesy to Matron. Nevertheless, he could not help looking at the pictures with the aid of James' torch. Dym was in nearly all of them. They were interesting pictures after all, Tony decided; they were too good to be thrown away. He would save them to show Mutti after the War was over. Was that figure by the bomber really Dym, though? He bent over the page, peering close.

"Tony, what on earth d'you think you're doing?" James' voice said, sleepily, in the darkness. "Reading, you crazy cucumber! Now then, you just chuck either your book or your torch across to me to be kept till the morning. Buck up, or I'll come and collect them both!"

Tony flung him the torch.

14

Music in the Air

FOR THE THIRD time Tony pressed the door bell. Somewhere inside the house he heard a long, lonely buzz, but nobody answered his ring. The tangled, weed-grown garden of *Querns* was very dark; it was full of wet rustlings and cracklings and flappings; unseen claws hooked him as he stood in the rose-covered porch.

Tony put a hand under his pullover to feel the cover of the blue exercise book hidden there. It was not quite full; but his latest entry contained information so important that he had considered himself justified in approaching the stranger at *Querns* without further delay. A stupid boastful new boy in the next desk had told him a secret really worth knowing: the exact position of a big ammunition dump for the Home Guard. Now, at the first opportunity, he had stolen down to see the man who might or might not be a spy.

By way of excuse for his visit, he had armed himself with a small purple handbill summoning the householders of Greltham St. Andrew to a preparation-for-invasion meeting in the parish hall; it had been abstracted from the packet that the printer had just sent to Thomas. Once alone with the mystery man, he thought he could tell friend from foe.

The garden gate clicked. Someone was coming up the

path. Tony hoped that the ghost was wearing his head. With heart beating faster than usual, he looked into the darkness.

"Well, I'm blessed!" said the voice of Police-constable Smith. "If it isn't one of you scamps from the *White Priory* again! Now look here, sir, this won't do. Ever since last January you lads have been haunting these grounds as if you were the headless man himself. Why, I sent three of you off in double-quick time not two hours ago! I shall have to speak to Mr. Ingleford, that I shall."

Tony held out the purple bill.

"Oh, you're taking those round, are you?" said the policeman, evidently surprised by Thomas' choice of messenger. "I understood from Mr. Ingleford that Miss Sally and the Girl Guides were taking them tomorrow. Well, you needn't leave one here, at any rate. The gentleman's gone away and the house is empty."

"I didn't know," said Tony. "Thank you. Good night." Hurrying homeward in the dark, he felt as if a weight had been lifted from his heart. A spider's web of plotting and planning had loomed before him; but now it was broken, the spider gone, the fly set free. In the relief of the moment he forgot that other secret behind the shut door of Dym's room. There was almost a smile on his face as he crossed the *White Priory* hall and went into the sitting room.

Then he turned crimson and could not tell which way to look.

They knew! They knew that he knew that they knew.

Amid a deep, watchful silence he sat down at the table and drew forward the books he had left an hour ago ostensibly for piano practice in the drawing room.

He did not need to be told what they had found. For the

past two weeks he had hardly ever stopped seeing mind-pictures of what their eyes had seen in the last hour: beautiful dark wood scarred and marred by the great clumsy letters that went to form the two words *Heil Hitler.* Fiery red, he waited for someone to speak. But after that moment of meaning silence, life went on again just as usual. "They're not going to say anything at all," he said to himself after half an hour of waiting. "They're going to leave it to Herr Dym because it is Herr Dym's business—and mine."

He did not like the thought of more waiting for an explosion; he'd had a fortnight of waiting already. But when he heard Herr Dym's voice unexpectedly in the hall, he would gladly have waited for a year. Summoning all his pride and courage, he set his teeth and put on a look of cool unconcern. The door opened and shut. Somewhere in his neighborhood he could hear Dym talking to Mortimer about the news from the Far East. Now Dym was telling Phemie that he had been allowed to see Roger Kitteridge. Now Dym was reading Richard's last letter. And now it was quite clear that he wasn't going to say anything either. None of them were going to say anything. Those words on the desk were going to be quietly ignored.

Dym had not gone back to his station when, a couple of hours later, Tony slipped off to bed, hoping to be under the clothes before the others followed him upstairs. But on reaching the attic landing he stood still in a patch of shadow, not wishing to see Judy who had come to pay Simon a visit. Simon, in bed with a cold, was listening to the end of a story.

"And so Dym said, please, would we not say a single word to Tony. And we promised, all except Porgy and Sidney Parker. Sidney said Tony ought jolly well to hear what people thought of him, and Porgy said he was dying

to tell Tony that he'd proved he couldn't be a German by
the awful hash he'd made of carving a few letters in wood.
Porgy said that a born German couldn't have done it so
badly 'cause wood carving is second nature to Germans;
they do it by instinct. Especially little wooden bears, Porgy
said. Dym said would they mind promising, just to oblige
him. So they promised they wouldn't say anything—"

Here, for some reason incomprehensible to Tony both
Judy and Simon went into peals of laughter. "You know all
the rest," said Judy at last, still giggling. "Mr. Bland's going
to see what he can do about mending poor Dym's desk. He
thinks he can put it nearly right again, but he's afraid it will
never look quite the same. He's furious with Tony. The
evacuées say it's lucky it wasn't one of them that did it—
they wouldn't have lived to tell the tale. Tony didn't know
that Dym was at home. He pretended he wasn't frightened
when Dym came into the room, but he was. And—"

"Bedtime, Judy," called Euphemia from below.

For some reason Judy obeyed the summons reluctantly,
lingering as though loath to quit an interesting sight. As
she went, Porgy and the four evacuées tore up the stairs and
into the attic, followed with more dignity by James. There
was a roar of laughter.

Curiosity drew Tony to the door. On the distempered
surface of the wall opposite his bed he saw a colossal face
roughly outlined in black paint. One glance was enough.
He retreated to the landing.

"Hullo, Tony!" shouted Porgy, catching sight of him.
"See what we've got here! Sid and I did him, for your
special benefit. Speaking likeness, what? Come and look."

"I'll never come in again," said Tony. "Nothing will
induce me to sleep in a room where the Führer is insulted."

"Insulted? Don't know what you mean. That's not an insult. It's a jolly good portrait."

"It isn't in the least like the Führer."

"Then how did you know who it was supposed to be?"

The question did not admit of an answer. Tony only said, "I'll never sleep in that room again."

"We won't have you in with us," said the evacuées.

"If yours were the only unbombed rooms in the whole of England I wouldn't share with you," Tony retorted.

"Come along, Tony," said James. "What's the use of taking any notice of Porgy? He did it for a rag, that's all."

"I'm not coming."

"If I get a sheet from the linen cupboard to hang over Hitler, will you come?"

"No."

The door was shut. Tony could hear a consultation going on behind it. Scraps of disjointed talk told him that Porgy did not want Dym to know that a certain promise had been evaded. By and by the door opened again, and the evacuées rolled Tony's mattress and bedclothes on to the landing. "There you are!" said Porgy with a magnanimous air. "You can manage without a bedstead for tonight. Taking it down and putting it up would make too much row at this time o' night; besides, you'll have come to your senses before morning, I hope. Sweet dreams!"

After the evacuées had gone chuckling to their own quarters, Tony undressed and lay down. At first he tossed restlessly, unable to sleep for the knowledge that he was being talked about in every part of the house. Next he began to feel that he was in the cellar-shelter once more. Then the darkness grew velvety and cloudy and quiet.

He had been asleep for ages upon ages when the screaming bomb fell on him. The scream of it was appalling, the crash terrific. Gasping, struggling, and half-smothered, he awoke. "Tony!" cried a voice he knew well. "Tony! You naughty boy, what are you doing here?"

With that, the bomb lifted itself and so gave him room to breathe. He clutched something that was unmistakably an arm in a woolen cardigan. Suddenly the landing was flooded with light. Steps were heard; faces appeared in doorways. "What is it?" Tony asked, only half understanding. "Where—what—?"

"I came upstairs to rub Simon's chest," said Euphemia crossly. "I didn't put the upper landing light on, for economy's sake, and I tripped over your mattress. I should like to know how you come to be here."

"Ask them," Tony answered curtly. He had been very much frightened and his hair was full of the camphorated oil intended for Simon's chest.

Turning, Euphemia caught sight of the face on the wall. She prudently held her peace.

"It's his own choice, Dym," said Porgy. "Nobody put him out. He just went, and he vows he'll never come back again."

Dismayed, Tony saw that Herr Dym was in the group on the landing. He had picked up the empty camphorated-oil bottle and was now searching for the cork.

"You can't stop there, Tony," remonstrated Euphemia. "It's not safe to sleep so near glass. And there's a terrible draught in that corner. You'll catch cold. You really must go back."

Tony clenched his hands on the mattress and put on a limpet-look of determination. "I will not go back."

Euphemia appealed to Dym. "Tell him he's got to."

Dym had found the missing cork. He fitted it carefully into the bottle as he said, "No, there's another way out. Tony can have the spare half of my room."

At that Porgy and the evacuées set up a howl.

"Take your sheets and blankets downstairs, please, Max. Jim, will you lend me a hand with the bedstead?"

Tony accepted the offer promptly because it seemed such a good way of revenging himself on everybody from Porgy to the doubtful and concerned Euphemia, whose protesting whispers he could overhear. He scrambled out of his uncomfortable bed, made a couple of hideous grimaces at his enraged family, and went off, trailing armfuls of bedclothes.

Ten minutes later Euphemia was bending over him as he lay hunched and sulky in his new surroundings. "Good night, Tony," she was saying gravely.

"Good night." Tony was brief and cold, too.

"It's very good of Dym to let you share his room."

Dym was not far off. He was emptying the oak cupboard and carrying most of the contents to a press in the other half of the room. Raising his voice that Herr Dym might hear, Tony said:

"It's your fault I've done what I did. I never should have thought of it if you hadn't put it into my head. You told the doctor that you wouldn't allow the evacuées to have Herr Dym's room for fear they would cut their names on the woodwork. That gave me the idea. It's entirely your fault."

Euphemia took a little time to recover from the shock of this unexpected charge. Then she said, "I'm sorry I put it into your head, Tony. But I can't take all the blame, I'm afraid. You're not a baby; you know right from wrong."

"Of course I do. Whatever serves Germany is right."

"Black can never be white, Tony."

"When it serves Germany, it can. Nothing that serves Germany is ever wrong."

"You've been taught that. But are you quite sure it's true?"

"All good Germans are quite sure it's true."

Euphemia stopped arguing. "Look what Dym's doing," she said. "He's turning everything out of that cupboard to give you a place with a lock and key for your own special treasures. You'd like to keep your *Jungvolk* uniform there, perhaps? Shall I bring it in?"

"Yes, if you like."

Carefully washed, mended and pressed, the uniform was brought from safe keeping in Euphemia's room and laid on a chair by Tony's bed. With a softened look Tony put up his arms and drew her down for a kiss. "Thank you, Phemie. I'm sorry I was cross. It was shock, I think. When you fell over me, I mistook you for a bomb. Yes, I did, honestly. The kind that's supposed to scream as it comes. A four-thousand-pounder."

They both laughed. She kissed him, whispering, "Tell Dym you're sorry, too. You are, aren't you?"

Tony's face clouded. He withdrew from sight beneath the blankets. When he peeped out again, Euphemia had gone and Dym's task was ended. The cupboard doors stood invitingly wide; below them he saw a heaped waste-paper basket. "Max," said Dym, "I've thrown away a lot of things for which I have no further use. You might like to turn them over. Keep all you want, and give the rest to Simon and Judy."

Grim silence answered him. He read the unspoken thought. "I'm not trying to bribe you into keeping your knife in your pocket," he said. "There's nothing in the basket worth calling a bribe. I shan't ask any questions afterward. Good night."

Tony did not move until he had heard Dym's bicycle going down the road that led to the airdrome. Then he got up, locked the door on the family, and once more donned the familiar uniform. He smiled as he looked at himself in the glass. "I thought I'd grown a lot lately; I shan't be able to wear this any more."

The uniform was neatly folded and laid at the back of the top shelf of the cupboard. The rest of the cupboard remained empty. A wave of self-pity ran over him as he thought of certain well-stocked cupboards far beyond his reach. Once he'd had everything; now, he had almost nothing. He turned his back on the heaped basket. Everything in it should be handed over to Simon and Judy before breakfast tomorrow; never would he stoop to receive gifts from Herr Dym. Never, never, never! That being clear beyond shadow of doubt, there could be no harm in obeying Herr Dym's recommendation to turn them over. That wasn't the same as keeping. He sat down on the floor by the basket.

Two hours later he repacked the basket for the fifth time. On the top lay a leather wallet and an engine. The wallet was just what he wanted for holding the pictures of Dym which he was saving to take home to Mutti. It had pockets and flaps innumerable, he could cut the pictures out with Phemie's scissors, and perhaps he might be able to coax her to find him a photograph of the *White Priory* and Herr Thomas and the rest.

He thrust the wallet hastily into the cupboard and took the shining model engine into his hands. Dym had once won a first prize at an exhibition of model engines; James had said so. This, then, was the engine. Tomorrow it should be Simon's, who would as likely as not take it to pieces in a silly attempt to find out how it was made. Tony felt suddenly sorry for the finely fashioned little engine. After winning such high honors, to come to such an ignominious end! No, it jolly well shouldn't. It should go back where it came from.

Roller skates came next. He knew what would happen if the twins had a pair of roller skates between them. They would take one skate each and make nuisances of themselves, roller skating everywhere and cannoning into everybody. They had better not see those skates. And they were much too young to make good use of the stamp albums and the books, the hand printing press or the paints. They would no doubt quarrel violently over the Scout's knapsack, and in wartime it was wicked to waste drawing paper on people who could not draw. Simon might have the dagger-shaped paper knife; no, he might not. If he poked an evacuée with it, the evacuée's mother would be very much upset. Judy could have the giant shell because girls liked ornaments to put on their mantelpieces; but how could he part with anything that murmured so enchantingly of the sea?

Tony put the key of the cupboard under his pillow. Tomorrow he would remove his notebook, diary and pictures of Dym from their hiding-place and put them with his new treasures. And tomorrow Simon and Judy should have what was left in the basket.

Back in bed, he amused himself by flashing James' torch on and off. Surrounded by dark paneled walls, he made believe that he was lost in a cave, haunted by mountain spirits who made strange music. Then he laughed at his own fancies. "It's the wind making that queer noise," he told himself. "No, it isn't. It's real."

He listened again, intently. Somewhere hard by he could hear the spirit-music rising and falling with the wind, wild, solemn, sweet. Crouching under the bedclothes to shut out the eerie sounds, he heartily wished himself in the attic where pretenses didn't come true. Then the howling of the air-raid siren drowned the delicate elfin strains. At first he welcomed it as a link with the human world. Then he grew impatient with its ugliness: he resented its power to silence beauty. When it died away, the music in the air stole forth, remote and mysterious as before. No longer fearful, he slept.

15

The Seventh Life

"WONDER WHAT'S keeping him quiet?" said Porgy, some days later.

Nobody could answer the question, for nobody knew that the treasures in the cupboard were a magnet, holding Tony fast. To take them with him was impossible; to leave them behind was equally impossible. So he stayed, though he did not feel very comfortable at the *White Priory* just then. He wrote in his diary:

> *They say nothing, but they look a great deal. The worst of them is Mr. Bland, who has spent many hours in repairing Herr Dym's desk. He does not speak to me, but he talks at me. Though there is no sign left of what I did, he told Mortimer that a hundred pounds had been taken off its value . . . We are having Easter holidays now. Simon is making an invention that he says will stop the war. It has two empty jam jars in it and some quicksilver and a good many bits of wire. They had roast lamb and rhubarb tart on Easter Day; it is a custom in some parts of England, but not everywhere. There was not enough sugar in the rhubarb . . . They watch me all the time for fear I should do more damage, much as they did after I meddled with the light in the boxroom. Even the twins watch me . . .*

It was the twins' watchfulness that at last obliged Tony to make use of his seventh life. He was looking at his

179

treasures one evening when he heard behind him an indignant noise that might have been a growl or snort. Turning quickly, he met two pairs of reproachful eyes.

"Tony," said Judy, "where did you get all those things? Did Dym say you might have them?"

Tony went pink. "Of course. Herr Dym said I could have what I liked. He didn't tell me to share. He said, 'Give Simon and Judy what you don't want.' "

"If Simon and I had been in your place," said Judy, "we'd have been ashamed to take as much as a bent pin from Dym. You know why."

The twins walked to the door, where they conferred in whispers. Judy was again the spokeswoman.

"We are not tell-tales, Tony," she said with dignity. "But we both feel that Dym ought to know how greedy you have been. He is coming home tonight. He has seven days' leave unexpectedly; we have heard him ringing Phemie up. When he comes, we shall be obliged to tell him what you gave us out of the basket. We are sorry to do this, but we think you deserve it."

In that moment of intolerable humiliation Tony felt that Nils and Inger stood avenged. Pride forbade him to throw himself on the twins' mercy. He slammed the door behind them and began to think hard. Soon everybody would know that he had been poor-spirited enough to profit by the generosity of the man he had injured. Later Herr Dym himself would know it. He could never face any of them again; beyond all shadow of doubt he could never face Herr Dym.

There was only one way out of the difficulty. He took it.

When he heard Dym's laugh ringing out of the darkness, Tony knew that only a few moments of freedom remained to him. He was on foot, having failed in an attempt to purloin the key of the bicycle shed; and he was walking between dark trees that loomed above him like giants with outstretched arms. The feathery-hedged road had hitherto been silent save for his own footfalls; when little whisking shapes scampered across it, their paws made no sound. Now the silence was unexpectedly broken by gay young voices, Herr Dym's among them. A word or two told Tony that he was saying good-bye to some friends. Peering into the gloom, the runaway could see a garden gate and the dusky outline of a house.

To turn back meant that he would be overtaken by an enemy mounted on a bicycle. To advance meant that he would almost certainly meet that enemy fair and square. A low fence on the opposite side of the road offered easy entrance to a field where he might hide until the enemy had gone by.

Climbing the fence did not prove as easy as he had thought, for some inconsiderate person had laced great awkward loops of barbed wire above the top rail evidently for the express purpose of baffling would-be intruders. At the cost of torn hands and clothing, Tony forced a passage through the biggest loop, then slipped, clutched at nothing, and found himself lying dazed and breathless at the foot of a steep slope.

Sitting up, he decided that he couldn't fight his way back to the road over a heavily barbed fence that leaned at a sharp inward angle over a high bank. If he did, there wouldn't be much left of his clothes and skin. Instead of waiting to climb out after Dym had gone, he would walk along the side of the field in search of a safer way out. The height of the bank was an ample shield: he was well hidden from seeking eyes.

He had not taken a dozen steps when the gurgling of unseen water and the sudden squelching of his shoes ankle-deep in mud warned him that progress in that direction was barred. Nothing remained but to turn toward the *White Priory* and walk on till the fence gave place to a hedge that could be scrambled through as soon as he judged that Dym had passed. To the best of his recollection, fence joined hedge about twenty yards away, near the spot where a cart track ran from fields to road.

He would not have noticed the cart track if a sentry had not been pacing up and down before the mouth of it, which was trebly barred off by a rope, a red lantern and a notice board that bore the words DANGER. ENTRANCE FORBID-DEN. Tony could guess what that danger might be, and he had an uneasy suspicion that those loops of barbed wire had not been twined about the fence without good reason.

The knowledge that he was on the wrong side of the loops was not agreeable, but he comforted himself with assurances that he must be safe because he was so near the sentry who had, of course, been stationed outside the danger limit. Better not let the sentry see me, though, he reflected. I expect he has orders to arrest anybody who disobeys the notice. Hope I'll find a decent gap before I get up to his post.

His hopes were disappointed, for he had to halt, dismayed, before another of the horrible streams that looked so delightful on picture postcards. Trapped between two watercourses, he ventured a little farther into the field in the hope of finding an easy crossing or a plank thrown from bank to bank. But the darkness was now so dense that he could find nothing. Alarmed by his own rashness he hurried back, caught his foot in a tussock, and fell heavily.

Picking himself up, he tried to return to the fence. However painful the struggle through the wire, it was preferable to night wanderings in the neighborhood of an unseen danger. He quickened his steps to a run, but it did not end at the sloping bank on which the fence stood. There was no slope, no fence. Taking out his torch, he half covered it that the sentry might not see. Before him stretched vast impenetrable gloom. He turned. The gloom was behind him too.

Still dazed by his fall, he could not make out what had happened. He ran wildly from left to right in search of one or other of the guiding streams. Both had disappeared. That meant that he had strayed, how he could not tell, into the heart of this marshy meadowland. Frightened, he took another irresolute step or two. Suddenly, at the third step, his heart began to beat in rapid jerky thumps. Danger was in the air. It was near; it was very close; it was almost touching him. If he moved, he would meet it. "Dym!" he screamed. "Dym! Dym, come!"

There was no Dym, there was nothing in the world save himself and an unseen Thing shrouded in vast blackness pierced by the tiny fiery eye of James' torch. He could not walk, much less run; his legs turned to stone as he stood. He screamed again, louder than before. Then his throat went stony too. Far off he heard the trickle of the streams, the call of a hunting owl, an angry human voice shouting, "Come back! Come back, you fool! She's due to go off. She's due to go off, I tell you. Any minute, she's due to go off. Come back, will you! Come back!"

Someone was running, running swiftly. A second torch gleamed in the darkness. By the twofold light Tony saw the Thing he feared. As an ice-cold shiver ran through him, he felt a grip that he knew. "Run!" said Dym.

Word and touch broke the stony spell. His hand fast in Dym's, he was running with all his might. As he ran, the Thing behind him bestirred itself. A shattering roar deafened Tony; the earth rocked under him; a wind that was not a wind flung him and his rescuer violently to the ground. "All right?" he heard Dym asking. "Are you all right, Tony?" He noticed, half-affronted, that for once Dym had forgotten to call him Max.

"Yes," he answered confusedly. "I think so."

His brother's arm was round him, lifting him to his feet. "Come along," Dym said. "Can you walk?"

Tony's knees were trembling under him. "Yes. Don't take your arm away for a minute, though. I feel funny."

He felt himself being guided across more grass and then down the ruts of a cart track. The red glow of a lantern could be seen.

"I'm afraid the sentry will be very angry with both of us," said Dym. "You needn't be scared. I'll settle it."

They came to the opening. Tony saw the sentry's face like a round white moon. "I thought you were a goner, sir," the sentry said, adding the "sir" with a jerk as if he had only just realized that Dym was an officer. Then he turned on Tony in a fury. "You'll hear about this, you will! You'll catch it, going poking round a delayed-action bomb as wasn't none of your business. What d'you suppose danger notices and red warnings are put up for, you young noodle? Next time you play this kind of trick you won't find a gentleman ready to risk his life fetching you out. Just you give me your name and address—"

"There won't be a next time," said Dym. "I'll take care of that. I'm his brother."

The eyes of the two men met.

"Well," said the sentry, turning away, "that'll do. Maybe I didn't see—nothing. Good night, sir."

Tony did not remember what came next. When he was able to think clearly, he and Dym were sharing a big chair in a room with a log fire. The chair was lined with newspapers. Tony thought this curious. "Is this the house of your friends?" he asked. "Why do they have newspapers on their chairs?"

Dym laughed. He took Tony's hand and turned it palm upward. "Because you're as black as a sweep, Max. So am I."

Tony's eyes went from his grimy hand to Dym's clothes. "I've spoilt your uniform, Dym," he said. "I—" Tears choked the rest.

"Nonsense! All we shall need is a clothes brush when we're dry. I should think that old bomb must have kicked up every atom of mud from the marsh! Got a nice pasting, didn't we? I wonder whether my face is as dirty as yours."

Tony could not answer; he was trying not to cry. The boom of the explosion had not stopped echoing in his ears, and he still felt as though some invisible monster were pelting him with lumps of flying mud. He saw Dym look up quickly. The kind protecting arm went round him again. "Shaky, aren't you?" said Dym. "You'll feel better by and by. John and Cherry are going to run us home in their car. He has used up his petrol ration, so he's had to go on a borrowing expedition. But he won't be long."

Tony neither knew nor cared who John and Cherry might be. He rested his head on Dym's muddy shoulder and lay staring at the rosy flames on the hearth. Presently he said, "Herr Dym."

Dym laughed in gentle derision. Tony smiled too. When

a vow of eternal silence had been broken, there was no good reason for keeping up forms and ceremonies.

"Well, Herr Max, what is it?"

"Only about the twins. They were disappointed with what was left in the basket."

"I told you to take all you wanted, Max."

"I know. I explained to them. But they still think me greedy."

"We'll soothe their injured feelings by rigging up a home-made telephone for them. Ginger and I made one, years ago. I came across the whole contraption the other day, stored in the garage. It wasn't so successful—we took it down, I remember, when Ginger and I were as hoarse as crows and the rest of the family deaf. But if you and I put it up at a safe distance from the house, say between the woodshed and the rabbit hutches—"

"The twins would be pleased," said Tony.

"You'll help me, then?"

"Yes."

"Thanks very much."

There was a long silence.

"I still have two lives," said Tony. "I will not use either of them while you are on leave. I promise."

"Thanks again."

"But I must not promise for always. I have not chosen—" He stopped, remembering in time that Dym did not know he had heard the story of the *Sword Chrysaor.* "I mean, I must go on fighting. I am not giving in."

"I understand. There's to be a temporary cessation of hostilities during my leave? After that, the balloon will go up? But don't you think we could be friendly foes in future, Max?"

"Yes," said Tony. "I think we could."

16

Friendly Foes

IN THE MORNING Dym and Tony put up the telephone for the delighted twins. In the afternoon they
helped James and Sally and Porgy with the potato planting.
Porgy stared when he saw Tony. "I thought you said wild
horses wouldn't drive you into doing any war work," he
said.

"I'm not doing work to help your war effort," said Tony
with great dignity. "I am planting the potatoes that I shall
require for my own eating next winter. That is allowable."

"Oh, quite," said Porgy, grinning. He said to James,
aside, "It's only an excuse for following Dym round. The
latest official communiqué from the frozen north announces
that the garrison has surrendered."

"I wonder!" said James.

"Well, he isn't wearing the black scowl that he always
puts on when Dym comes home. That scowl's a mistake, if
he only knew it."

"Why?"

"It brings out a strong family likeness to Margaret. Haven't you noticed that Margaret and Tony have much the
same kind of temper—dour and sulky, with a strong dash
of spitfire? Vera was saying the other day—"

"Here, hold on!" said James. "That's enough. Who
wouldn't be stiff and sulky in Tony's place? He can't talk

about the Eckermanns to us, and he won't talk about life in Germany for fear of letting out something he shouldn't. He's in a ghastly fix—and if you could change places with him, you wouldn't come out of it any better than he does."

Tony did not hear what was said. He was busy trying to make out the meaning of the dialogue carried on in distant screams between Simon and Judy.

"A for Annie calling flare-path. A for Annie calling flare-path. May we taxi up and take off? May we taxi up and take off? Over to you. Over."

"Hullo, A for Annie. You may taxi up and take off. You may taxi up and take off. Over."

"B for Bobby calling flare-path. B for Bobby calling flare-path."

They had gone half through the alphabet before Tony realized that they were pretending to be bombers taking off on a night flight. Sally groaned. "They'll go on like that for hours, Dym," she said. "You'll be sorry you ever gave them that telephone."

After the darkness and horror of the night before, Tony was glad to be in the quiet brown field under the pale-blue sky. He liked the scribbling sound of lark song, the rough crumbiness of the earth between his fingers, the patient hours of plodding work. "Shall you plant potatoes again tomorrow?" he asked as they went home to tea.

"Not tomorrow. You've heard about the corner of waste land that Thomas has been ordered to plow?"

Tony nodded. "The District Committee says it must be cropped. James says they are a pack of idiots; it won't even grow ragwort!"

"Well, orders are orders in wartime. And Thomas hasn't a man for the job."

"James or Sally could have done it, if they weren't so busy with the potatoes. And I could have done it if I'd known how."

"D'you want to learn? I'll teach you."

Tony hesitated. "If I learn, it is that I may not have to learn later, when—" He stopped. He had meant to tell Dym that he wanted to prepare himself for *arbeitsdienst* but, after being on friendly terms for a whole day, the words refused to be spoken.

"When what?" said Dym, with a twinkle that told Tony he had guessed the answer.

"Oh, it doesn't matter. I should like to learn."

"We have six days left," said Dym. "What else shall we do?"

They plowed the waste land together. Those were good days. About the workers the hedges whitened with blackthorn, primroses and violets starred the banks, leaves and fronds and ferns flung out green clasping hands and tiny clinging fingers. Nests of blue and speckled eggs were hidden in the bushes. Fox cubs peered out of holes. Prickly mother hedgehogs took their babies for a walk. Over hill and dale blew the keen cleanness of the spring wind.

The evenings were good too. Family fun was all very well, but when he was at home Dym belonged to too many people. In field and meadow it was possible to talk to him, to ask him questions. At home, he had to be shared. Besides, conversation was not easy in a room that was positively crammed with human ears; whose owners always looked as though they remembered that one of the speakers had vowed never to speak to the other again. And that was tiresome indeed, inasmuch as it had now become necessary to satisfy a thirst for information. Unluckily, Dym was not fond of talking about himself, even in the few moments when the two of them were alone. Answers had almost to be dragged out of him.

"You've never had to bale out, have you, Dym?"

"No, I'm not a member of the Caterpillar Club."

"At school they call you an air ace."

"That's nonsense. We don't have air aces in Bomber Command."

"Are there air aces in Fighter Command, then?"

"Not really. Bomber or Fighter, we're part of a big team. And the ground crews are just as important as the flying crews. Every bit."

Tony tried again. "What do you feel like when you start on a raid?"

"Funny inside."

"And afterward, when you're on your way?"

"Too busy to think."

"Sidney Parker says you're mad to get at 'em—I mean, at us."

"No. It's a horrible job that has to be done."

Once, rummaging in Dym's desk, Tony drew out a silver cross with ribbon striped in violet and white. "What's this?" he asked, though he was almost sure of the answer.

"That? Oh, that's my D.F.C.," said Dym.

"D.F.C.?"

"Short for Distinguished Flying Cross," said Dym.

"And you've got two bars to it. Bill told me."

"Yes."

"It is like the Iron Cross? Ludwig has that."

"Much the same."

"What did you get it for? And the bars?"

"Oh, for being a good boy, I suppose, like little Jack Horner. You've heard of him?"

"Yes," said Tony, "he took a plum from a pie, in the English nonsense verses for babies."

"So did I," said Dym.

Making a hero of Dym was not an easy task. He did not look like a doughty warrior, either then or on the last day of his leave, when he and three of his friends played croquet on the damp green lawn in the teeth of a bitter April wind. The friends had never played croquet before. They seized the mallets and insisted on playing a wild game with rules of their own invention, though Euphemia stood at the garden door, scolding, her red hair tossed by the wind.

"You silly, silly boys, this isn't the right time of year for croquet. You'll be frozen; you'll all catch your death of cold. Put the hoops away at once and wait till the summer comes."

They looked at her a little oddly, Tony thought, as if they wondered whether there would ever be a summer. Then they laughed, waved her a defiance, and went gaily on with the game. It was not quite over when Euphemia again appeared in the doorway. "A telephone call for you, Dym—for all of you. Report at once!"

Ten minutes later, they were on their way. Euphemia and some of the family went down the drive to see them off. Tony walked last, apart from the others. Leaning against the iron gate, he stared at the blue woods on the horizon. Somewhere in the wet fields he could hear the cuckoo's throaty cry.

"I've left my possessions in an awful muddle, Phemie," Dym said as he kissed her. "I was searching for something I wanted. I turned everything upside down and had no time to put it straight. Don't spend hours in sorting and tidying, please. James will shovel the lot back in two ticks."

A voice from the gate spoke, crossly, but with a queer little note of reproach in it. "Phemie needn't ask James. I can do it."

"Thanks very much, Max," said Dym. "Then I'll leave it to you."

Throb-throb-throb through the darkness. Tony knew the meaning of the deep, purposeful hum that could never be confused with the irregular *thrumming* of the *Luftwaffe*. It was as he had feared, then: Bomber Command was going out. Dym was up there, high out of sight. The hands that had brought beauty out of ivory and catgut and wood were guiding a great aircraft now; the gay young voice was silent, to save oxygen; the eyes that had looked on the fair earth would soon see the night sky spotted with red and orange fire. It was only a few hours since he had seen Dym pause abruptly by a blackthorn hedge on his way home from plowing, break off a twig and go home studying with curious intentness the curves of the inky bough, the exceeding fragility of the white petals. It wasn't very long ago that Dym had been teaching him an English folk song:

> *Cold blows the wind tonight, sweetheart,*
> *Cold are the drops of rain.*
> *I never had but one sweetheart*
> *And in greenwood she lies slain.*
>
> *I'll do as much for my sweetheart*
> *As any young man may;*
> *I'll sit and mourn all on her grave,*
> *A twelvemonth and a day.*

He could see the laughing face almost as plainly as if Dym had really been in the room; no, Dym was not laughing now but was looking straight ahead, gravely steadfast as he had looked on that far-off snowy night in the train.

If Dym never came back?

Outside the window the strange music wailed a dirge. Tony felt as though he were sinking into measureless depths of blackness. Dym gone, never to come again! The thought was unbearable. Yet once Tony had said deliberately, "May you never come back!" The words sounded like an evil spell. He shuddered, then tried to reason with himself. After all, it was by no means certain that Dym was on ops tonight. He had returned safely many times since the spell was laid: why trouble about his safety on this particular flight?

Reasoning was useless. However hard Tony tried, he could not banish mind pictures of the giant bomber hit, staggering, on fire; of Dym struggling to the last to bring his aircraft safely home; of Dym giving his crew the order to bale out; of a gray sea opening to engulf him in foam. That would be the end of Dym who, only that morning, had stood full of life in this very room, had done surprising gymnastics on the great beam, had whistled like a blackbird as he dressed, had knelt down, like James or little Simon, to say his prayers. Tony sprang out of bed. One could at least tell God that the curse had been taken back. One could pray.

He rose from his knees, comforted. Stumbling in the darkness, he went over to Dym's desk and groped about till he had found what he wanted. Treasure in hand, he climbed into bed and nestled down with Dym's flying cross pressed to his cheek.

When he woke, dawn was on its way. But he did not wait for daylight before carrying out a resolution made in midnight hours. There was only one place in the world for a spy notebook that had power to hurt Dym and the people Dym loved. It must find a last resting place at the bottom of the well below the hole in the beam.

He fumbled at the back of his cupboard, drew out a blue exercise book, and pattered barefoot down the corridor. The book, bent in half, slid through the opening. He heard it swishing and flopping as though it were making a kind of Alice in Wonderland descent of a tunnel. He started at the sound of a creaking door. If Margaret happened by ill luck to be getting up early, she might tell Thomas that she had seen him throw something through the hole. Thomas had forbidden the younger members of the family to throw anything more down the hole; it wasn't ten days since he had threatened to block it for good and all, the next time he caught anyone misusing it. The others would find it hard to forgive the one who deprived them of a hole of legendary fame: a quick retreat was advisable. Tony turned and fled.

Safely back in his room, he took pencil and paper and set to work to compose some viola music for Dym, who had complained that there was little to be found. The fairy harp, sweet and plaintive as ever, was playing again; he thought that he could weave some of the haunting notes into a tune. Some day he must ask Dym what made the music in the air. He hadn't asked yet because it did not always play; at such times he was half afraid that it hadn't been real after all. And he couldn't ask the others because they had made fun of Paddy, who owned a family banshee and had heard leprechauns laughing in his garden. They shouldn't have a chance to make fun of him! He bent, absorbed, over his self-appointed task.

At breakfast time Sally said, "What have you done to your face, Tony?"

"Me?" said Tony, who was eating porridge very thinly sugared. "Nothing."

"You've got the queerest mark on it," said Sally. "It looks almost like a cross."

17

Banned Area

"MAY I HAVE some of my money, Phemie?"
"What do you want it for?"

"I want some music manuscript," said Tony, lowering his voice that Porgy might not hear. Porgy had a great contempt for music and its makers.

Euphemia whispered a word or two to Judy, who ran upstairs and returned with a small brown packet.

"I've no idea how much it ought to cost, Tony. I only know that the war has made paper frightfully dear."

"Sixpence will be enough, thanks," said Tony.

He watched her untie and retie the brown packet, which she laid at the side of her machine table. The handle flew round again, whirring as it went. Inch after inch of striped calico crawled under the needle.

"Phemie?"

"What is it now?" mumbled Euphemia, her mouth full of pins.

"I'd like to tidy your workbasket. May I?"

"You're the only tidy-minded boy I've ever met! Yes, do."

Tony sat down on the floor at her feet, turned the basket upside down and began to rearrange the contents. Presently he made, unobserved, a neat little brown-paper parcel with a cotton reel inside and Christmas string tied round about. Later, a hand took two stealthy journeys to the side of the machine-table. The first time it went up empty and came down full; the second time it went up full and came down empty.

"Oh, Tony, how nice my basket looks!" said Euphemia, much impressed.

"Doesn't it?" said Tony complacently.

He was walking upstairs with his spoil when a name came to him out of the mists of memory, unbidden. "That's where Michael lived!" he said to himself. "I've remembered at last, after all these months."

Hurrying to his cupboard, he looked at the map on the back cover of his diary. The name was clearly marked on a bulging part of the East Coast. A tingling of excitement ran through him. I have the money and I have my last two lives and I've remembered the name of the town—I must be meant to go. Uncle Laurie and Auntie Nell will help me. At least, Auntie Nell will. I'm not so sure about Uncle Laurie. He paused, looking down at the sixpence in his hand. But I won't go till I've finished that viola music for Dym.

Tony saw Michael before Michael saw him. Michael was sitting on the garden wall, his eyes on the ships in the bay. He was older, taller, more serious. As Tony approached, the seriousness changed to puzzled interest, as though the sight of another boy was a welcome but surprising novelty. Then he sprang off the wall with an incredulous cry. "Max!"

"Mike!" Tony answered.

For a minute or two the sun-shimmer on the sea seemed to fill earth and sky as well. When it faded from his eyes and brain, he and Michael were both on the wall with their arms round each other's necks. Michael was saying, quite coolly, "I didn't know the invasion had begun. Our wireless is out of order, so we haven't heard the one o'clock news. Where did you land?"

"The invasion hasn't begun," said Tony. "I am alone."

"How on earth did you get here?"

The uncomfortable question had to be answered. Better to tell Michael the worst now, than to have it inexorably dragged out of him later by Michael's father. "Last January," he said, "there was something in the newspapers about a German boy who was carried off from Norway. Did you see it?"

"Yes."

"It was me," said Tony hardily. He tried to disentangle himself from Michael's arm, but Michael held fast. "I'm sorry to trouble you, I only came to find out whether any of you could remember the names of Vater's business friends. I thought possibly Mr. Cavendish might have heard Vater speak of English correspondents. That's all I want. I know quite well that you won't care to have anything more to do with me, but it wouldn't hurt you just to tell me—"

"Max, don't be an idiot," said Michael.

"Uncle Laurie will be furious with me, anyhow." Tony's voice trembled; it was no longer defiant. Ten minutes ago the cool, sarcastic Englishman had been a shadowy figure belonging to the past. Now he was real again, like his son.

"No, he won't. Truly he won't, Max. I promise for him. He'll understand."

There was a long pause, broken by Michael. "You haven't told me how you got here, Max. Why didn't you come sooner?"

"I hadn't finished the viola music for Dym," said Tony.

"I mean I forgot your address until it came into my head suddenly one day last week."

"But where have you been living since last January? Who's Dym?"

"I've been sent to live with an English family named Ingleford. Dym is one of them. He's in the R.A.F., a flying officer. They lost a brother once, when he was a baby. They think that he was stolen by a German lady who had no children, and, because I'm rather like them to look at, they think that I am—"

"Then it was true!" Michael cried.

"What was true?"

Michael's thin face crimsoned. "You remember old Frau Brand in the little house at the end of the road? Years and years ago, the summer when we were six, she told Mummy that she had good reason for believing you to be English, not German. And then she shut her mouth up tight and wouldn't say another word, ever. Mummy never knew what it was that she had heard about you, and, of course, she and Daddy couldn't ask. D'you remember we were away in England for three months that summer? We shouldn't have gone back to Germany if I hadn't been ill again. Mummy didn't tell Geoff and David and me till last Christmas, when we were talking about you and wondering what you were doing. She and Daddy never dreamt you were stolen. How could they? But they did think it was quite likely you had been adopted without letting everybody know."

He thought that Tony was either lost in dreams or had failed to follow his rapid speech. A repetition, made in German, was interrupted halfway. "They needn't have thought that," said Tony, still staring out to sea. "It is the Inglefords who have made a mistake. But it will be put right after the war."

"Tell me how it all happened," said Michael.

The telling took a long time. When it was over, Michael pinched the cold rough stone of the wall as hard as he could. "It sounds like a cross between a fairy tale and a nightmare," he said. "I can't believe I'm awake." And then, in a whisper, "Does Tante Anna know that you're with the Inglefords?"

Tony nodded. "Dym told me that a letter had been sent. But I don't know who sent it or what was said. Dym tried to tell me, but I wouldn't listen. It was when I wouldn't speak to him."

"You could ask him now."

"What good could it do me to know? Dym said the letter was kind. That's all I cared about."

"Did Herr Eckermann or Tante Anna write to Dym?"

Tony turned his face away. "I don't know."

"Did they write to you?"

"No."

Michael thought, but did not say, That's funny.

"It isn't," said Tony, reading the thought. "I'm not a prisoner of war. I'm supposed to be English. Prisoners of war can get letters through the Red Cross, but I can't. Don't let's talk about it any more. Is Auntie Nell at home? And Uncle Laurie?"

He was not looking forward with pleasure to the interview with Uncle Laurie; nevertheless Michael's words struck a cold chill into his heart. "They're not here now, Max; they're hundreds of miles away, doing a war job in—a dangerous place where they can't have us with them. I'm here all the time, except for an odd day or two, now and

then. I'm living with Uncle William and Aunt Louisa.
Geoff and David spend their holidays with another uncle—I haven't seen them since Christmas."

"Oh-h!" said Tony, slowly. "I see."

Michael sat silent while Tony rearranged his plans.

"Well," he said at last, with a sigh, "I don't know that it
makes much difference, my not seeing them. That is, if you
can help me. D'you know the names I want?"

Michael said, very reluctantly, "I only know one, Max,
and I'd ever so much rather not tell you what it is. I think
you ought to go back to the *White Priory*. Honestly, I do.
Why not write to Daddy from there? If he can help you in
any way, I know he will."

"I'll write to Uncle Laurie if your name's no good," said
Tony, who knew that any help given by Uncle Laurie would
certainly not take the form of a list of names. "Go on,
Mike! Here's a pencil and paper."

Michael wrote down a name and address. "You know
that frightful special tonic I always used to have? Just before we left for England Herr Eckermann told Daddy the
name of the only place over here where we could get it. The
firm's still in London, though I don't suppose Herr Eckermann's friend is at the head of it now. What are you going
to do next, Max?"

"Find a night's lodging somewhere," said Tony. "Then
go by train as far as what's left of my money will take me,
and walk the rest of the way."

"But—" began Michael, and stopped. "Here's Uncle
William coming," he added in an altered tone. "He'll want
to know who you are. No, no, keep quiet! You'll have to face
him—you can't escape."

One swift scared glance told Tony that Uncle William

was an older and sterner Uncle Laurie. "Ha! Entertaining
company, Michael?" he heard him say, with a note of surprise in his voice. "Who's this?"

Michael hesitated. "It's someone I used to know years
ago, Uncle. He's come to see me."

Tony was not surprised to see Uncle William's eyebrows
lift in Uncle Laurie's manner as he listened to the awkward
reply. "Indeed! And how did you contrive to find your way
into a banned area, young man?"

Tony named a town on the edge of the banned area. "I
happened to be in Garford today, for a few hours. So I took
a bus. Nobody asked any questions."

"I don't suppose anybody would," said Uncle William,
"since the only afternoon bus between Garford and Thar-
rington is run for children attending the Garford schools. I
suppose the conductor didn't notice that you weren't wearing a school cap. So that's how you got in, is it?"

Tony thought Uncle William too clever. He began to
feel that he disliked Uncle William.

"Well," said Uncle William, "it doesn't really matter
how you got in. What does matter is how you'll get out. Do
you realize that the next bus doesn't leave till early tomorrow morning? How do you propose to return?"

"Walk," murmured Tony.

"It's twelve miles."

"I have money. I can pay for a night's lodging if I get
tired."

Uncle William's unpleasant look told him that he had
tripped up among wartime rules and regulations. "Don't
you know that no one under fourteen is allowed to spend
the night in a banned area without permission from the

police? Don't your people know— You mean you came without leave?"

Tony felt that Uncle William was the most disagreeable man he had ever met. He was silent.

"Does your family have a phone?"

"Yes, but—"

"Very well, then, you'll shortly have the pleasure of telling them that you're stranded here for the night. As you're a friend of my nephew, the police will probably expect me to take charge of you."

Uncle William's voice showed that he had a poor opinion of his nephew's taste in friends. It also showed that he thought the friend's proper place was in the station cell.

"I shall have to report your presence in my house. Name and address, please. Write it down."

Tony had very little hope that he would be able to escape without revealing his identity. However, he wrote down the name and address that he had chosen for himself.

"H'mph!" said Uncle William. "German hand, this. At school in Germany, eh? That where you met Michael?"

"Yes, sir."

"H'mph! Got your identity card with you?"

"No, it's at home."

"H'mph! But you're English?"

"I'm a British subject," said Tony.

Curiously enough, this way of putting it appeared to rouse Uncle William's suspicions. "Oh, you are, are you? Welsh, Irish, Scotch or what?"

"English."

"Then why couldn't you say so straight out? Here, Michael, write this chap's name down for him in a decent round hand. Sergeant Stubbs won't be able to read his scrawl."

Michael took Uncle William's pocketbook, which had opened and shut again. He fluttered the pages as if seeking for something. "Anywhere will do. Be quick!" said Uncle William. "Hullo! What's this?" He swung about, glowering at Tony. "You call yourself Arthur Harris on one page, and my nephew calls you Max Eckermann on another. Now you'll kindly explain—"

Tony explained. Uncle William was the kind of person from whom it was not wise to withhold explanations. "Stay there till I come back," said Uncle William, pointing to the wall. "If you let him go, Michael, it'll be the worse for you."

He strode off. Michael and Tony sat down again on the wall. Looking across the fields between them and the water's edge, Tony could see barbed-wire entanglements, lines of concrete blocks, interlaced iron poles. Beyond the defense works lay the sea, sad-colored in the fading light. Dark ships made a broken line right across the bay. As they moved steadily northward, their barrage balloons floated high overhead, like gigantic silver elephants gamboling in the sky. "Convoy," said Michael.

"First I've seen," said Tony.

"Queer things come ashore sometimes," said Michael. "Eggs and tinned food and matches and onions. Once it was dolls, hundreds and hundreds of dolls. But that was a long time ago."

They followed the convoy with their eyes. Then they talked again, chiefly about Tony's adventures. Michael seemed unwilling to speak of his own. "Nothing happens to me," he said. "I just go on living here because I've nowhere else to live. I've no friends. Most of the boys here have either been evacuated under the Government scheme or sent to live with their relations. There are a few left—you saw them this afternoon—but, unluckily, Aunt Louisa doesn't like them. She says they aren't suitable companions for me. And I can't go to school with Geoff and David because of being so wretchedly delicate."

"Aren't you any stronger?" Tony asked. He knew that the Cavendishes had made their home in Germany so that Michael might be constantly under the care of a famous doctor.

Michael shook his head. "Not much, but don't tell Uncle William I said so. He's a doctor too! I'd give a lot to be able to go to school. How'd you like to do lessons with an old clergyman of ninety in the shade? He's very kind, but he keeps on forgetting my name. Now tell me about Gantry's and the school where your brother teaches."

They talked on. Uncle William did not return until the sea was a velvety blackness, hovered over by the long silvery fingers of searchlights. "I've settled everything with your eldest brother and the police," he told Tony. "You will stay here for the night. Tomorrow someone will come to take you home."

"Who is coming?" Tony asked, not without hope that it might be Dym.

Uncle William did not know. It was plain that he did not care either. Tony understood that he was that rare and uncomfortable thing, a visitor in disgrace.

He and Michael had their supper in a corner of Uncle William's surgery. "There's nowhere else," Michael told him. "We've got officers billeted here. The house is as full as it can be."

The talk over the supper tray continued in whispers.

Without a word being said on either side Tony knew that
this was not the sort of house where one made a noise. It
had glossy paint and shining floors and severe furniture.
The other people in it matched their surroundings.

After supper they made their way to Michael's slip of a
room, which was just big enough for Michael's bed and
Tony's mattress on the floor. Michael was still unwilling to
talk about himself. No, he hadn't any pets. No, there was no
place where he could do carpentry. No, he hadn't many
possessions with him; they were stored. Would Max please
show him the bit of flak from Dym's aircraft again? And
would Max finish telling him how Dym made a landing
with a retracted undercarriage and one wing nearly shot
away?

Tony finished the story, which was interrupted toward
the end by a tremendous explosion that made the house
leap on its foundations. "Only a mine," said Michael, "lucky
it wasn't any nearer. The last one smashed most of the
windows and blew the front door in. They go off now and
then, generally after a heavy sea. Sometimes they're touched
off by dogs or cows that have managed to get into forbidden places. Not cats. Cats have too much sense. But Uncle
William's dog went out one day and never came back. You
weren't hoping for a sea bath tomorrow, were you? 'Cause
you won't get one."

"Why not?" asked Tony, though he could guess.

"It would end like that if you did!" Michael waved an
arm in the direction of the recent noise. "Hullo, there's the
siren again! I've heard it five hundred and fifty-six times since
the beginning of this year. Now tell me some more about the
White Priory. You haven't said much yet about James."

The telling lasted till Tony, tired out, fell asleep in the

middle of a sentence. Waking with a start at the sound of distant heavy gunfire, he was surprised to hear a choked-back sob somewhere near him. He listened, and heard it again. This time there could be no doubt that Michael was crying.

Sleepy though he was, Tony knew at once what had happened: the sight of him had reminded Michael of the old days when they both had a home. And he could not help admitting to himself that what Michael had now was a good deal less homelike than the *White Priory*. It was probable that Michael, alone in this cold, aloof house, actually envied him his place in the rough-and-tumble life of the Inglefords. "Mike, don't," he said compassionately. "Is it so bad here? Aren't they decent to you?"

Michael had himself in hand in a flash. "It's all right. They're very kind, really. It's only that—well, it doesn't matter. Sorry I woke you."

"It was the guns; it wasn't you. Would you like to have my bit of flak for keeps? Dym will get me some more."

"Sure you can spare it? Thanks awfully."

The flak changed owners. "Mind, you're not to tell Mother or Daddy," Michael warned him. "They'll be writing to you, and I'm sure they'll try to see you if they can. But you're not to tell them anything that might worry them. Their work's terribly important. You can't work when you're worried. And there's nothing for them to worry about, nothing. If you tell them anything, Max, I'll scrag you. Honestly, I will."

Tony tried to think of something comforting to say. "When invasion comes, you'll have to move out," he observed, looking at the small suitcase, ready packed, that stood by the chest of drawers. "It would be a change."

"It would," said Michael, "but I don't believe it's ever going to come. We expected it last year, and I daresay we shall expect it next. If you'll promise not to tell anyone, I'll tell you what I was thinking about. I was only wishing that I could go to Mortimer's school; I'd like to be somewhere near you. But if I suggested it to Mummy or Daddy, they'd guess what I've been trying hard never to let them know."

"I could mention it in a casual way in my letter to them," said Tony. "If I told them about Mortimer's school after I'd mentioned that Dym's in the R.A.F., I don't see how they could guess. And they might ask questions about the school of their own accord. You never know."

"It's not a bad idea," said Michael, much cheered.

"And anyhow," said Tony, "you and Geoff and David will all come and stay with us in the summer hols, won't you?"

"I'd love to," Michael answered eagerly. "But it isn't arranged as easily as all that. My people don't know your people and, even if they did, I don't suppose Miss Ingleford would invite three more boys!"

"I could work it," said Tony confidently. "I can work a lot of things. If Phemie thought it would make me happier, she'd invite all the lions and tigers from the zoo. There's really oceans of room. We can easily squash up a bit tighter than at present. If Dym comes for me tomorrow, we can settle everything." He would not allow himself to think that his escort might be Mortimer.

It was Michael's turn to laugh. "You're running on too fast, Max. Dym mayn't be able to come tomorrow—and what about that last life of yours? Not much use inviting us when you don't know whether you'll be at home to meet us, is it? Had you forgotten?"

"Yes, I had," said Tony. And he sighed.

18

Ticket to London

WHEN HE FOUND the railway ticket to London lying in the road, Tony was in two minds about picking it up. Phemie had not yet invited lions and tigers to stay at the *White Priory*, but two giraffes and a tank of water-snakes were shortly to be evacuated to Gantry's from one of the smaller zoos. Then there were the white rabbits with ruby eyes that Thomas had just given him; they might pine if he went away. Besides, he and James and Sally were very busy, planting potatoes for lazy Mr. Cramp down the road, who had promised them a leaky old boat by way of payment. Really it seemed absurd to put aside all these interests in order to search for an unknown Herr Möller on the bare possibility that he had escaped internment! But Tony took the train just the same.

"Hurry up, sonny; don't you hear the barrage? Best get down to the shelter quick. 'Tain't a good time for star-gazing, not when there's bombs about."

The old woman in rusty black paused at the top of the flight of stone steps that ran down beneath the church. Tony eyed the dark hole distastefully, then looked again at the bright flashes in the sky, heavy now with unseen wings. The rise and fall of the siren was dying away, and the guns

209

were beginning to open up. Clearly, it was prudent to take
cover. He followed his guide.

The steps wound into the heart of the earth as if they
led to the haunts of goblins and trolls. But no rocky cave or
jeweled subterranean palace awaited him on the other side
of the screened door. He stood in a large room with other
rooms leading out of it. Light came faintly from behind
black-paper shades. The air smelt of mould and disinfectant and damp clothes drying. All round him were bunks
with people lying in them. Other people were walking
about and talking. Children ran up and down.

Tony's old woman was friendly. She pointed him to a
vacant place on a wooden bench near her bunk, saying,
"You're not one of the reg'lars. Your ma'll be fine and
anxious, knowing you're out in this."

Some explanation was evidently expected. Tony said, "I
came to London to find a business acquaintance of my
father. But—the street was bombed last week, and there's
nobody who can tell me anything."

"Gave you a bit of a shock, I reckon," said the old
woman. "Poor lad!"

She was an inquisitive old body, Tony discovered. She
wanted to know more than he was willing to tell. He was
rather glad when she went off to talk to a friend; but before
long she was back again, bobbing about in a vain attempt to
catch the eye of a clergyman who had just come down the
steps. "That's the Vicar," she told Tony. " 'Im or one of the
curates comes every night for prayers. I'll 'ave a word with
'im afterward."

Then beneath the muffled thunder of the guns the Vicar
gave a brief talk. A prayer followed: the *Lighten our darkness*
that Tony had heard Sunday after Sunday at the evening

service in the little gray church. The roar of the barrage blotted out the rest.

When the service was over the old woman hobbled forward and accosted the Vicar. Tony had a suspicion of what she was going to say. When he heard what sounded uncommonly like "You take my word for it, mister, that child's run away from 'ome," the suspicion became a certainty. On the whole, he was glad that she had guessed the truth: there was no longer any need to perplex himself with thoughts about the future. He would be returned to the *White Priory* again, like a bad penny, that was all.

The Vicar and the Shelter Warden came to his corner and took one look at him. "The game's up, young man," said the Warden.

"Yes," said Tony thankfully. "Do you want my name and address? My brother's telephone number is—"

The Warden asked questions. After the answers had been taken down, the Vicar asked, "Will you come to breakfast with me at the Vicarage? I can't ask you to spend the night there; you're safer here. I'll call for you in the morning."

He was gone. The Warden gave Tony a blanket smelling of camphor and disinfectant, and showed him how to make himself a bed out of two benches put together, with his coat for a pillow. From her bunk Tony's old woman entertained him with long stories about all the gentlemen whose offices she cleaned. He grew drowsy in the middle of her ramblings.

It was morning. The guns had ceased, and the shelter was emptying itself. Tony's companion was tying a little fur tippet round her neck. The Vicar was beckoning to him from the stairs.

He had breakfast with the Vicar and the two curates in a room with a bucketful of soot on the hearth, brought down by last night's bombing. "We'll not be needing the sweep this year; that's one comfort," said the housekeeper as she brought in coffee, porridge, bread and shrimp paste. He had come on an unlucky day, they told him; for they had already eaten their week's bacon and their month's jam, and had lent what was left of their margarine ration to friends in difficulties.

Tony was disappointed to find that he was not to be kept at the Vicarage till he could be fetched. Instead, it had been arranged that he should travel with a party of children who were being evacuated to his own village. As soon as breakfast was over, he was hurried off to join them at a great railway station, where a harassed teacher promptly bundled him into a compartment with a dozen other boys and girls. His ninth life had come to an ignominious end.

At first his companions took no notice of him. Having parted from their parents an hour ago in the school buildings, they had no farewells to make and nothing to do but enjoy themselves. As the train went out they sang *There'll always be an England,* followed without a second's pause by *Daisy, Daisy, give me your answer, do.* For the rest of the trip they laughed, screamed, sang, tried to climb into the rack, raced up and down the corridor, devoured bags of buns and sandwiches.

Thomas was on the platform at Greltham St. Andrew, waiting to receive the evacuated children. James and Sally stood behind him, trying to look as though they were not there. "You're to come home with us," James said briefly. "Come on."

Nobody spoke until they were alone in a lane between hedges white with may. Tony had passed through it twenty-four hours earlier; but in that short time the green bracken balls had uncurled a little more, and the delicate fern of the cow parsley and the broad blunt leaves of pigweed and wild angelica were further out. The cold sweet air had a tang in it; twitters and chittering came from every tree. "Well!" said James, explosively. He was red to the tips of his ears, and his face was stiff.

"You're not to be cross with him, Jim," Sally murmured.

"I'm jolly glad you've come to the end of your nine lives, Tony," said James. "We've had enough of dancing about the countryside in search of you. And this last affair is the limit, absolutely. However, it's a comfort to remember that next time you run away you'll pay for it. Dym always keeps his word. Where'd you spend last night?"

"Air-raid shelter," Tony answered shortly.

James' wrath melted suddenly into a grin. Then Judy and Simon appeared through a hole in the hedge. "Oh, Tony, you were an idiot to choose yesterday for running away!" they cried. "We had the best raid we've had yet. You haven't told him, James? Sally, you haven't told him?"

"What's happened?" Tony asked. "Is the house down?"

"No. But we've got the biggest bomb-crater in England," said Simon and Judy proudly. "The Army has been measuring it, and a very nice sergeant says so. It's in the nine-acre meadow. Thomas is going to leave it just as it is, and me and Simon are going to begin tobogganing down it on a tea tray directly Phemie thinks it's safe. She's frightened at present—thinks there might be a bit of something unexploded somewhere. She says you never know."

"I want to turn it into a lovely sunken garden," said

Sally, "with purple and white aubrietia and crocuses and snowdrops and hyacinths and golden basket growing all over the sides, and a goldfish pool at the bottom."

"Much better grow tomatoes in it," said James. "If you helped me, Tony, we could grow enough to feed the village if invasion comes. Porgy's a lazy beggar; he doesn't want to help. Would you?"

"I might," said Tony.

They went into the meadow, looked at the huge gaping hole, and made their way home. "Phemie!" shrieked the twins, at sight of Euphemia. "Phemie! Tony spent the night in an air-raid shelter. A very dirty one."

"Go upstairs this minute and have a bath," said Euphemia. "Put your clothes outside the door. You're to change every stitch you have on."

"But I'm hungry," argued Tony. "Must I? Can't I have my dinner first?"

"Certainly not. You'll find a piece of carbolic soap on the right-hand corner of the shelf where the hot-water cans are kept."

Euphemia's nerves had been shaken, Tony decided, by the fact that the biggest bomb-crater in England was uncomfortably near the *White Priory*. He went off meekly. When he came downstairs again, his dinner was ready on a corner of the long table. Euphemia was sitting in the window seat with her hands in her lap, idle on a Saturday, idle for the first time since he had known her. He lifted a dishcover and saw that she had saved him a generous wedge of treacle tart. Treacle, almost as rare as gold! Moved by gratitude and some pricks of conscience, he stole up to the quiet figure by the window and looked at her under his eyelashes. "You never said you were glad to see me back, Phemie. Aren't you?"

"You're a naughty boy," said Euphemia wearily. "This is the ninth time—and we were terribly anxious about you last night. You're such an expense, too, with all this running away. Do you ever think how much all these telegrams and police messages cost? That ticket you took had to be paid for, too. It belonged to the sister of an evacuée in the village; she came here crying because she had dropped her ticket and didn't know how to get home. Of course we knew where it had gone. That sort of thing is stealing, Tony, though I know you don't think so. And Dym simply can't afford to pay these extra sums."

"I've used up my nine lives now," said Tony.

"That's just the worst of it, Tony—"

"You didn't give me time to finish," said Tony. "I was going to say that I don't suppose I'll bother to run away again. I've had enough."

A few days later Tony woke up hot and tired and cross. He did not know why he felt cross. Dym and half a dozen of his friends had spent the evening at the *White Priory;* there had been talk and fun and laughter, and he had gone to bed in the highest spirits. Now, nine hours later, he hated everybody.

"Hurry up, Tony; you'll be late for school," said Euphemia when he at last dragged himself to the breakfast table. "Why, what's the matter . . . oh, Mortimer, just look!"

Mortimer looked, pulled Tony's collar down, looked again. "Measles!" he said. "That comes of spending the night in an air-raid shelter."

Somebody asked, "German or English measles?"

"You don't suppose Tony would condescend to the English kind, do you?" said Mortimer. "German, of course. Go back to bed, Tony."

When Euphemia came up with a breakfast tray, Tony was crying. "What is it?" she said, horrified. "Head bad?"

"No."

"Are you disappointed about feeding the water-snakes? You were telling Dym that it was your turn to feed them today."

"No!" sobbed Tony again. "It wasn't fair of Mortimer to say that. I can't help what kind of measles I get. He might just as well blame me for having been kidnapped. I couldn't help that either."

Then, too late, he tried to dodge Euphemia's kiss. "Don't, Phemie!" he cried sharply. "D'you want to catch measles too?"

"I forgot," said Euphemia. "What you said pleased me so much that I forgot."

Tony thought this out. "I didn't realize what I was saying. I meant that he might just as well blame the real Tony. Of course I'm not the real one."

"Only *ersatz*, eh?" said Euphemia. "Don't think about it any more. Mortimer didn't mean to hurt your feelings. It was a joke."

"I like Dym's jokes better than Mortimer's. Dym wouldn't have said it."

"If we all thought before we spoke, there'd be no more wars," said Euphemia wisely. "Never mind, Tony, it's a shorter measles than the other kind; that's one good thing. You'll soon be downstairs again."

But he wasn't. The next morning she looked at her patient with startled eyes. "Tony, there's another rash coming out on your chest, a different rash."

"What do you think it is?" Tony asked.

"English measles," Euphemia answered.

"And the queer thing about it," she said afterward to her family, "was that Tony actually seemed glad!"

The second illness was much worse than the first. It was not until some days later that a very limp and languid Tony said, "Shall you be writing to Dym soon, Phemie? I've got a message for Jacob."

There was an odd silence. Tony raised himself on his elbow, startled. "Has anything happened, Phemie? To Jacob, I mean."

"Jacob was killed last week," said Euphemia. "When you see Dym, don't say anything about Jacob. They were great friends."

At first Tony could not believe that he would never see Jacob again. Jacob had always been kind, had helped him with hard passages in his violin and piano practice, had approved the viola music he had composed for Dym, had encouraged him to try again. Jacob had been at the *White Priory* on that last evening, and had again been perturbed because Euphemia couldn't and wouldn't keep still while he was playing. "Next time I come," he had said, "you, Miss Euphemia, will not be permitted to manufacture those detestable khaki and navy socks that occupy your entire leisure time. You will not be allowed even to work for the deserving but neglected members of the Royal Air Force. Instead, you shall sit with your hands folded—folded, mark you—and listen to the *Air on the G String.* I insist. Positively, I insist."

And at the end of the evening he and Dym had made plans, airy ambitious plans, of all that they would do after the war. Euphemia had laughed at the planners. "What boundless energy you have, Jacob!" she had said.

Jacob had turned—Tony could see the dark, curly head and sparkling eyes quite plainly—and smiled at her. "Madam," he had said, "if I had a thousand lives, I could fill them all."

Suddenly and for no apparent reason Tony's mind went back to a wooden notice board that he and his cousin Fritz had passed every day on their way home from school. Framed on that notice board were newspaper pages with articles and pictures scoffing at the Jews. Then he remembered his notebook—certain early pages held Jacob's name surrounded by the contemptuous words he had first seen on the board, and he recalled with satisfaction that Thomas had fulfilled his threat of blocking up the hole in the beam: it had been closed the very day he threw his notebook down, after Euphemia had caught two of the evacuées throwing each other's caps into the well. Now there was no shadow of danger that Simon and Judy, fishing with a hook and all the string in the house, should even bring that hateful book to the light of day.

Jacob was killed last week. How queer it sounded! *They were great friends.* That was true enough. Once they had linked Tony with their dream plans for the days of peace.

"What shall we do after the war, Jay?" Dym had asked. "Make music, with Max to help us, or help to build the brave new world?"

And Jacob had answered solemnly, "I don't see why you say 'or.' I say 'and.' " But Jacob was dead, killed last week.

He would make no music, would build no brave new world.

When the secret spring moved under his fingers, Tony could hardly believe that he had found the lost entrance at last. There was something uncanny about the blackness behind the parted panels; he did not like being alone with it. Running to the door, he called the family. Thomas answered the call. Together they went through the opening and stood looking round them by the light of Tony's torch.

There was no hidden treasure in the room, which was bare of furniture and very dusty. Thomas pointed to some marks on an unpaneled wall. "That's where the door into the passage must have stood. This was the window space. All right, Tony, I'll have it opened up for you."

"Won't it cost a lot, in wartime?"

"Wartime's no excuse for not keeping one's word. I promised that the room should go to anyone who could find it. As soon as you're out of quarantine, Tony, I'll get a man to put in the door and window. You could distemper the walls and stain the floor yourself. Get Dym to help you."

Tony guessed why Thomas wanted busy Dym to be busier still: hard work would drive away sad thoughts. He nodded to show that he understood.

The news of the discovery soon spread. After school the rest of the family came into the passage to shout their comments through the door. James said, "Good for you, Tony. Porge and I will make you some bookshelves if we've time."

Sally said, "Phemie's going to give you her dear little red table. I'll work a tablecloth for it."

Mousie said, "It's funny that a person who has run away nine times should be the one to find the room rather than people who never ran away in their lives."

The eldest evacuée, who was disappointed, said, "It's the way things happen in this world."

And Simon said, "Now it will be easier to fit the Cavendishes in, if they come here for the summer holidays."

"Lots easier," agreed Tony.

The coming of the Cavendishes was the chief topic of conversation at his first meeting with Dym who was quieter than usual, but otherwise unchanged. Tony was not much surprised to find that Dym had not only written to Uncle Laurie and Aunt Nell but had seen them and lunched with them.

"What did they tell you?" he asked, half defiantly.

Dym put the question aside; but held out tempting possibilities of a future in which the Cavendishes might once more play a large part in Tony's life. The doctor-uncle had liked what he saw of Mortimer and had recommended that Uncle Laurie make inquiries about the school where he taught. It was very probable that Michael would be sent there to be near his friend. It had been arranged that the young Cavendishes should spend the latter half of the summer holidays at the *White Priory*. And it had been suggested that, when Uncle Laurie and Auntie Nell spent a week's leave in Wales, with their boys, Tony might join them there.

"But that's all in the air at present," Dym warned him. "For one thing, they don't know whether they will get leave or not. And, for another, we'll have to see how you go on. I must be quite certain you've given up running away before I let you pay a visit to two of the nicest people I've ever met.

You'd completely spoil their hard-earned holiday if you ran away in the middle of it."

Tony said in an injured voice, "I haven't run away for ages."

"No, it's difficult with a thermometer in your mouth," Dym agreed.

Whereupon Tony flung himself on Dym and they rolled over and over on the floor till they upset the only pot of distemper the Tamley Market decorator had been able to spare them from his scanty wartime stock. Sobered by this mishap, they scraped the floor clean and went on with their work.

Tony was spending the first night in the room that was his very own. He liked its shape and the furnishings that were either homemade or drawn from Phemie's stores in a dry cellar. He liked it so much that he had to stay awake to admire it. Would Ginger, he wondered, admire it too, or would Ginger be as scornful as Sidney Parker? Downstairs on the hall table lay a pink telegram, announcing that Ginger would arrive on leave tomorrow. Down in the depths of his heart Tony looked forward to seeing Ginger again. Already he had made Phemie promise that she would never tell Ginger that he had thought there was fairy music in the air outside Dym's window. How Ginger would laugh at anyone who was silly enough to mistake the sounds of an aeolian harp, set up by Dym himself, for the playing of English elves! It was lucky that nobody but Phemie and Dym knew of his silliness, for one had pledged herself to silence and the other had too much sense to talk.

The music stole forth again, sweet as before. As Tony listened, it carried him back to a day long ago when he and

Mutti had tramped through the vineyards above Heidelberg; he saw again the golden sun, the purple grapes, Mutti's kind, smiling face, the blue, blue sky over their heads. They had picnicked among the vines and had come at nightfall to a little hotel or *Gasthaus*. But they had not gone indoors at once; it was so pretty in the dark garden, where a group of men were singing to the accompaniment of a guitar and an accordion. Some of the hotel guests were there, listening. He could see them now: elderly man, elderly woman, young man. English, all three of them.

Mutti hadn't seemed pleased when they strolled into the grounds. She didn't speak against the English as so many people did, but she never cared to talk to them or be with them. She had made a little restless movement and had whispered something about going in; but Tony had pulled her down, pleading, "Not yet, Mutti, not yet;" and they had stayed under the dark trees with stars peeping through the interlaced boughs. The music had had the fairy quality of the wind-harp's songs without words, something too of the mysterious beauty of Easter singing heard in the streets at midnight long ago.

When it stopped, the young Englishman had whistled some of the airs again, softly, to amuse his old companions. He whistled beautifully; it was like listening to a bird in the darkness. The silvered water, the arms of the tossing black trees, the vine-scented night, the bird song from the unknown Englishman—these things had made an enchanted hour. He had been sorry when the English people moved on and he and Mutti went up the garden into the bright light of the hotel.

While Mutti signed her name in the big book he had stood thinking hungrily about supper, when suddenly Mutti had given a little cry and had dropped the pen. It had rolled all down the page, splashing as it went, and they hadn't stayed at that hotel after all. Mutti had made some confused explanations about a mistake, and they had walked miles and miles to a horrid little hotel—and, very early the next morning, they had gone away by train to spend the rest of their holiday a long, long way off.

Tony sat up in the darkness, clasping his arms round his knees. "I think I'll tell Dym," he said to himself. "Yes, I will. I'll tell him tomorrow."

19

What Happened When Ginger Came Home

MUCH TO THE satisfaction of the younger Inglefords and the four evacuées, Ginger's return was on
a day when they spent the afternoon doing extra prep at
home because their classrooms were being used by other
classes. This arrangement gave all except Tony a chance of
going down to the station to meet the train. "You mustn't,
Tony," Euphemia said firmly. "The wind's in the east and
it's awfully cold—you'll only get pneumonia if you hang
about that draughty station for nobody knows how long."

Tony was quite content to stay at home; he felt a little
shy about meeting Ginger. Besides, he wanted to write a
letter to Richard. Euphemia, who found difficulty in making the twins write occasional letters to the half-forgotten
soldier brother in the Middle East, had gone so far as to
pay Simon and Judy threepence for a blotty letter. Tony had
very little doubt that he could coax threepence out of her
too, which was worth having, when one had exactly nothing at all.

He went up to his room, and hunted for his neglected
blue exercise book. A sheet from this would do for notepa-
per. He opened it with a superior smile, feeling years older
than the boy who had begun it all those months ago. As he
looked, the smile vanished. Eyes wide with horror, he gazed

at what he held as though it were a gift from some evil fairy. This was not his diary; this was the book that should by rights have been lying at the bottom of a ninety-foot well. How had it come back again? How could it have come back?

"I—must have thrown—the wrong book—down the hole," he told himself, thinking it out in little jerks. "I—must have thrown—the wrong book—"

There was a limping step in the passage. He drew back, clutching the book to him.

"Tony," said Margaret's gruff voice, "I want you to help me with the— Why, what's the matter?"

"Nothing," said Tony.

Her fierce dark eyes went to the book in his hand. "What have you there that you don't want me to see?" she asked.

Tony lost his head. Darting past Margaret, he ran downstairs and made at top speed for the kitchen range. Margaret, though lame, was swift. He had barely thrust the book under the hot coals when something not unlike a whirlwind was upon him, flinging him aside. Frantic, he saw the blue covers held high in the air by Margaret's tongs. He made a wild grab at them, but only succeeded in tearing off a small piece of flaming paper.

"I never trusted you," said Margaret scornfully. "I've always thought you were spying. I knew there was something behind the show of friendliness you've made lately. I'm going to read this through before I hand it over to Dym."

At the last word Tony flung himself on her, fighting tooth and nail for his property. All in a moment—he could not tell how or when it came to pass—he found that he was fighting not Margaret alone but most of his family and all the evacuées—kicking, scratching, wrestling, hitting and screaming. There was a red mist before his eyes and room for but one thought in his mind: whatever happened, Dym must not see what he had written in that book.

As he fought, it seemed to him that he had somehow or other been carried out of the *White Priory* kitchen and set down again in the gun room on board the battleship, savage and frightened amid a host of enemies. For Ginger's face was close by. He faltered in bewilderment—and the battle came to a sudden ignominious end.

The prisoning hands that held him were certainly those of Ginger. But, as his senses cleared, he saw Thomas by the door and knew that, after all, he hadn't been spirited out of the kitchen. Besides, he could hear Margaret's angry voice growling out her story somewhere quite near.

Thomas' kind eyes were troubled. "I think you'd better go to your own room for a bit, Tony," he said unhappily. "We can't have scenes like this, you know."

Tony wanted to say "Don't tell Dym," but the words would not come at his bidding. When his captors pushed him toward the hall, he did not resist. For some time after the key turned in the lock he crouched on the floor, feeling as sick and shivery as on the night of that fierce struggle in the wynd. From the ominous stillness in the house he judged that the family had gathered in one room to discuss him and his crimes. Then he heard the evacuées talking in the garden. A gleam of comfort came with the knowledge that they hadn't been invited to share the discussion, though they had poked their noses into the fight.

When the conference in the sitting room broke up Tony listened dumbfounded to sounds of laughter coming from

Dym's room. He lifted himself from the floor and took a chair to the other end of the room, where he sat looking dolefully down at his arm, which he had burnt badly in a stumble against the range at the beginning of the fight. The pain, hardly noticed at first, was becoming worse every minute; it kept him from thinking connectedly, and sent what thoughts he had flying in the oddest directions.

Instead of wondering what his own fate would be, he found himself remembering a queer little boy with round owllike glasses who had come to the *Jungvolk* meetings two summers ago, a little boy who was also named Max. It was whispered that the other Max had spied on his own father and had reported him to Hermann "for treasonable activities." But nobody knew for certain whether Max had done it or not, though they all knew that the Secret Police had gone to Max's home and taken his father away. "There's only one loyalty," Hermann had said, "it's loyalty to Germany." That meant that no questions were ever to be asked.

And now everybody at the *White Priory* would always feel about Tony as he had once felt about Max. They would think in their hearts what Mousie was saying in a loud voice outside the door, "You are a traitor and a spy. Do you hear, Tony? You are a traitor and a spy."

"He's a spy all right," Bill was heard to say, "but I don't know that you can call him a traitor. After all, he thinks he's German. If he knew he was English, then he'd be a dirty traitor."

The face of the other Max seemed to glitter palely out of the paneling. In a kind of frenzy Tony shouted, "Go away! Go away!" He was not sure whether he was speaking to the face or to Mousie and Bill.

"Don't make such a row," said Bill. "We've brought you

your tea, that's all. We're leaving it outside, with the door unlocked. Run for it, Mouse! Come on!"

They ran as if in fear for their lives. Tony rather thought that they came back after an interval to eat up the untouched tea, but he had no spirit to open the door and bounce out. He sat holding his injured arm; there was nothing else to be done. Now and then little waves of terror ran over him as he recalled what he had written about Jacob. Whatever else Dym forgave, he wouldn't forgive that. He would never speak to a traitor and a spy again.

When the long-awaited quick light footstep sounded in the passage, the boy on the chair dared not look up. He knew that Dym had entered the room, had crossed it, and was standing at his side, but he could not raise his head to meet the eyes of Jacob's friend. Then Dym spoke. "Why, what's wrong here?" he asked. "What's the matter with your arm, Max?"

He heard his own voice answering from a long way off. "I burnt it." The words wobbled up and down as though he were going to cry.

"Let me look."

Tony gathered all his courage together. "No. It does not matter. I would rather you did—whatever you have come to do."

Dym's voice was gentler than Tony had ever heard it. "I came to talk to you, Max, but I'm sure you can't listen while your arm is in that state. You will let me put something on it? I'll be very careful. Or would you rather I called Phemie?"

Through white lips Tony murmured, "You."

Dym's hands were swift and dexterous; they had tended burns far worse than Tony's. In a few seconds cool lotions and dressings brought a gasp of relief.

"That feel better? Able to talk things over?"

"Yes."

Dym laid a battered blue exercise book on the table. "Thomas can't read German," he said, "so I looked this through for him. You understand, Max, that I had to do it?"

"Yes."

"There were two pages that it wasn't necessary for me to read. Margaret had seen them. She told me that there was no military information in either of them; they merely gave your private opinions of people you had met. Those pages were and are no business of mine. I haven't read them, and I don't want to know what you wrote. That quite clear? I don't want to know."

As the words were spoken, the blackest clouds rolled out of Tony's sky. Only Margaret knew what he had said about Jacob, but Dym did not know and would never, never know.

"Thank you, Dym," he said humbly.

"Now for the rest," said Dym. "I can't think that we've been lax in letting you make your various discoveries, for you have found out only those things that couldn't very well have been hidden from any intelligent boy who had been taught to use his eyes and ears. You've managed to pick up a good deal that would have been useful to the other side in the event of an invasion. It was sensibly and cleverly done; you're a credit to whoever trained you. But—"

Tony pleated Sally's tablecloth nervously between his fingers, dreading what he might hear next. When it came, it surprised him.

"You haven't made any entries in your book for months," Dym was saying. "The last entry, which is partly torn off, was written in March. If you don't very much mind telling me, I should like to know why you stopped."

"I—" began Tony. Then a horrid recollection caught him by the throat. "What's the good of telling you why I stopped when everybody thinks I've started again? Margaret told them she'd caught me with the pen and ink all ready. Didn't she tell you?"

"Yes, she did. And I told her that you had too much sense to do secret service work with your door wide open. You see, I couldn't help thinking there might be some other explanation. Is there one?"

"It's no use explaining," said Tony. "If I said I wanted to tear out a sheet of paper for a letter to Richard, you simply couldn't believe me. You'd think I was making it up."

"Hadn't you better try me?"

The explanation came then, upside down and inside out. "I thought I'd write a letter because Phemie gave Simon and Judy threepence for writing to Richard. And I took my diary out of the cupboard to tear out a sheet because I'd stopped writing it. I was tired of writing diaries. But it wasn't my diary. I'd thrown my diary down the hole in the beam early in the morning of the day Thomas sealed up the hole because he said he would, next time anybody threw anything down except a depth-pebble from the jam jar which he didn't mind and then Bill and Pat threw each other's caps down and Bill's mother wrote to complain. I threw it down because I was sick of writing it. The last entry, which I tore off, was the most important. I know where there is an ammunition dump. And—but I didn't know till—"

"Steady, steady," said Dym. "That's rather a ropey take-off, isn't it? Now begin again."

Tony told the whole story.

"So that's all, Max? Quite sure you've nothing more you want to tell me?"

Tony did not answer at once. At last he said, "I've told you everything about the ammunition dump, and you've read all the rest for yourself."

"I know. But is there anything else you'd like to tell me—anything not connected with your book?"

The used pages of the blue exercise book were all torn up and burnt in the empty fireplace; it was, Dym said, "a secret and confidential document" that could not be put with salvaged waste paper. As Dym spoke, Tony was busy gathering up handfuls of black ash and scattering them through the window.

Again he failed to answer the question. He said, quickly and nervously, "I wish you'd explain why you laughed just now, when I told you how I took my book down to *Querns.*"

"Did I laugh?"

"You looked as though you were trying not to."

"I was wondering what sort of reception you'd have had, Max, if you'd found the old fox in his den?"

"You mean that he wasn't a German agent?"

"He most certainly wasn't."

"You know something about him that James and Porgy don't know?"

"I know that James and Porgy are two uncommonly fine geese, and you're a third. No, no, you won't get any more information out of me, however diligently you fish. Besides, it's time we went downstairs, isn't it?"

Tony shrank back. "I don't want any supper. I'd rather stay here."

"If you wait till tomorrow morning you'll have to face

them alone," Dym reminded him. "Better get it over while I'm here. And it isn't so awful, really. When you've told Thomas you're sorry, that'll be the end of it; we'll all arrange to forget the past."

"Ginger won't forget," said Tony, quivering.

"Nonsense. It would take a good deal more than this to spoil Ginger's leave. Come along."

There was nobody on the stairs, nobody in the hall. Tony was grateful to the family for keeping discreetly out of the way. They knocked at Thomas' door. It swung back, revealing everybody. The room was full of light, and round eyes. All the eyes looked at him and then hastily pretended not to have seen him. Dry-lipped and speechless, Tony shrank against Dym, who spoke at once. "Thomas, Tony wants to apologize to you and to Margaret for what happened this afternoon. Some of the entries in his notebook were not good form. He apologizes for those too."

Tony felt as though he had stumbled into a nightmare. He could not think what had brought the entire household into Thomas' room at an hour when Thomas was usually to be found alone, busy with billeting letters. Afterward he learnt that his family, anxious not to embarrass him on his first appearance in their midst, had delicately but mistakenly withdrawn themselves into Thomas' room, where they were watching Ginger unpack the birthday presents that had been saved for him. But in those painful minutes Tony only knew that they were round him, all staring at him. From somewhere in his neighborhood came a satisfied whisper, "He's been thoroughly blitzed!"

Dym turned his head and looked at the speaker, who appeared to shrivel. Somebody moved closer to Tony and took his hand for a quick second. That was Sally. Someone else glanced at him out of the corner of an eye. That was James. Their support was comforting. It helped him to say in a low voice, "I'm very sorry, Thomas."

"Won't do it again, eh?" said Thomas. "All right. We'll say no more about it."

"I think we all ought to know," said Dym, "that Tony of his own free will told me what he had written on the page that was torn off. He could easily have kept that bit of information to himself."

Tony knew why Dym said nothing whatever about the secret that the torn page had held. Only the elder members of the family must hear of the discovery he had made; it could not be mentioned before anyone who was likely to chatter. He had himself promised solemnly that he would never, never reveal what he knew.

"There's something else," Dym went on quickly, "something that escaped notice in the first excitement. All Tony's notes were made in the early days of his return home. By far the greater number belong to the weeks when he was still entitled to think of himself as a German. Only one entry was made in March as against six in February and fifteen in January. In April he thought he threw the disused book down the hole in the beam, intending to get rid of it for good. Unluckily he threw his diary into the well by mistake—"

Disbelief was written large on some faces. No one spoke, but Tony knew they were thinking that his defense wasn't good enough.

"He had two exercise books exactly alike," said Dym. "As he was tired of writing his diary, the mistake wasn't discovered till this morning when he thought he'd use one of the blank pages in the diary exercise book for writing a letter. That's the whole story. Tony knows he can't prove the truth of it without taking down the house to get at the well. He won't feel hurt if you can't join me in believing that what he has said is true."

Tony felt Sally's hand grip his for the second time. Margaret was the first to speak. Her gruff voice said unexpectedly, "Yes, Tony did throw a blue book into the hole. I can tell you when he did it, too. It was the day Thomas blocked the hole, the day after your seven-days' leave ended, Dym. I heard somebody moving about in the passage early in the morning, and looked out to see whether Tony was running away again. I saw him, but he didn't see me."

For the first time since he came to the *White Priory,* Tony felt that it might be possible to like Margaret. She was cross, suspicious and aloof, but you could count on her to play fair.

"That was the date Tony gave me," said Dym.

There was a murmur in the room, a pleased murmur. They were glad, actually glad that he was not as blackly guilty as they had thought! Tony did not know which way to look. Thomas rose from his chair so suddenly that he upset Simon and Judy, who were on the arms of it.

"I'm going down to have a look at White Blaze," he said to Tony. "You'd better come too."

20

In Freedom's Cause

ON THE LAST day of Ginger's leave Dym entered the hall of the *White Priory*, where he was met by a pair of excited twins. "Tony's been machine-gunned, Dym," they cried in important voices. "At school, in the playground. He was taken to the hospital first, and then he was brought home. He was hit twice, in the shoulder and in the leg, but he wasn't killed."

Halfway up the stairs, Dym paused for a second look at the battered and disheveled Simon. "You're all right, Simon? You weren't hurt?"

Simon blushed and hung his head. "I wasn't there. No, nobody was hurt 'cept Tony. He says he didn't like being the only one; it made him feel conspicuous."

Dym ran up to Tony's room. Tony, feeling much better now, looked at him with an awed but slightly complacent grin. "They got me, Dym."

"Hard luck, old man."

Then he put his hand lightly on the bandaged shoulder. "No, not hard luck at all. You've been wounded in Freedom's cause. It's an honor."

A tinge of red came into the boy's face. "I'm rather glad I'm hurt, Dym. It—sort of—makes up for what I did."

"That's another way of looking at it," said Dym.

"Now I'll tell you how it happened," said Tony. "We

were just crossing the playground on our way back from gym when, quite suddenly, Burton—not the Burton whose brother was killed in Greece but the other one—said to old Badger, 'Sir, there's a Jerry! and old Badger said, 'What? Where? Bless my soul, so it is! Lie down, boys.' And then all in a second—"

He moved restlessly, crimsoning.

"I'll get Phemie to tell me the rest by and by," said Dym. "Think about something else. What are these four shillings doing on your pillow?"

"They're what's left of the money I had for being machine-gunned," said Tony. "Thomas gave me two-and-six, but that went to help pay for the gramophone records James and Sally and I are giving Ginger for the gun-room gramophone. Ginger gave me five shillings, but I had to give a shilling to Simon and Judy. They said it wasn't fair I'd had so much; they'd have been machine-gunned gladly for half a crown. So I gave them sixpence each to keep them quiet, but if ever they're machine-gunned and Ginger gives them five shillings they're to pay me back."

"We didn't have a Scotch great-grandmother for nothing!" said Dym as he added a contribution to Tony's depleted hoard. "Now just you lie down and keep quiet." Dym left the room.

James' voice sounded in the passage outside. "Congrats, Dym."

Congrats! Tony sat up in bed so suddenly that he hurt his shoulder and fell back among the pillows, wincing. Ginger's voice joined his brother's. "And from me, old chap. I say, is it true that you're posted near Olive and Basil? Does that mean you're going to the new hush-hush place at—"

Dym said, "S'sh!"

"Well, if you're near Olive and Basil you'll be near young Olaf's school. You'll try to see something of him, won't you? I know the dears have done all they could, but they are aged company for a kid, aren't they? And—"

Dym said "S'sh!" again. The three moved away.

Tony knew what it all meant. There was no longer a Flying Officer George Dymory Ingleford, D.F.C. He had been promoted, and with promotion had come a change of stations, a change that would bring him into the neighborhood of the old cousins who were so fond of him. It would bring him into Olaf's neighborhood too. Olaf made friends easily, and Olaf would gain by another's loss—

When Dym returned later he was dismayed to find Tony restless and feverish. "What's up, young fellow?" he asked.

"You're a flight lieutenant now," said Tony wearily, "and you're posted—"

"But I'm not posted to the Far East or even to the Middle East, you little owl. I'm still going to be somewhere in England. What about the seven days' leave that's due to me in your summer hols? Remember the plans we made?"

Tony nodded. "You're going to take me to stay with Uncle Tony and his family because they want to see me. And then you'll take me to Wales and leave me with the Cavendishes."

"Well, what's wrong with that plan?"

"Nothing. It's wizard," said Tony.

He tried to put away jealous thoughts of Olaf. Dym mustn't on any account guess that he had them. "It's my fault that Olaf is in England at all," he told himself. "He would be in Norway if it wasn't for me. I oughtn't to mind—I oughtn't to mind."

Dym said, with a twinkle, "I shall miss you a little. Not much, of course, about twice as much as I shall miss Bill."

"That's not much," said Tony. But the sore place in his heart was healed, though the drumming in his head went on. He pressed his face hard against the pillow. "Sometimes it's the witches' dance that I keep hearing," he said. "You know, Dym, the witches' dance from *Hänsel und Gretel*. Sometimes it's the dance of the trolls in *Peer Gynt*. Sometimes it's both, mixed. And all the time it's a marching song we used to sing in the *Jungvolk*—"

"Which one?"

"It begins: '*Und liegt auch von Kampf in Trümmern*—' "

"*. . . Die ganze Welt zu Hauf,
Das soll uns den Teufel nicht kümmern wir pfeifen drauf;
Wir wurden weiter marschieren, wenn alles in Scherben
    fällt,
Denn heute gehört uns Deutschland, und morgen die ganze
    Welt,*"

Dym finished the song.

*Though the whole world lie ruined around us after the day
    of war,
What the devil do we care? We don't give a hoot any more.
We will go marching forward, though everything fall
    away,
For the world will be ours tomorrow, as Germany is today.*

"You know it?"

"Yes, I know it."

"I'll never get to sleep till I've stopped hearing it. Tell me something to take it away."

"We've nothing like that," said Dym with a wry little smile. "*Rule, Britannia* is quite polite."

"Don't want anything like that. Want something quiet." Dym sat down on the side of the bed and took the hot hands into his cool, firm clasp. "I'll tell you what James and Sally and the evacuées sing, shall I? It won't be new to you; I daresay you've sung it yourself since you came to England."

"If you mean a sort of song written by a man who thought he could see angels, I know it. We have it a lot at school prayers. Old Badger likes it. Yes, go on."

Dym repeated the lines:

> *"And did those feet in ancient time*
> *Walk upon England's mountains green?*
> *And was the holy Lamb of God*
> *On England's pleasant pastures seen?*
>
> *"And did the Countenance Divine*
> *Shine forth upon our clouded hills?*
> *And was Jerusalem builded here*
> *Among these dark Satanic mills?*

"You understand what the verses mean?"

"I've been told. There's a legend that Jesus came to England when He was a boy. St. Joseph of Arimathea used to sail to Cornwall, trading for tin from the mines. Once he brought Jesus with him. And that's why the poet didn't like the black mills and factories that were spoiling the places where Jesus had walked. It was all rather horrible in the days when Blake was alive. They used to send cartloads of children from the London workhouses to work in the mills."

"You've made good use of your all-too-often-interrupted schooling," said Dym. "Now suppose you tell me what came next?"

Tony raised himself from the pillow. "Old Badger said it was a vision of a better England. Listen!

"Bring me my Bow of burning gold!
Bring me my Arrows of desire!
Bring me my Spear! O clouds, unfold!
Bring me my Chariot of fire!

"I will not cease from Mental Flight,
Nor shall my Sword sleep in my hand,
Till we have built Jerusalem
In England's green and pleasant land."

When he came to the end Tony suddenly felt shy. He added in a great hurry, "I don't see how you can build anything with a sword."

"Well, it isn't the best of instruments, perhaps, but there are times when it has to be used. Do you remember those men in the Bible who built the walls of the earthly Jerusalem and fought their enemies at the same time, one hand doing the work and the other hand holding a weapon? Doesn't it say, *For the builders, everyone had his sword girded by his side, and so builded?* Blake may have meant something like that."

"You can tell me that story presently, if you have time," said Tony. "I don't know it. Who were the enemies that Blake was fighting? The mill owners?"

"Exactly the same enemies that we're fighting now, Max:

the powers of darkness enslaving the souls of men. The battle is always going on, though the foe takes different shapes at different times. England and her Allies aren't just fighting the Axis countries—they're fighting the evil spirits that have laid hold of Germany and Italy and Japan. It's a far bigger fight than most people realize. Those powers are responsible for what's happening today; a hundred years ago they were responsible for what happened in the dark Satanic mills, and two thousand years ago they crucified Christ.

"Blake's song isn't really a song for England alone," said Dym. "It's a song for every land. We're all building the unseen Jerusalem together. But the powers of darkness don't want to see a time when *the earth shall be filled with the glory of God as the waters cover the sea.* They think that a smashed and tortured world is a prettier sight, and so they won't allow Jerusalem to be built in England or anywhere else. That means that every country has got to choose between God and the devil. Yes, and every man, woman and child has got to make the same choice too."

Tony said slowly, "You think that England has chosen God's side?"

Dym answered, almost in the words he had heard before, "I believe with all my heart that my country is on God's side in the struggle that is going on now. The awful part of it is, Max, that our hands aren't as clean as they should be."

"You didn't want the war. I used to think you did, but—"

"God knows we didn't want it. But they say that, in the years before the war, we drifted away from Him and thought of nothing but the things we could get out of life. I don't know how far that's true—I'm not old enough to judge. But this I do know—it's written down for all men to read—there have been times in our history when we fought on the side of the powers of darkness, when we did what was cruel, treacherous, mean, lazy, shabby. And now, when we want to be strong to fight for the right, half the world taunts us with the shady places in our past, and our misdeeds rise up like grim specters, mocking us—"

Tony, very red, murmured, "Like when I found that, after all, I hadn't thrown my notes into the well—there's a boy in my form who keeps a newspaper cutting about me, and shows it to the others."

"Uncommonly like that," said Dym. "Well, there it is, Max. The powers of darkness are making yet another attempt—perhaps the biggest they've ever made—to cast down and destroy the City of God."

"They can't do it, can they? That other hymn says they can't."

"What other hymn?"

"Margaret's found another tune to it," said Tony.

"You mean:

> *"Glorious things of thee are spoken,*
>   *Zion, city of our God;*
> *He whose word cannot be broken*
>   *Formed thee for His own abode.*
> *On the Rock of Ages founded,*
>   *What can shake thy sure repose?*
> *With salvation's walls surrounded,*
>   *Thou mayest smile at all thy foes.*

"No, they will never do it; you needn't be afraid. They'll be defeated in the end."

"Even if we lose the war? I mean, even if you lose it?"

"We're not going to lose it. But, even if we did, this war is only part of the struggle between good and evil. You don't suppose God would accept defeat? He will win."

"But why doesn't He stop the war? He could, couldn't He? About three good big earthquakes would stop it easily."

"Perhaps it's because He has made us men, Max, not dolls that can't lift a finger of their own accord. But I don't really know; I'm not in the Operations Room, you see. All I do know is that the world has a Chief who was victorious when the powers of darkness struck at Him with everything they had. He has the plans today. The darkness won't last forever. There's a splendor beyond."

Dym stopped abruptly. "That's enough; I've talked too long. Good—"

"No, please! Not yet. You were going to tell me a story about men who built the Bible Jerusalem with golden swords."

"Golden swords?"

"I was thinking of the sword of *Chrys*—" Tony muffled the last two words hastily in his pillow. "I mean, I'm a little mixed somehow. Please tell me. Oh, Dym, I've been machine gunned— I do think you might!"

And Dym did.

21

Tony into Frank

ONE SATURDAY afternoon, toward the end of the summer term, Tony sat on a stile by the roadside, watching for Simon and Judy, who would join him in a game of Commando raids as soon as they could escape from picking black currants under Margaret's keen eye. He had been waiting impatiently for ten minutes, hot and tired and cross.

There was no Dym stationed near the *White Priory* now; there was no Ginger at home on leave; for three days there hadn't been any Euphemia either. After two years of war she had gone for a week's rest in the house of a friend. The three days of her absence seemed as long as a century, Tony thought, and there were four more days to be dragged through before she came back again.

Margaret had made a strict and grumpy substitute and, on this particular day, she was grumpier than usual because old Great-aunt Desdemona was ill, Vera had left to join the Women's Auxiliary Air Force, and Thomas could not find enough workers to pick his black-currant crop. Margaret had driven the entire family into the fields willy-nilly and was doing her best to keep them there till teatime.

Picking black currants was a detestable form of war work, Tony decided gloomily. He put his elbows on his knees, cupped his chin in his juice-stained hands, and shut his eyes to keep away the little shiny black blobs that still danced in front of them. "I'm browned off," he told himself.

When the small dark car drew up beside him, he observed without interest the quiet, middle-aged man who looked out of it. "This is the Tamley Market road," Tony began mechanically, supposing the stranger had lost his way. But the words were waved aside. "You are Anthony Ingleford? You live at the *White Priory*, Greltham St. Andrew?"

"Yes," Tony answered, in mild surprise.

"Ah, then you're the one I want," said the man. "I've been told you speak German. Would you mind translating this German letter for me? It's very short."

Tony had once before been asked to translate a letter written by a German hospital nurse on behalf of a wounded prisoner of war. He nodded, holding out his hand for the sheet of paper. Then all the color left his face.

"Well," said the man, "what does it say?"

In a voice that quivered, Tony read aloud:

"You may safely trust this gentleman, Max darling. He is a friend who will bring you back to us.

Mutti."

The door of the car slid open. "Are you coming?" asked the man.

Like one in a dream, Tony got in. As the door slid gently to, he caught a glimpse of two little blackened faces, peering at him from the bracken in a dry ditch. His Commando troops, stalking their leader, just too late! Huddled on the floor at the back, he felt the car begin to move.

Far away in January a motorboat had carried him off to a land where he had changed from Max into Tony. Now in

July a motorcar was carrying him to where Tony would
again change into Max. For the moment, nothing seemed
real. Life itself had become a thick white mist, pierced here
and there with twinkling points of light. Out of the mist a
voice spoke, a level monotonous voice. Tony could not tell
whether the speaker was English or German. "I am your
mother's agent," the voice said. "She has persuaded your
father to allow her to attempt your rescue now, instead of
waiting to claim you in person after the invasion of England is accomplished. He thought it would be wiser to wait,
but your mother could not wait. Did you think she had
forgotten you? Never! But a rescue is not easy to arrange;
besides, the shock of losing you made her ill—"

Tony's own voice said breathlessly, "She isn't ill now?
She's better?"

"She's as well as you could expect when she is fretting
her heart out for her boy. I have undertaken to smuggle you
out of England. While certain nations remain neutral, there
are ways of doing it even in wartime. We've a good start,
haven't we? I never dreamt I should light on you alone, so
easily. When will you be missed?"

Tony wondered whether he should mention the small
heads that had popped out of the ditch. Without knowing
why, he decided to hold his tongue about them. "Not later
than teatime at five," he said. The mist surged round him
again, thickly. Somewhere, a long way off, he heard the
agent still speaking.

"Now listen, my boy. You are no longer Anthony Ingleford or Max Eckermann. Today you are Frank Richardson.
You understand? Your name is Frank Richardson! You live
at the address given on this identity card." He handed Tony
a card. "As you see, your home is in an evacuation area? You

know what that means, don't you? It's a dangerous part from which children have been sent away. You and your sister Doris have been evacuated under private arrangement to your relations. You, Frank, have been sent to live with your Uncle Fred, otherwise Frederick Halliwell, your mother's brother. And I have just had a telegram from your father—here it is—asking me to take you home at once as your mother is very ill."

"*Lucy dangerously ill pneumonia can you bring children urgent. Richardson*" Tony read from the pink slip. He laughed suddenly and tremulously. "Mother has been ill," he said.

"That will make it easier to remember," said "Uncle Fred." "We're on our way now to collect your sister Doris, who is staying with your Aunt Emma in—well, if anyone asks questions you just leave it to me to answer. Aunt Emma's name is Bates, Mrs. Bates. She lives a good way from here; we shan't reach her home before black-out, and we shall spend the night there. What's your sister's name? Right. And mine? Your aunt's? Right. You know what to say if we should be asked for an account of ourselves? Good. Say as little as possible, though, and, whatever you do, don't speak to me in German. No, not even when we are alone. Now suppose you memorize the names and addresses on your identity card and mine. Where's your old identity card, by the by?"

"In my gas mask," Tony said slowly.

"What! you carry your gas mask in a country lane, do you? First boy I ever met—"

Tony flushed. "I never carry it at all, except to school. We have to take it then, always. But we were warned that the Army will have a drill today. They may be using tear gas—"

"The drill's been cancelled," said Uncle Fred. "If it hadn't
been, I shouldn't be here. Don't want too many nosy park-
ers shoving their heads into the car to ask for a sight of our
identity cards. We prefer not to attract attention, you and
I." He laughed, but Tony did not laugh with him. "Put your
new card into the place where you keep the old one," he
said, "and give the old one to me. You won't need it any
longer."

Tony felt strangely unwilling to obey this sensible command. When a fumbling search in the gas mask case re-
vealed no card, he was glad. "It isn't there, after all."

"Try your pockets."

Tony fumbled again, and shook his head. He did not tell
Uncle Fred that he had just remembered where the identity
card was. His wallet of secret treasures had gone with him
to the Commando-raid game, tucked carefully into his
shirt, and inside the first flap was the identity card, doing
duty as "sealed orders." He had to have sealed orders when
he was leading a Commando raid. And, curiously enough,
he felt strongly disinclined to surrender them when bidden
to do so.

"Come," said Uncle Fred, "if you have it on you, you'd
better get rid of it. Look again."

Suddenly Tony became sharply and unreasonably determined not to part with the only bit of himself that was still
Anthony Victor Ingleford. Still sitting on the floor, he
made another prolonged but unsuccessful search; then, by
way of pacifying Uncle Fred, he detached the metal identity disk he had brought from Germany and handed it over.
"I've got this," he said, "perhaps you'd better take it."

"You will need it again," said Uncle Fred, "but it will be
safer in my keeping for the present."

There was no suspicion in voice or manner; nevertheless Tony had an odd fancy that there were eyes in the back of Uncle Fred's skull. He turned his own head away that he might not see them boring right through pullover and gray-flannel shirt to his precious wallet. Why, he asked himself, had he been so unwilling to part with a British identity card that he would need no longer, so overready to part with a German disk that he would need again? He could find no answer to the question.

For a few minutes Uncle Fred remained silent, driving fast but not so fast as to attract notice. In those minutes of silence the mist cleared from Tony's mind. Its going left him sore and resentful, as if he had been unfairly dealt with. He found himself remembering what Judy had said at dinnertime that day, after Margaret had hurried her into making a choice between two left-overs of pudding, "You hustled me and bustled me till I hadn't time to think. I've chosen jam roly-poly with scarcely any jam in it—and now I wish I'd chosen raspberry tart!" Uncle Fred, he thought, had treated him much as Margaret had treated Judy; he hadn't allowed him a moment in which to make a cool, free choice. He wondered what would happen if he said that he had changed his mind about coming. Uncle Fred was quite an ordinary man, but the back of his head did not look promising.

"It's a pity you had to leave the Inglefords without a chance to say good-bye," Uncle Fred said carelessly. "I daresay you're sorry about that. They were kind to you, weren't they?"

"Very kind."

"Ah, just so. Well, you shall write them a letter of thanks as soon as we reach Aunt Emma's house tonight. That is, if you think your mother wouldn't object to your writing. By the way, what is your mother's name?"

"Frau Eck—"

"Aha! Caught you there, my boy!"

"Mrs. Richardson, I mean," said Tony, discomfited.

"That's better. If you really want to write to the people who tried to deprive you of your name and your nationality, you may do it. I give you my word that your letter shall be posted as soon as you are safely out of England."

"I think I won't write," said Tony miserably. "There doesn't seem anything to say."

"I agree with you," said Uncle Fred. "If my son had been stolen from me, I shouldn't care to think that he was on friendly terms with the people who took him. Good boy!"

The words frightened Tony a little; he couldn't tell why. They also served to remind him that he wouldn't be able to tell Mutti much about his life in England. Not that he didn't trust her—but walls had ears, and it was important that Tante Bettina should never know that he had done war work at the *White Priory*. Why, his hands were still stained with the black currants that were going to be made into syrup for orangeless British babies, and there was a shilling of his wages in his pocket at this very moment! Thomas was a just man; he didn't make his relations work for nothing; they were paid at the standard rate for their fruit picking.

"Still, they seem to be a jolly family," Uncle Fred allowed generously. "I heard about them when I was making inquiries. Always up to what are known as larks. Two of them, I understand, kept an elaborate and painstaking watch for months on the house of a famous member of the British Secret Service, under the impression that he was a German agent."

Tony turned pink. So that was why Dym had laughed at the story of his visit to *Querns!* He no longer wondered that, for many weeks, James and Porgy had cycled to and from school by a road that did not lead past the scene of their former spy hunting.

"Very funny!" said Uncle Fred. "There is also a young naval lieutenant, given to practical joking, who seems very popular in the village—"

"He isn't a lieutenant; he's only—" said Tony, putting up a hand to feel whether his wallet was safe. There was a treasured letter from Ginger in it, beginning *Dear Spitfire.* "You're mixing him up with my other brother, Dym—"

"Your what?"

"With Dym, I mean."

Uncle Fred grunted. "You'd better forget that you ever had any brothers, Frank Richardson. This Dym is in the R.A.F., isn't he? What's his rank?"

"Flight Lieutenant," said Tony proudly.

"Which Command?"

"Bomber Command."

"Where's he stationed now?"

There flashed into Tony's memory certain words spoken in the passage on the night of the machine gunning. "I don't know the name of the station," he said.

"You needn't be cautious with me, you know," said Uncle Fred.

Tony felt uneasy. He said in a subdued voice, "It's the truth."

"You never write to him, then?"

"Yes. But Phemie—Fräulein—Miss Ingleford posts my letters inside hers to save paper and stamps."

"And when Dym writes to you, he also saves an inch of paper by omitting his address. I understand. Are you the only one who has been prudently kept in the dark?"

Tony thought of Porgy and Mary and Mousie. It was intolerable that anyone should think that they knew what was kept from him. He answered indignantly, "No."

As the word left his lips he knew that he had blundered: Uncle Fred had learnt, quite easily, that the secret of Dym's whereabouts was shared by very few. But he made up his mind that one blunder should not be followed by another. Uncle Fred might like to hear that Dym's station was not far from Orrington Magna, where the old cousins lived, but Uncle Fred wasn't going to hear it. Nor should Uncle Fred be told that Dym had been posted to a hush-hush place in which secret and important work was being done. Conscious, however, that the invisible eyes were on him again, he tried to find an excuse for his silence.

"If I should be caught," he said, "it would be awkward for me if the police found out that I had been giving information. That is so, *nicht wahr?*"

"Take care!" said Uncle Fred.

Tony could not tell whether the warning was double-edged. While he was still wondering whether there was any sinister meaning behind the simple reminder not to speak German, Uncle Fred's thoughts took another jump. "What do you suppose would happen," said Uncle Fred, "if you were caught running away? You have done it a good many times, haven't you? Mr. Ingleford's patience must be nearly exhausted."

"Thomas never—I mean, Mr. Ingleford always says I'd better be left to Dym. I'm Dym's responsibility."

"And what view would Dym take of the matter? What would he say?"

Tony gave a reluctant answer. "He said I could run away nine times without being punished, but the tenth time I was caught there would be a really serious row. And this is the tenth time I've done it. At least," said Tony, remembering his visit to Rond Cross Hospital, "it's got to count as the tenth time."

"Have you any idea what he meant by a really serious row?"

Tony nodded.

"And what sort of discipline will you get from Dym?"

"I—" Tony stopped quickly. He had meant to say, "I was going to stay with friends in Wales if Dym thought I could be trusted not to run away any more. Now he'll say he can't trust me." But he suddenly remembered that the less he said about Auntie Nell and Uncle Laurie the better. People who were engaged on secret war work wouldn't want a German agent to know where they had planned to spend their leave. He said falteringly and with a downcast air, "I don't know for certain what he would do."

Uncle Fred said in a kind voice, "Never mind, my boy. You're quite safe now. You'll never see him again."

Tony's chin dropped. He knew that Uncle Fred expected a reply, but he could think of nothing to say. When Uncle Fred's real eyes turned to look at him, he went very red and looked down. And, although he did not speak, it was as if he had said loudly, "That's not the kind of thing I want to hear."

He was sure the man had read his thoughts; but all Uncle Fred said was, "You'll get cramp if you sit on the floor any longer. Get up and sit in the right-hand corner. You're not likely to be recognized at this distance from Greltham St. Andrew. Besides, no one has any reason to suspect you of driving away in a car. Tell me how you managed to run away before."

Tony told some of his adventures, not because he wanted to talk but because it was wise to oblige Uncle Fred in any harmless way. His voice rang in his ears like a cracked gramophone record that was slowing to a full stop. Then something clicked inside him, and not another syllable would come out.

"Go on," said Uncle Fred.

Tony made a great effort. A soundless little whisper said, "I can't."

"You need your tea, that's what's the matter with you," said Uncle Fred. "Can you open that basket in the other corner for me?"

Tony opened the wicker hamper, and they had tea as they drove slowly along. It reminded Tony of his first meal with Dym in the train, though Uncle Fred, unlike Dym, carelessly dropped the thermos flask after he had halted for a moment to pour out their tea. He laughed at his own clumsiness. "No tea for me!" he said, looking in mock dismay at his empty cup. "If you hadn't already started yours, Frank, I should have made you go shares!"

Tony thought that Uncle Fred hadn't missed much, for the tea was so sweet it was almost undrinkable. Only the fear of offending Uncle Fred enabled him to gulp it down. Afterward he felt sleepy, so sleepy that he could not keep awake long enough to finish the slice of sandy, wartime cake that he had toyed with throughout the meal. Sleepy though he was, he had a confused fear that Uncle Fred might steal away his wallet. Slipping it out of his shirt, he pushed it under the cushions. Then he crept further into the corner, pillowed his head on his arm, and slept.

At first his sleep was disturbed by queer dreams: Uncle Fred was turning his pockets out and talking, talking, talking in the same steady, monotonous voice. As far as he could understand, Uncle Fred appeared to be preaching a kind of sermon to someone who ought to be thankful for a chance of getting out of defeated England into victorious Germany. Tony interrupted the sermon once by saying that he thought it was time for him to do his homework now, and, when Uncle Fred asked him, laughing, what his lessons were that night, he said that his prep had been excused because he had been machine gunned by a Jerry. Later he fancied he had asked to be taken back to the *White Priory,* for Uncle Fred's voice, fuzzier and more distant than before, said that he had made his choice and must stick to it; there could be no going back. Tony tried to protest; but wave upon wave of sleep rolled over him, drowning him deep, deep down for ages and ages.

And then somebody—not Uncle Fred—roared at him, "I say, am I right for Orrington Magna?" As Tony started out of a cloudy unknown depth, the air about him vibrated with echoes: *Orrington Magna—Magna—Orrington Magna —am I right for Orrington Magna?*

Tony stared round him, puzzled and blinking. It was night. The car had halted at the entrance to a major road. Framed in the front side-window was a young face with a glimmer of Air Force blue above and below it. Uncle Fred was saying "yes" as if in answer to a question. Now the car had shot across the major road, leaving the face behind. For a moment Tony's pulses galloped and thrilled. *Orrington Magna! Orrington Magna!* He knew that the words had a meaning for him, but he could not think what it might be. His head fell forward and he went down again under the waves of sleep.

The house door opened. As soon as it shut behind him, Tony was conscious that, although he still stood on English soil, he was in Germany again. Yet there was no Party notice board or photograph of Hitler in the narrow entrance hall, nor was there anything particularly German about the furniture of the small ugly sitting room into which he was led.

For a few minutes he sat by himself on a prickly chair covered in black horsehair, gazing at the large framed reproduction of *Dignity and Impudence* over the mahogany sideboard. At home—no, at the *White Priory*—they always said that Thomas and Judy looked exactly like Dignity and Impudence when they sat next to each other at table.

"You like that picture?" said Uncle Fred, entering with a tray.

"We've got it at—" said Tony. "I mean, I've seen it."

As Uncle Fred put the tray down beside the big aspidistra, an enormous spider scampered out of the leaves and began lowering itself to the brown tablecloth by its thread. Tony, shrinking in his chair, felt as though he were a fly that had, somehow, been caught in a mesh he could not break.

He did not feel hungry for his supper of herring, bread and coffee, eaten in Uncle Fred's company. The sight of his own face in a mirror on the wall did not please him. It was white and scared and it looked as though he had been crying. The house was uncannily quiet. Once he heard a cough in the passage. Uncle Fred got up and went out, shutting the door behind him. In the moment of his absence Tony parted the leaves of the aspidistra and poured his coffee into the flowerpot. Uncle Fred had sweetened the coffee with a white powdery sugar-substitute that gave it the same taste he had disliked in his tea. He had contrived to swallow the tea, but he did not think that he could possibly swallow the coffee. Uncle Fred's disappearance was almost providential.

Much to Tony's distress, a very untoward accident marked the moment of Uncle Fred's return. Just as the low voices in the passage stopped speaking, a nervous movement of his hand flicked the spoon out of the bowl of sugar-substitute. When Uncle Fred re-entered the room, Tony was in the act of putting back the spoon, for all the world like a greedy guest who had helped himself in his host's absence to a precious wartime delicacy. It did not appear to be a case where an explanation would improve matters. He hid his flaming cheeks behind his empty cup. Uncle Fred smiled.

"Ah, that's better!" he said. "I'm glad you're beginning to feel more at home. Now what about bed?"

Tony followed Uncle Fred to a small bedroom. "There's no black-out curtain here," said Uncle Fred, "so you must manage without a candle. You'll have just enough light to undress by; tumble into bed as quick as you can. You might as well give me your shoes—they'll need cleaning. No, no, you can't clean them yourself. Aunt Emma doesn't like boys in her back kitchen. I'll have them done for you."

Tony stooped to unfasten his shoes. As he did so, his

wallet fell with a bump on the floor. There was a very curious silence. Then Uncle Fred held out his hand for the shoes. "Thanks," he said. "Good night, Frank. Sleep well."

The door shut. Tony stood alone, clutching his wallet and wishing that he hadn't been so stupidly sleepy when he refastened it inside his shirt at the end of the journey. He felt sure that both he and it were in danger. At some unknown hour in the night Uncle Fred would steal in silently to take it away. When it was gone, there would be nothing left of the boy who had once been Anthony Victor Ingleford. There would be only Frank Richardson, dressed in the well-worn clothes that he could see hanging in readiness over the back of a chair; and then, later, there would be Max Eckermann again. If Tante Bettina and the cousins ever came to know what was inside the wallet, then Max Eckermann would have a most uncomfortable time.

With a glance of mingled fear and defiance at the keyless door, Tony sat down on the side of his bed and hastily made a little parcel of his dearest treasures. If worse came to worst, Uncle Fred might have the wallet, but he should have nothing else except the snapshots of Porgy, Mary, Mousie and the school giraffes. They could be spared and might serve to act as a blind.

This done, he looked about for a safe hiding place. The treasure could not be hidden under his pillow, for that was the first place Uncle Fred would search if the emptiness of the wallet made him suspicious. Other hiding place there was none. The room was as scantily furnished as a prison cell.

He opened the window and leant out, peering round in search of broken brickwork or comfortable cluster of knotted ivy. The wall was disappointingly bare, but a little to the left of his room, some four or five feet lower, he could see, dimly outlined, the flat roof of a porch. I could jump down —if I made myself, he thought, and then I could easily hide the parcel under some of those broken bits of tile that are scattered about. I don't believe he'd ever dream of looking there. But what's the use of thinking about it? If I did manage to jump down without smashing myself up, I couldn't possibly get back!

The jump was undoubtedly awkward and the result of any failure so dangerous that he was not sorry to be relieved of the necessity of making it. The roof hiding place being now out of the question, Tony decided that he could not do better than lay his parcel on the window sill behind a half-open casement. It was a poor hide, but it was the best at his disposal. After all, people didn't usually put their valuables outside their bedroom windows: the chances were that Uncle Fred might not search the ledge.

But Tony did not at once leave the window and obey Uncle Fred's command to tumble into bed. Still holding the parcel, he studied his surroundings with close attention. From the porch it would, he thought, be possible for a boy with stout nerves to drop to the ground. The garden beneath was not large; it was a grass patch bordered with flower beds and ending in a long fowl house with a wired-in run. A gate in the fence on the left led into what looked like woody meadowland. Clouds were dark overhead, and trees were waving in the wind. He said to himself, with a laugh that did not feel like a laugh, "I'm somebody that I've never been before, somebody between Tony and Max, somebody called Frank. I wonder who I'll turn into next."

22

The Making of a Choice

THE SOMEBODY called Frank looked into the garden. Its rustling wavery darkness made a background
on which pictures of the life before him stood out plain.
First of all he saw the old house in the wide, quiet road,
with the Cavendishes' house next door to it and Tante
Bettina's close by. Mutti was standing in the doorway, her
blond face radiant, her arms stretched out to greet him.

The picture faded and re-formed. Now he was in the
sunny playroom that had fairyland scenes and fairy animals
painted round the walls by a famous designer when he was
a little boy. From the playroom he stepped straight into a
line of moving figures, and saw himself staggering along as
he had staggered that day last summer when Hermann had
been so angry with him for not being able to march eleven
miles with a heavy pack on his back. He could see the very
bend in the road where Hermann had stood, the plum trees
on either side, the dazzle of sunshine overhead, a blue-
aproned old woman gathering raspberry leaves from her
garden to be dried for use as tea.

Hastily dismissing that picture, Tony saw himself and
Mutti, holidaying in Salzburg with peasant dances and
songs, or afoot in green Bavaria with its enchanted castles
perched high on craggy hills—and now cosily at home
telling each other stories of witches and kobolds and char-

coal burners' huts in the forest. No, those delights belonged to peacetime and the days of long ago. If there were any spare minutes for either of them, he would be telling her tales of his gallant war service in England: how he had sung *Deutschland über alles* in an English church; how he had shown lights to guide the German aircraft, how he had cut *Heil Hitler* on their priceless desk, how he had run away ten times. Of course, there were those stories that he wouldn't be able to tell.

Then a young face flamed into life on that dark background. A thin face, with wild red hair. Tony leaned against the window, unable to meet James' accusing eyes. James didn't know, he told himself. Dym would have understood, but Dym was far away, very far away at—Orrington Magna!

Out in the garden starshine glittered and voices began calling again insistently, "Orrington Magna—Orrington Magna—I say, am I right for Orrington Magna? Orrington Magna?" Tony could put a meaning to the words now. Orrington Magna was where the old cousins lived, Cousin Basil and his sister Olive; it was the place near Olaf's school and near the—no, let him not think those words where Uncle Fred might overhear his quietest thoughts.

The pictures flashed and faded. He was looking now at a white, wintry world. As he looked, the snow melted and the dark earth stirred and changed. Primroses gleamed on the banks, daffodils and American currant danced in the breeze, bluebells spread sheets of sapphire in the woodlands. Slowly the oaks began to turn golden, the beeches shook crinkled satin leaves out of tightly rolled buds, the birches flung a leafy rain about their silver trunks, and the chilly lilac opened the lower buds on its white and purple pyramids, as if feeling its way cautiously in the cold new world. Cuckoos called above the marshes with pale cuckoo-flowers, yellow

kingcups and bulrushes that were rougher than brown vel-
vet. Turtle doves *turr-turr-turred* in the trees. Fields sprang
to swaying, grassy life. And through every sight and scene
moved Thomas, big, silent, patient, with his dogs and his
horses about him. It would be queer, not belonging to
Thomas any more. Queer, and not very nice.

"Coming round with me today, Tony?"

"No, never again." How odd it sounded! He was glad to
see Phemie instead of Thomas, Phemie with her sandy
wisps of hair sticking out as she bent to kiss him good
night the evening before she went away. "You'll try to help
Margaret while I'm gone, won't you, Tony boy? She'll have
such a lot to do. I shan't stay longer than a week. I promise." Phemie's promises were always to be trusted.

There were no pictures of Margaret that he wanted to
call to mind, for she was like an accusing conscience, glowering at him with angry dark eyes. And there wouldn't have
been any pictures of Mortimer either if he hadn't remembered that Dym was fond of the quiet, colorless brother
whose life had been broken in the Four Years' War long
ago. Mortimer had gone out to fight when he was hardly
more than a schoolboy; he had come home to drag wearily
through a semi-invalid life, glad to earn a living by teaching
in a small school for delicate boys. When you looked at
Mortimer, you felt that war was cruel, so cruel you found it
hard to believe Ernst and Hermann when they said it was
glorious. There were lots and lots of people like Mortimer
in the world, people who suffered because other people
thought war glorious.

Looking into the night, Tony waited for what he should
see when the lights went up. But the dark eddying shadows
looked like stormy waves.

Again a picture rose upon the darkness. Tony was crouching behind a chair in Dym's room. The sunset made red lakes in the sky as Dym sat talking to the others about the sword *Chrysaor*. All that Dym had said came back to him. Then he saw the passage with its brown matting. He was speaking to somebody with a small eager face framed in red hair. "I shall never choose *Chrysaor!*" he was saying. Well, hadn't he kept his word to Sally? Soon he would be in the country where—what were Dym's words?—"the sword *Balmung* is forced into every hand." But might not Dym be mistaken?

At his first coming to England, seven months ago, the English had told him that almost everything he had learnt at home, at school, in the *Jungvolk* and from the radio had been wrong. Wasn't it probable that when he went back to Germany he would find that he had been deceived? Once more Germany would be the great, brave, splendid nation fighting for the living space that she needed; once more England would be a false and greedy foe. No, no, Dym had not deceived him; Dym would never deceive anyone. But Dym had himself been deceived.

What a din the radio was making, to be sure! Then, with start and shudder, Tony found that the noise was within his own weary head. There was no radio on downstairs; the house and its mysterious occupants were quiet. He shook himself, as if to shake away the clouds left by heavy, bewildering sleep. But he could not rid himself of the voice. It made him listen and, as he listened, he felt that he was in a dark place being drawn ever nearer to some unseen Power more terrible than the danger that had lurked in the marshes long ago. And as it drew him it spoke.

Germany calling; Germany calling.

Tony saw no more pictures, for he shrank from guessing what might happen next. It was enough to know that a boy who would choose *Chrysaor* must face danger, open-eyed.

Germany calling; Germany calling. If only England would call too! He listened, but England did not call. He listened again. No, there was no counter-summons to Germany's imperious call: Tony could hear only the thumping of his own heart and the nervous tap of his fingers on the window ledge, where they were beating out a rhythm that he had often heard of late—*dot-dot-dot dash, dot-dot-dot dash, dot-dot-dot dash.* It sounds like someone knocking at the door, he thought. Someone knocking— He broke off as the ears of his mind were filled with the opening bars of a great and stately music. "The beginning of the *Fifth Symphony*," he said to himself, startled, "one of the V Army's signs—and Morse code V, that's another—I'm making V signs—I mustn't—" Crimson with alarm, he stayed his hand. But he could not stay his heart. *Dot-dot-dot dash*, it beat; *dot-dot-dot dash, dot-dot-dot dash*, as though it spoke the code language of the secret army of oppressed peoples all over the earth.

Dot-dot-dot dash, dot-dot-dot dash, dot-dot-dot dash. The noise was so loud that he was afraid Ernst would hear it. For he was in Germany now, facing Ernst in a room that might belong to the Gestapo headquarters. And this time he was not a prisoner taken in England but a boy who had returned to Germany of his own free will, who knew the whereabouts of an ammunition dump, who could give a clue to the position of a hush-hush place, who held in his hands many lives and one life that was dearer than all. "Stand there, Max," Ernst was saying. "Answer my questions. Keep nothing back." Tony shrank from that picture, shuddering, as he had shrunk from the other. Betray the Inglefords? Betray Dym? They were England, all the England that he knew.

Germany calling; Germany calling.

England remained mute. But his own heart beat out the Victory sign.

Crossing to the table, Tony pulled out a pencil and searched among his treasures for a piece of paper. As he did not like to use the back of Mutti's note, he chose an Ingleford family group snapshot and turned it face downward. Then he wrote:

I can't come.
Your loving Max.

He filled the empty space with X's for kisses, then snatched up his wallet, thrust the remaining treasures into it, and made one bound for the window sill. For a moment he stood clenching his hands, gritting his teeth. Then he sprang, swaying perilously on the edge of the porch roof, and fell forward with a thud. Crawling back, he lowered himself over the edge, hung by his hands, and dropped.

It was a long drop that jarred every bone in his body and sent a sharp thrill through one foot. Heedless of the pain, he darted across the garden, through the gate into the meadow. Somewhere behind him he heard a door open. His name reached him in Uncle Fred's level tones: "Frank! Come back at once!"

Tony had to fight against obedience. Uncle Fred's voice ran through the air like a lasso, encircling him, dragging him back, forcing him into surrender. For a full second he paused in terror, then fled blindly as fast as he could go. Words that reached him told that Uncle Fred was not alone. "You take that side—I'll try the right—" Looking over his shoulder, Tony saw two dark shapes that were men, and a third that might have been a woman. Two men, to say nothing of Aunt Emma! He could never escape, never, in this fearful game of hide-and-seek, without any friendly den at the end of it. Yes, there was a den in—Orrington Magna—Orrington Magna—if only he could run harder with a stab in his foot and a stitch in his side.

If he were caught, what would Uncle Fred do to a boy who had changed his mind about going to Germany, a boy it was dangerous to let go free? Uncle Fred's house was lonely—all sorts of things might happen to a boy in a lonely house—funny to think that there ever had been a time when he ran away from Ginger and Dym! He wasn't caught yet, though the chase was hot. One of the pursuers had fallen down, Aunt Emma he thought. Now Uncle Fred had halted. No, it was the man on the other side of the meadow. He was flashing a pocket torch into the hedge as if he thought something was moving there. Then the man said, "Got you!" The thing that had been caught flew out of the hedge cackling *Twark-twark-toowark* in wild affright. It wasn't me after all, Tony thought, with faint surprise; it must have been a fowl that had escaped from the fowl run. I've had more practice—in running away—than most fowls. And he sped on.

He did not know what happened after that. When he came fairly to himself, he was crouching in ferny gloom, his forehead and hands wet and clammy, his heart thudding as though it meant to jump out of his body. He knew that his hiding place must be a wood, for he could see the glimmering of tall tree trunks and smell the woodsy scents of bracken and dead leaves. But he had no notion how he

THE MAKING OF A CHOICE

came to be there. Behind him was a confused remembrance of running and twisting and dodging in the darkness, of tumbling over roots and catching his foot in rabbit holes and rolling down banks and falling against haystacks. His clothes were torn, his socks were gone, his injured foot ached abominably. Worst of all, Uncle Fred and his companions were in the wood too, rustling and sighing high up in the treetops, trampling fallen twigs underfoot, pushing their way through the undergrowth. The air-raid siren hadn't driven them away, nor the lurching of German aircraft, nor the whistle and crump of a bomb. He could see, a long way off, the horrid glow of the pocket torch seeking, seeking. Tony shut his eyes and sank motionless under the ferns.

Raising his head, he saw that the torch glow was still in the same place. Then, for the fraction of a second, it was darkened as if some object had passed across it, and at the same time he heard the zipping of a motorcycle that might very well belong to dispatch rider or military patrol. Somewhere near the torch, then, was a road. People walked on roads; cars drove on them: that was the use of roads. If he could reach a road, he might be able to find someone who would help him. But how could he get to the road when Uncle Fred's ally was blocking the way with his torch? He looked again. The torch was steady but dim. Perhaps it was not a torch. No, it was an opening in the wood. As he gazed, another motorcycle zipped across.

Tony had only one thought in his mind: terrifying though the passage was, he must reach that opening at all costs. With a swish of parted bracken, he was off again, stumbling, tripping, lashed by twigs and clutched by briars. His breath came in sobbing gasps that were easy for Uncle Fred to hear, and his foot felt as if red-hot needles had been stuck into it. Once he barely bit back a scream as a long tree-arm stretched out and caught him by the shoulder. But the opening was growing larger and larger; it was coming nearer, nearer, nearer. Something huge with heavy wheels was lumbering past it. An army lorry—another—another. They would all have passed long before he could hail them from the stile that he could now see in the gap; there was no sense in hailing them while he was still in the wood. Though his shouts might attract the notice of Uncle Fred, they wouldn't be noticed by men who were singing lustily:

> *"What's the use of worryin'?*
> *It never was worth while;*
> *So pack up your troubles in your old kit-bag*
> *And smile, smile, smile."*

Tony swayed against the stile, flung one hunted glance into the undergrowth behind him, and jumped. Then all fear died, for, a few yards down the road, one of the lorries had come to a halt.

Three or four men belonging to it were clustered about the bonnet, engaged in giving advice to the driver, who was anxiously poking about inside. Tony made for the back of the lorry, which stood invitingly open. With a spring and a scramble he landed on the floor.

It was better this way, he told himself. If he asked for a lift, the soldiers might refuse to take a boy who was so plainly a runaway. While he was trying to make them believe his story, Uncle Fred might rush out of the wood to claim him. The soldiers would believe Uncle Fred. Besides, he didn't want to remain on the road where Uncle Fred could see him, no, not even for a moment.

Tony looked about. The lorry was empty save for a

couple of boxes, a coil of wire, a large brown-paper parcel, and a heap of camouflage nets with brown and green tags sticking out. Tony flung himself down in a corner, pulled a camouflage net over him, and lay gasping for breath, too tired to move. Soon a clatter outside warned him that the soldiers were about to move off. They tumbled in again, and, when they had settled down on the floor, two of them went to sleep while the other two unconcernedly lifted up their voices and sang:

"John Brown's body lies a-mouldering in the grave,
John Brown's body lies a-mouldering in the grave,
John Brown's body lies a-mouldering in the grave,
But his soul goes marching on.
Glory, glory, hallelujah!
Glory, glory, hallelujah!
Glory, glory, hallelujah!
But his soul goes marching on."

They sang other songs as well, but they returned again and again to *John Brown's Body*. Tony was glad they did, for the triumphant marching rhythm made him feel that he was free. But he had no inclination to show himself. He wanted to put as many miles as possible between him and Uncle Fred; he was desperately ashamed of the story he had to tell, and he was so very, very tired. The singing soldiers grew tired too; they fell silent at last. One of them, casting about for amusement, spied the parcel and began to open it.

"You let that alone, Jack," said his friend.

"Shurrup!" said Jack. Then his face fell, his eyes bulged in his head, and he dropped the parcel as if it had burnt him.

"What's the matter?" asked the other soldier sleepily.

Tony couldn't hear Jack's answer, but it appeared to electrify the man for whom it was meant. "The Major's washing!" he repeated in a hollow voice. "What's the Major's washing doing here?"

"What's the good of asking riddles at this time of night?" Jack said crossly. "What we've to do is get it back to him before he misses it."

The two sleeping soldiers were prodded awake and obliged to take their share in an anxious consultation. Before long, Jack made a suggestion that turned the listener under the camouflage net cold with horror. "If Bill's got enough juice in the old bus," he said, "I reckon the best thing we can do is to run her back lickety-split to that wood where we stopped to do a bit of tinkering. I know a fellow on the searchlight post across from there. He's a good sort, is Bert Stokes. He'd get this parcel handed over to the Major's batman before the Major's had a chance to miss it."

All but Tony agreed that this was a happy way out of the difficulty. The Major's beautiful shirts having been thrown out of their folds by the exploring Jack, it was further resolved that the man with the cleanest hands should re-pack the parcel in the light of the lorry's head lamps while she was being turned. Before Tony had made up his mind what to do next, they hallooed to Bill to stop, and were all tumbling out at the back pell mell. This was Tony's chance. Without waiting to see whether Bill was willing to under-take the double journey, he slipped quietly out, ran a little way down the road, and climbed over the nearest gate. To be alone again was unpleasant, but anything was better than going back to the dangerous neighborhood of Uncle Fred.

As soon as he heard the lorry moving off, panic seized Tony. Leaving the safe company of the soldiers had been a mistake, an idiotic mistake. Probably Uncle Fred was following the lorry in his car and when he met the lorry coming back, he would know that his nephew wasn't in it. Then he and the other man and Aunt Emma would search on both sides of the hedges and go into all the fields. You couldn't escape from Germany—you never escaped—

It was cold in the field under the night wind. Bats whirred past him; wild things whisked through the grasses at his feet. A large white owl sat on the roof of a broken-down shed, gazing at him in solemn surprise. He could see it clearly, for the clouds had swept past, and the moonlight shone serene. He took a few more irresolute, frightened steps, then felt the earth sloping away under him. The last year's bomb crater beneath him was seeded over with wild flowers and grasses: all moon-silvered to ghostliness. For a resting-place, this was as good as any. Uncle Fred would search the owl's haunt; he wouldn't search a bomb crater.

Tony lay down, his hands behind his head, to watch the white shafts of light roaming across the sky, twisting, interlacing, making light pools far up in the clouds. Once a red object like a fairy chandelier hung glittering beneath them. The guns barked at it savagely, drowning the hum of enemy aircraft. Then guns and aircraft became quiet. Faraway, so far that he could hear no sound of firing, he saw the pin-point lights of anti-aircraft shells bursting overhead. Then the *All Clear* rang out, shrill, steady, sweet. The pale beams stopped weaving their patterns on the sky loom; the winking lights vanished. Tony said his prayers lying down because it seemed safer. After a time he slept.

23

The Last Crash Landing

WHEN TONY WOKE, it was Sunday morning. He was stiff and blue with cold, dew drops were shining in his hair, and he was very hungry. Worse still, his foot was hurting him badly.

For nearly two hours he sat shivering in the dawn. Gold ruffled the gray; furrows of red stirred the gold. Soon the whole sky was a mingling of rose color and deep, still blue. Young rabbits came out to feed. Their little white bobtails scampered past him; their small brown bodies were full of eager life. Tony made his plans as he watched them, but he did not leave his hiding place until voices and bugle calls told him that the world was fully stocked with people who were not Uncle Fred.

When at last he limped painfully down to the road, a passing milkman offered him a lift in his cart.

"Where are you going?" Tony asked.

"Pebberton Green," said the milkman.

"Is it near Orrington Magna?"

"Sixteen miles." The milkman looked at Tony's bare feet and tattered clothes. "Run away from your billet?" he asked, with a grin.

Tony disliked being taken for an evacuée who had failed to settle down in somebody else's house. "No," he answered curtly.

The milkman took another look at him. "School, then?" he suggested.

Tony did not want to tell the whole of his story, but he saw that he must tell some part of it if he wished to keep the inquisitive milkman from handing him over to the police. "I've run away from home," he said, red and sulky, "but I'm going back. Two cousins live in Orrington Magna. I shall stop there on my way."

"I've a brother living in Orrington Magna," said the milkman. "What are your cousins' names?"

"Dr. Fairleigh and Miss Fairleigh."

The names appeared to satisfy the milkman, who nodded to show that he recognized them. "Well, it's a good thing you're come to your senses, that's all I can say. There's no place like home, you know. There's a bus leaves Pebberton Green for Orrington Magna somewhere about one o'clock. Churchyard Corner, it starts from. Got enough cash to see you through, son?"

"Yes, thanks. I can manage all right."

"It's a bit early to ask anybody for breakfast," said the milkman, "but I daresay Mother Dawkins'd find you up something in about an hour's time. I'll show you her house as we pass."

Tony did not see how his money could be stretched to cover breakfast as well as bus fare. But he kept his perplexity to himself. His nine lives had cost his family a good deal in one way and another; they should not be called upon to repay another loan.

"If you're Dr. Fairleigh's cousin," said the milkman, as they halted at Churchyard Corner some minutes later, "you'll be some relation to the Flight Lieutenant G.D. Ingleford they talk about such a lot. He's a cousin too, I've heard."

"I'm his brother."

"Good for you." The milkman became suddenly respectful, and he drove off smiling, making a V sign. Tony returned the salute from his perch on the churchyard wall.

But he felt small and depressed when he was alone again, with no chance of getting either breakfast or dinner. Hunger brought gloomy thoughts in its train. He began to wonder whether his family would be pleased to see him again.

The thought, too, of Mutti waiting for him in vain was so painful that he sought refuge from it in thoughts that were just as gray. Dym was going to be angry; Dym was going to punish him by depriving him of the holiday that had promised to be so delightful: first the visit to Uncle Tony and then those seven glorious days with Geoffrey, Michael and David, playing on the white sands of Wales, climbing the purple mountains, bathing in the blue sea that was not grimly fenced off like the sea on the East Coast. He deserved to be punished, he knew—but not that way; that was too hard. Auntie Nell and Uncle Laurie belonged in part to the old life that was gone forever. If he could see them, the sight might help to cure the dreadful gnawing pain deep down in his heart, the pain that stabbed him when he thought of Mutti all alone.

The hours went by with lagging feet. When church goers went down the path, Tony followed them. There was something odd about a boy who sat on a wall hour after hour: if he stayed in his place during the time of service, people might start asking questions. So he crept into a pew at the back, where his clothes could not be seen.

It seemed to be a special service, a thanksgiving to God for a great deliverance. Looking at the boarded windows and roof, Tony could guess what the deliverance had been. He followed the service till they came to the first hymn. Then he put the hymn book down on the book rest and stood with bent head. Not even poor playing on a dreadful little organ could entirely destroy the beauty of *Austria*. All the congregation sang heartily except the boy near the door.

He did not hear the rest of the service, and was at first only dimly aware that something out of the ordinary was about to happen. Then he knew what it was. He stood stiffly to attention, staring blankly ahead, terribly afraid of meeting any human eye. He wished all the other people on the far side of the moon. He hoped nobody could hear him singing. But he sang.

The last notes of the *National Anthem* died away, and the congregation went home to their Sunday dinners. Sitting on the wall, Tony nearly died of hunger as he smelt the good smells wafted from inhospitable cottages on the other side of the green. By the time the bus arrived he would have welcomed a slice of Tante Bettina's turnip pudding with gratitude. He was thankful to leave Pebberton Green; it was, he thought, the most selfish village he had ever met.

The bus joggled comfortably on its way. He shared a seat with a woman who carried a basket of red currants and a bag of onions. The conductor came to collect the fares. "Tired, Ted?" said the onion-woman, looking sympathetically at the man's drawn gray face. "You've a right to be tired, with all the fire-watching, nights."

The bus rumbled on through the lanes. Behind the hawthorns and blackberry hedges Tony saw the ripening harvest fields, churches nestled among trees, park lands where sheep were feeding, green water meadows where dark-haired rushes bowed ceaselessly to their images mirrored in the stream. Scraps of talk floated to him from time to time. Some words lingered in his mind; others drifted past like thistledown.

Then the conductor's hand touched his shoulder. "You wanted to be put down near Dr. Fairleigh's, didn't you? That's the house, over there."

"Thanks. 'Morning."

" 'Morning."

Tony went down a side road, pushed open a gate, and went slowly up a broad graveled path between rockery walls, purple and gold with summer climbing plants. At the top of the slope the path divided, one fork leading to the house and the other to a wide stone terrace bounded by a low wall. And standing on the terrace, with face turned to the broad sweep of countryside, was a slight figure in Air Force blue.

"Dym!" said Tony to himself.

He hadn't expected to meet Dym so soon. He had thought that Cousin Olive or Cousin Basil would ring Dym up at the hush-hush place to tell him that the wanderer had returned. All his carefully prepared speech of explanation and apology vanished out of his head, leaving him nothing but the remembrance that he was a troublesome young brother who had run away for the tenth time.

He stood still, craning his neck for a sight of the elder brother's face. Dym was grave, a little sad; he had the air of one who had failed in a task he had set himself to do. Although he did not look angry or even stern, Tony hesitated before approaching him. At last, his heart beating jerkily, the runaway's bare feet stole softly over the sun-warmed stones. Dym did not move or turn his head.

"George," said the runaway, in a scared whisper. He used this name because he felt that this was undoubtedly what Dym would call a state occasion. "Please, George, I've come back."

Dym wheeled about with astonishing suddenness. "Tony!"

The one word was enough. Tony flung himself into his brother's arms and felt them close round him tight. "Hold me so I can't get away!" he said, and found himself queerly rejoicing in the steely strength of those scarred wrists.

"Well, is that enough for you?" Dym asked, releasing him with an odd laugh.

Tony nodded, struggling to keep back quite incomprehensible tears. "I've left my shoes and my gas mask behind and I've lost my socks," he said, anxious to get the confession over.

"Doesn't matter," said Dym. Slipping an arm round the tattered gray pullover, he drew Tony down beside him on the terrace wall. Without speaking, Tony held out Mutti's note. Dym read it gravely, but made no comment.

You could see a long way from Cousin Basil's house. Below his hilly gardens stretched mile after mile of well-ordered farm and park land softly rising and falling to the horizon line that cried as always of the sea almost within sight. The trim boundary hedges gave the landscape the look of a gigantic chessboard running up hill and down dale, Tony thought, as his eyes rested on the green and golden squares. He put his head down on Dym's arm with a contented sigh.

"What's wrong here?" Dym asked, taking a dusty foot into his hand.

"Screwed it a bit," Tony answered. "Had to take a long drop from a roof."

He hoped Dym wouldn't ask any more questions yet awhile, and Dym didn't. "I'll get Basil to see to it by and by," he said. "They're having a Sunday afternoon nap at present—Basil, Olive, and their old Emily. All except me."

"Are you spending the day here?" Tony asked.

"Yes. I couldn't go in search of you this time, old chap. I'm not allowed to be more than a certain distance from the station; I'm liable to be recalled at any minute. Thought I'd rather wait here for news. It was pretty grim, waiting."

"You wanted me to be found?" Tony asked.

"What do you suppose?" said Dym. "But I'm a thousand times gladder that you found yourself."

"Shall I tell you what happened?"

"Not yet. I'm going to give you something to eat first. Hungry?"

"If there's any unrationed food I could have, please," said Tony. "I'm starved."

"Don't remember what we had for lunch," said Dym, "but I daresay we can find something or other."

Tony was surprised that it was possible to forget what you had had for lunch. When the refrigerator door swung open to disclose cold chicken and cherry tart and custard, his surprise changed into a feeling of guilt. It seemed wrong that he should be about to enjoy his dinner so much when Dym hadn't enjoyed it at all.

Dym set him a meal at one end of Emily's kitchen table, and made coffee for him on the gas stove. Only after he had been washed and fed did Dym say quietly, "You'll have to tell your story to the police, I'm afraid. Will you let me hear it first?"

Telling Dym was as easy as could be, for they shared Emily's armchair, in the warm sunny kitchen with its canary's cage and scarlet geraniums and rows of shiny metal dishcovers. But telling the policeman, that Dym summoned by telephone, was a very different matter. It meant much questioning, some gruff indignation, a long-distance call to the Greltham St. Andrew police, and an announcement that Tony must hold himself ready at any moment to identify Mr. Frederick Halliwell, so called. When the policeman's big boots tramped down the path, Tony did not know whether he was a convicted desperado or a small mushroom under a steam roller.

They were in Cousin Olive's drawing room now; its pink carpet soft beneath his bruised feet. Dym smiled comfortingly at the culprit. "That's safely over. Bit of an ordeal, wasn't it? I wonder whether they'll catch Uncle Fred?"

"Think they will?"

"I doubt it. If you could find your way to the house again, you'd probably find that Uncle Fred and his surroundings have undergone a remarkable transformation. You wouldn't be able to identify anybody or anything. There's a bare possibility that the police may trace the airman who asked the way to Orrington Magna, and the soldiers whose lorry you boarded. But the first man mayn't remember which road your car took, and the second lot may not want the Major to hear what happened to his washing and the Army petrol."

"They were awfully scared of him," said Tony.

"Just so. On the whole, I fancy Uncle Fred will be left in peace."

Tony was not sorry to hear it, for he had no desire to

meet him again. He turned the conversation. "Are you going to ring them up at home?"

"Didn't you hear me asking the constable to let them know? I thought it would save a second long-distance call. Perhaps Phemie may ring up after seven, when we get the cheap rate."

"Phemie?"

"She's at home again. Came back unexpectedly last night because she felt in her bones that things weren't going too well without her. She's actually found someone to take Vera's place—the old Nannie we had long ago is going to have one of the farm cottages for herself and her husband. You'll be in clover, Tony; you were her special favorite."

Tony smiled.

"And that leaves Vera's room free for the Cavendish boys when they come back with you after the week in Wales."

Tony stopped him there. "Are you going to let me go to Wales, Dym? I thought you'd say you couldn't trust me—"

"I think I can. Anyway, I'm going to try."

"But I've lost all my lives; you said that if you caught me running away ten times—"

"When I said that, I never for a moment imagined I might one day be called on to keep my word. It'll be a lesson to me not to make rash vows. As it happens, you've scored. I didn't catch you, nor did anybody else. You came back of your own free will."

"Yes," said Tony, greatly relieved; "I did. Then this time doesn't count?"

"No, you scamp, it doesn't, as far as I am concerned. I daresay you'll hear about it later from James and Porgy. When Phemie last rang me up she said they'd been out all night following some mysterious clue of their own. They're not back yet; nobody knows what's become of them."

But Tony did not trouble about the coming vengeance of the unskilled detectives, James and Porgy. He said in a whisper, "I came back because I—chose *Chrysaor*."

"*Chrysaor?*"

"The sword *Chrysaor*. You told Sally and the others about the sword *Balmung* and the sword *Chrysaor*, the golden sword that the Knight of Justice carried. You said you hoped I would choose *Chrysaor*. And I did."

"I'm very glad." He laid his hand lightly on the younger brother's arm. Suddenly Tony found himself crying bitterly, passionately. "Mutti! She wanted me—she was sure I would come to her—and I didn't go—I stayed."

It was a long time before he could make himself stop crying. When he was quiet, Dym said, "You'll see"—he paused, and then went on, almost as though he were forcing the words out through clenched teeth—"Mutti again."

"Shall I?"

"Of course, after the war. I'll"—again he paused—"I'll take you to see her, some day."

"Will you really? You don't want me to—to hate her?"

Dym's face was very white. "No," he said, controlling his voice with difficulty, "that wouldn't make things any better. There's hate enough in the world already. You're not to blame for loving the woman who stole you from your father and mother. She wronged them cruelly—but we've got to forgive. No, go on loving her, Max."

A long shudder went through Tony. "There's something else I want to tell you, Dym. I nearly told you a long time ago. But I couldn't tell you after my spy book was found. You wouldn't have wanted to hear it then. The others wouldn't have been pleased, either. I thought that I'd better not tell, ever. But I must tell now that I've chosen *Chrysaor.*"

He could get no further. "Well, what is it?" Dym asked. "Not afraid to tell me, are you, Max?"

"No, not you. It's the others," faltered Tony. "They'll say —or they'll think—I'm a traitor."

"Leave the others to me, Max."

"I'm not Max," said Tony, with a wrenched sob. "I'm Tony!"

"That's what I thought," said Dym. There was a moment's silence, then he said gently, "Tell me what you mean, old man."

"I didn't know for certain," said Tony, "it wasn't as wicked as that. It was only that I—sort of knew, it's been coming back to me. There was a long time ago when I was small. I think it was when we were living in Japan. One Christmas Eve I had a gray furry monkey among my presents. I called it Toni. Mutti said she did not like that name; it was an ugly name. She wanted me to call the monkey Willi; she said that was a much better name for a monkey. But I wouldn't call him Willi; I said his name was Toni; then, one night, I took him to bed with me as usual and in the morning I woke up and he wasn't there. Mutti searched too. She was very sorry for me and she took me to the shops to buy a doll—she said she'd seen a very nice one called Hans. But I had a queer feeling that, somehow, the monkey was lost because I'd called him Toni. I didn't ask any questions; I just felt it. That was the beginning."

"Go on."

"Then there was a day when I came home early from school. I was six then, and I could write a little. I saw a photograph of me lying on Mutti's table with Tony written on it. It gave me a queer feeling that I was like the gray furry monkey. I can't explain the feeling any better than that. So I wrote my own name under the Tony—then I rubbed it out because I heard Vater coming. Mutti didn't notice what I had done. When she came into the room she put the photograph into an envelope. I never saw it again, and I forgot about it because then Mutti and I went to the seaside.

"After that nothing happened, except that I used to say 'Tony' to myself sometimes; I didn't know why—"

"Nothing more to tell me?"

"There's a queer story that I meant to tell you on the day my spy book was found," said Tony. "I couldn't tell it, afterward. You went to Germany once with Cousin Basil and Cousin Olive, didn't you? Look, I'm going to write down a month and a year on this bit of paper before I tell you the story. And when I've told it, you write a month and a year and a place on this other bit. Then we'll look at them to see whether they agree."

As he told the story of the moonlit concert in the dark hotel garden, he saw the light of memory kindle on his elder brother's face. Without a word, Dym wrote some words on his paper. They put the two pieces together and looked at them. Neither spoke. Through the window Tony could see a Spitfire scribbling white trails high in the air. Somewhere a bugle called. Out in the garden white butterflies danced on the lavender spikes. Dym gathered the papers together and put them into his pocketbook. He rose.

"That's all for the present," he said. "Now look here, you're tired out. I'm going to tuck you up on the sofa for a rest and, while you're asleep, I'm going to wake everybody ruthlessly and callously out of their Sunday snooze, and tell them what you have told me. When you wake up, you needn't make any explanations of any kind. See?"

Tony did not think that he should sleep but, in a very few minutes from the shutting of the door, he slept soundly, his wallet clutched tight in one hand. After a time a restless movement sent the wallet to the floor. Dym, returning, picked up the scattered treasures. As he did so, the young man's face changed oddly. Coloring almost guiltily, he restored the wallet to its owner and then stood looking down at the unconscious face. Tony stirred in his sleep; a troubled quiver showed round his mouth. "*Chrysaor,*" he murmured, and then, anxiously, "Dym?"

"It's all right; I'm here," said Dym.

At five minutes past seven that night, the telephone bell rang. Tony answered the call. "James Ingleford speaking," said the voice at the other end.

"Hullo, Jim," said Tony.

"Is that Tony? How on earth did you get there?"

"Yes, it's me," said Tony sedately.

James, being struck speechless, lost part of his three-minutes-for-a-shilling. He said presently, in a weak voice, "The twins vowed you'd gone off for good with a German spy. D'you mean there's been all the recent fuss for nothing? You were only hitch-hiking to Orrington Magna to see Dym?"

Tony would have given much for the power to say "Yes." "No," he said, with something of a pang. "I ran away. But I changed my mind and came back."

There was another pause while James digested this piece of news. "If you don't deserve to be shot down in flames!" he said at last. "What does Dym think of this performance?"

"I came back, I tell you. I wasn't caught. Dym understands."

"I never met anyone like you in my life," complained James. "You get away with everything. What's been happening?"

"Can't tell you over the telephone," said Tony primly. "The police wouldn't like it if I did. Ask Phemie. She knows."

"Ask Phemie! Porgy and I are sixty miles from home at this moment," said James. "We followed what we thought was a very good clue, but it led nowhere. Before we started cycling sixty miles back, we thought we'd find out how things were going. How many more times do you intend to do this will-o'-the-wisp stunt, I'd like to know?"

"No more times," said Tony. "You can tell Sally that I've chosen what she hoped I'd choose. I daresay she won't mind telling you what it was. And I'm not coming home till Dym brings me when he gets his leave. Cousin Basil said I'd made another crash-landing and I'd better stay here till my foot's better. I've hurt my foot. Dym says I'm a specialist in crash-landings. Cousin Olive says I can help her with her bees and rabbits and tomatoes. She's growing them to help the food supply."

"How can you help if you've hurt your foot?" James asked suspiciously.

"I couldn't cycle to school on it, but I can scramble round. I say, you might as well tell Phemie that I've lost my gas mask and my shoes and a new pair of socks. Break it gently. And I shall want my ration book and some clothes."

"I don't see why you couldn't come home till the end of term," grumbled James. "When you do come, you'll be flying off again to stay with Uncle Tony and the Cavendishes, and then all the rest of the hols you'll be having your precious Cavendishes here—"

"You want me?" Tony asked, surprised. "You've got Porgy and Simon."

"Cousins are cousins, when all's said and done," said James darkly. "You're better than no one. Sally thinks so too."

It was evident that James was in a depressed frame of mind. "What are you doing now?" he added. "Where's Dym?"

"The cousins have gone to church. Dym's playing, and I'm writing letters. I've written to Michael and—"

He paused, for it was not quite possible to tell James that he had written to ask Olaf to tea on Wednesday. "I'm just going to write to Ginger's captain," he ended.

"What!" said James. "I say, your adventures haven't turned your brain, have they? What are you writing to him for?"

"Because he asked me to," said Tony. "He said that if ever I changed my mind about hating England, would I let him know? And I said I would."

James whistled. "You've got a pretty good nerve, young Anthony. However, it's your funeral. Does Dym know?"

"Of course. He thinks it's a good idea."

"Well," said James, "you'd better speed the pen. The pips have sounded twice, so I shall have to pay two bob for this interesting conversation. Hope you're worth it. 'Night, old chap. See you soon."

" 'Night," said Tony.

He went back to his letter. After such a long day it was not easy to compose the mind for writing. His thoughts strayed first to suppertime and then to the march that Dym wanted him to compose. *Salute to Adventure* was the theme

Dym had suggested, and he had promised that the station band should play it if it was good enough. Between the sentences of his letter he drew bass and treble clef signs on Cousin Olive's blotting paper, thoughtfully. Dym's soft playing of *Jerusalem* had kindled a flame within.

"Finished?" said Dym, swinging round on the piano stool.

Tony held out the letter. "You may see it, all but the postscript," he said shyly. "The postscript is rather private." He put his hand across the lower half of the sheet. The letter ran:

> *Dear Sir:*
>   *You asked me to tell you when I changed my mind about England. I have.*
>   *Yours respectably,*
>   *A.V. Ingleford*
> *P.S. I have also changed my mind about Dym. I would follow Dym over the edge of the world.*

Dym smiled. "Short and sweet, like a donkey's gallop. What's in the mysterious postscript? Sure I mayn't see it?"

"No, you mayn't," said Tony, his hand still over the words. "What about the rest, Dym? Is it tidy enough to send to him? And is it good English?"

"It'll do," said Dym.

About the Author

"TELL ME A STORY," are the first words Constance Savery remembers saying. Though her clergyman father supplied her with "books galore" as soon as she could read, she could never get stories enough to satisfy her love of them. She soon took to making up her own. These were sometimes acted out with "paper dolls cut out of my mother's pattern books," sometimes written out or told in her head or while she walked around "the house or garden pretending to play a solitary game of bat and ball." She went on to write some fifty books, nearly all for children. Three of Miss Savery's sisters also became writers due no doubt to the close and creative family environment with its plenitude of books.

Constance Savery, eldest of five sisters, was born in Froxfield, Wiltshire on October 31st, 1897. Later the family moved to the city of Birmingham. From Birmingham she went to Somerville College, Oxford. Recently, just before her hundredth birthday, she was the guest of honor at an Oxford event celebrating the 75th anniversary of degrees for women. Previous to her year, though they took full university courses and passed all the examinations, women did not receive diplomas as full members of the University. She wrote, "I had done nothing whatever to deserve being a guest of honour except to outlive all the other women in the first group that was admitted to degrees! It was a very grand occasion for a very insignificant person."

Sixty years' worth of young readers would doubtless challenge this claim to insignificance. Though her first book was published in England in 1929, it was not until the publication of *Enemy Brothers* in 1943 that Constance Savery was introduced to American readers. She soon became known as a gifted and sensitive author on both sides of the Atlantic, excelling in the portrayal of warm personal relationships between characters. The satisfying conclusions of her books arise from her deep sense of faith and goodness and from her love of a good story; they uplift the reader with a sense of hope, escaping the snare of the moralizing or overly sweet tale.

Constance Savery spent her last years in the town of Stroud, of which she wrote, "It may amuse you to know that long ago Stroud was an important town. Most of the red cloth for British army uniforms was manufactured there." On March 2nd, 1999, Miss Savery died at the age of 101. Her gift of sensitive, thoughtful writing will continue to be appreciated by many new readers.

LIVING HISTORY LIBRARY

The Living History Library is a collection of works for children published by Bethlehem Books, comprising quality reprints of historical fiction and non-fiction, including biography. These books are chosen for their craftsmanship and for the intelligent insight they provide into the present, in light of events and personalities of the past.

TITLES IN THIS SERIES

Archimedes and the Door of Science, by Jeanne Bendick
Augustine Came to Kent, by Barbara Willard
Becky Landers, Frontier Warrior, by Constance L. Skinner
Beorn the Proud, by Madeleine Polland
Beowulf the Warrior, by Ian Serraillier
Big John's Secret, by Eleanore M. Jewett
Enemy Brothers, by Constance Savery
First Farm in the Valley: Anna's Story, by Anne Pellowski
Galen and the Gateway to Medicine, by Jeanne Bendick
God King, by Joanne Williamson
The Good Land, by Loula Grace Erdman
The Hidden Treasure of Glaston, by Eleanore M. Jewett
Hittite Warrior, by Joanne Williamson
If All the Swords in England, by Barbara Willard
Jamberoo Road, by Eleanor Spence
John Treegate's Musket, by Leonard Wibberley
Madeleine Takes Command, by Ethel C. Brill
Nacar, the White Deer, by Elizabeth Borton de Trevino
The Mystery of the Periodic Table, by Benjamin D. Wiker
Philomena, by Kate Seredy
The Reb and the Redcoats, by Constance Savery
Red Falcons of Trémoine, by Hendry Peart

Continued on the following page

Red Hugh, Prince of Donegal, by Robert T. Reilly
Shadow Hawk, by Andre Norton
The Small War of Sergeant Donkey, by Maureen Daly
Son of Charlemagne, by Barbara Willard
Sun Slower, Sun Faster, by Meriol Trevor
The Switherby Pilgrims, by Eleanor Spence
Victory on the Walls, a Story of Nehemiah,
      by Frieda C. Hyman
The Wide Horizon, by Loula Grace Erdman
The Wind Blows Free, by Loula Grace Erdman
The Winged Watchman, by Hilda van Stockum
Year of the Black Pony, by Walt Morey